RIVKA'S WAR

a novel

For Judy and Helman,
With gratitude for
loving memories. Come
back to camp!,
With love
Marilyn Oser
5/23/13

RIVKA'S WAR

a novel

MARILYN OSER

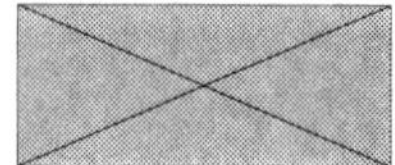

Mill City Press, Inc.
212 3rd Avenue North, Suite 290
Minneapolis, MN 55401
612.455.2294
www.millcitypublishing.com

ISBN-13: 978-1-62652-050-9
LCCN: 2013906523

Cover Design by Kristeen Ott
Typeset by James Arneson

Printed in the United States of America

for Mary Lou, always

A Note to the Reader: Historical maps and a glossary of foreign-language terms may be found on pages 257-265.

Prologue

On the Eastern Front, 1917

PEERING INTO THE black: useless. No information to be had there. You have to move by inches, as if with feelers on the soles of your feet. Falling shells illuminate the trench, but little can be seen in this smoke-fouled light, a ghastly flickering brilliance less comforting even than the darkness, for it exposes your silhouette to enemy snipers. Rivka is engrossed in the placement of each step and in the information it brings her: wet or dry, slippery or spongy or solid. In front of her moves the Lieutenant Colonel, and in front of him, Natalia Ivanova Tatuyeva, her latest and best friend. At her back is the adjutant to the Lieutenant Colonel, and beyond him, Olga Stepanova Redzvenka. Up and down the line, a *verst* in each direction, they file into place: boy-girl-boy-girl, rifles at the ready, every nerve alive, every fiber awaiting the fateful word.

A sudden hand on her shoulder, warm breath at her neck. She jumps, startled. Lieutenant Filippov's pocked face swims into view. "Drink," he says, extending a metal thimble that brims with clear liquid.

"What is it?"

"Shhh—vodka."

"Our *Natchalnik* approves?" Their Natchalnik, their commander, is a strict disciplinarian who permits her girls no latitude. Vodka is outlawed in Russia and has been since the outbreak of war in the summer of 1914.

He laughs, a low growl. "Yashka? Her orders. Truly Yashka's. Now, be quick about it. Drink up."

Rivka downs the tasteless, bitter liquid in a gulp. Fire plunges from her throat to her belly. Filippov proceeds along the row, refilling the tiny cup for each soldier. Rivka rests her cheek against the damp, rough wall of the trench. A faint odor of spring and its loamy fields still clings to the disturbed earth. "Lord God," she prays, "God of Abraham, Isaac and Jacob, shield of our fathers, king of the universe, protect me this night; guard us all, for we are women unaccustomed to fighting. Yet here we stand, in defense of our country. Have mercy on us in life and in death. And may our sacrifice be for good."

She speaks this in a mixture of Yiddish and Russian, but switches to Hebrew for the ancient prayer of Jews, whispered low so as not to be heard by the *goyim* nearby. "*Sh'ma Yisroel Adonoi eloheinu, Adonoi ehod.*" Hear, oh Israel, the Lord our God, the Lord is one.

The sky behind her lightens. Three AM, first hint of dawn. The muscles in her calves twitch. Her heart races. Any moment now will come the signal to go over the top, to attack the German army in their trenches one hundred meters across no-man's-land....

Part I

Women of Valor

A woman of valor, who can find? Her worth is beyond rubies…
She girds her loins…and makes strong her arms…
She is clothed in…fine linen….

Proverbs, 31:10

I

December 1914
Nachum

THESE COLD NIGHTS, she had taken to sleeping in the kitchen near the stove, but the fire had gone out. A foul smell woke Rivka. The room bore the iciness of an hour long after midnight and just as long until dawn. She had curled herself into a tight ball under the heavy quilts, where the odor found her, infiltrating her dream like the stench from a roomful of cholera cases (or so she imagined, for she'd never yet witnessed the cholera) or from the butchered intestines of a diseased pig (ditto). The smell was warm and moist and accompanied by a *huff* and then a *huff huff* that might have been the ponderous gentile butcher in his low hut, bending over the hideous porcine entrails.

She opened one eye, the one not jammed into her feather pillow, and it was met by an eye only inches from her own: an alien, dark-fringed, grayish eye with a horizontal black pupil thin and straight as the slash of the *shoychet*'s knife. A damp nose began rooting itself into the bedding.

"Gitteleh, what are you doing?" The little nanny goat had no business here. Were they peasants, to live among animals? She must have escaped from the pen, but how? And how had she gotten into the house? The goat gave another malodorous snuffle as the girl gathered the bedclothes around her shoulders, and then followed her to the back door, which was standing wide open.

Wary, Rivka peered out into the night. The moon had risen and was pouring its silvery light onto the patchy snow. Nothing moved. A dog barked in the distance. An owl hooted. There's such a thing as too quiet, too still. But if a pack of marauders were hidden in the shadows, surely her neck hairs would be standing on end, warning her. She stepped into the night and whispered to the goat to follow. Down at the bottom of the yard, next to the outhouse, stood the wooden shed where the animal ought to have been penned. Light was coming from inside, the faint yellow flickering of someone's lantern. Who?

Silent as her heroine Yael when slaying the Philistine general—now, what was that general's name?—Mischa would know. She should have thought to waken him. She shouldn't be out alone in the dead of night, a girl of thirteen. She shouldn't be creeping silent as the biblical Yael upon God-knows-who doing God-knows-what. She hesitated, and the little goat prodded at her fingertips. No sense turning back now—was there—when she had the advantage of surprise against the intruder. No sense turning back (was there?) when she had a plan to arm herself with Papa's axe, hanging on three nails just inside the door.

An unearthly screech ripped the night in two. Electrified, Rivka flung open the weathered wooden door, hurling herself into the shed. Her hand, grasping for the axe, grazed wall instead. Why wasn't it where it always was kept? But over there on the ground some eight paces in front of her, Papa's axe lay on the scattered hay, fans of dark droplets spattered across its blade. Next to it squatted Mischa, his arms held out like he was about to break into the *kazatzke*, the dance of the Russian chair.

His mouth foamed words, but no sound issued. His eyes were hollowed in the lamplight, his forehead and cheeks pallid. The right fist came up wrapped in his left. His lips trembled. "I did it," he cackled.

Rivka moved toward him. Methodically, he opened the fist just in front of his face, raising the pinkie, next the ring finger, next the third. From the socket of the next, blood splattered and ran down, bathing his hand, his arm, his shirt, blood that wanted to feed his trigger finger, no longer there.

"I did it," her brother repeated, before fainting dead away in her trembling arms.

IN THE WOMB, Mama always said, Rivka and Mischa carried on like Jacob and Esau, scuffling and punching, and everyone expected the younger to come out grasping the heel of the elder. The younger, Rivka, came out breech and nearly killed poor Mama, for her head and shoulders were larger than Mischa's. If dominance was what they struggled over during the nine long months of pregnancy, then Rivka proved the winner—Papa said—for she started out the larger and stronger twin and remained so. Tall, rangy, raw-boned, with straw-colored hair and cornflower eyes, she was pronounced by the *yentas* in their *shtetl* to be as big a loser for her strength as Mischa was for his delicacy. He'd been sickly as an infant, ate halfheartedly, grew slowly, and he remained small and slight with dark hair and extravagantly fringed dark eyes. He should have been the girl, it was whispered, and Rivka the boy. The twins never minded what busybodies said. He was happy being a student, star of the *cheder*, while she prefered exploring the fields and woods surrounding their village.

When Mischa was called to the Torah as a Bar Mitzvah, Mama blushed with pride. Some boys merely recited the blessings before and after the reading, which was cause enough for celebrating with honey cake and sweet wine following the morning service. For Mischa, Mama and Rivka baked *bobka* and *rugelach* and *mandelbrot*, and they set out *shnaps* alongside the wine. This princely celebration was fitting because he read the entire Torah portion, a long and important one, relating how Moses led the children of Israel through the parted waters to freedom. When he chanted "*Who is like unto thee O Lord among the mighty? Who is like unto thee, glorious in holiness, fearful in praises, doing wonders?,*" the women behind their *mehitzah* forgot their chatter. Falling silent, they sat motionless, listening. Mama wept. No boy ever in the hundreds of years of Jewish life in their village had read the entire portion himself and the haftorah as well. Maybe no boy even in Rovno, the nearest city.

Rivka nearly wrecked things, dashing outdoors as he came to the final blessings, vomiting up her guts in the snow. Sobs shook her. But everyone knew how close the twins were, inseparable all through childhood, so they jumped to the conclusion it was the nervous strain, the fervid devotion to her brother that must have overcome her. "A waste of tears," they consoled, patting her hand. "This boy does better than the rabbi."

They all believed he would grow up to be a great sage, study Talmud in a top yeshiva and bring renown to their little community. Little did they suspect that Mischa was not the least bit interested in Judaism. It was the study of languages he relished. Sometimes Rivka watched him studying, his body unconsciously twisting into the shapes of the letters before him on the page. Alphabets intrigued him. Their sounds delighted him. Already he'd learned the Hebrew, Cyrillic and Greek alphabets, and he was teaching himself the Roman. Finding out how distant speakers framed the world in their languages was what he wanted to do most of all. A *yeshiva bukher,* a scholar of Torah, he wasn't, but only his sister understood this—and she wasn't telling.

The summer following Mischa's Bar Mitzvah, Rivka began menstruating, and news reached the Pale of Settlement of a war about to break out against the German and Hapsburg Empires. Of course, there was no connection between the two events, except in Rivka's mind. One morning in late July, she showed Mama the smear of blood in her underwear. Mama smiled and kissed her, and then slapped her face. Rivka recoiled from the sharp, stinging blow. Blood rushed to her cheek. "What, Mama?" she cried.

Mama shrugged. "It's tradition," she said.

Later that same day they learned that Russian soldiers were being mobilized to invade Austria and Poland. And Papa informed Mischa he must choose how they would incapacitate him. This, too, it appeared, was tradition. His parents would not make the choice for him, since he would have to live with it the rest of his life. Papa as a boy had lost the toes of his left foot, for a soldier must march, and no one can march without his toes. Berel the drayman was missing an eye, the rabbi his two pinkies.

Pinkies seemed the smart choice. You could do almost anything without your pinkies. But it was rumored that when the Tsar's Army would come through taking recruits and line up the Jewish boys for inspection, lost pinkies were no longer sufficient. Near Berditchev, it was said, two boys had been taken despite this disability, boys with not a wisp of hair yet on their upper lips. No Jew would last long in a Russian regiment, proclaimed Papa. He'd be dead before a year turned over.

Nonetheless, most boys of Mischa's generation were answering the call, going off to become heroes. How else, these volunteers argued, could Jews ever expect to receive full Russian citizenship? They marched up the street, dazzling in new uniforms, the little girls skipping along beside them, throwing flowers in their path, maidens Rivka's age darting forward to wish them well, then dashing back to their gates. Mischa's friend Nachum volunteered to go. "Jews are not draft dodgers. Jews are loyal Russian subjects. We must demonstrate this to the Tsar and to the people," he told Mischa.

"They'll treat you like shit," Mischa said.

"At first, maybe. But when they see how I'll fight, they'll learn to respect me, and that's how you change things, one person at a time, by your behavior, slowly, over time."

"Slowly over time never changed things before."

"This time will be different."

News of the front trickled back with the draymen who'd been conscripted to transport men and matériel to the frontier. Russian armies were swarming into enemy territory, pushing back the Austrian and German troops fifty versts, a hundred versts, more. In no long time, they gained the banks of the Vistula River and were threatening Warsaw. Could the day be far off when they would sweep into Berlin? Troop trains rolled through from Rovno day and night, the cars filled to bursting with young men in uniform—more riding precariously on the roofs. They waved and called out to anyone nearby, especially girls walking along the road, as did Rivka every day, bringing Papa his lunch at the factory. "Come here, honey, give us a kiss!" She blushed to the roots of her hair.

At the frontier, they had to deboard for other trains of a different gauge. Supplies, too, had to be reloaded onto equipment that could ride the German rails. Before long, cars and men were backed up many versts, waiting. The countryside was soon stripped of horses and wagons, conscripted on the spot for military use. Papa was only able to retain his by arguing that his bootmaking factory performed a vital war service. Others were not so lucky. One cold day, Berel the drayman brought some wheat westward beyond Brody and ended up having to walk back.

The way back was clogged with refugees whose homes had been destroyed in the fighting. Some were peasants: the women and girls in their brightly colored babushkas, the men bareheaded, with wind-tossed yellow hair. Then Jews, whole shtetls of them, uprooted and driven from their homes in the occupied towns of Galicia in Austria-Hungary. They came with what they could carry on their backs, looking bewildered and vacant, their staring children backing away when Rivka offered a piece of bread. They moved together under guard of a few soldiers. It was for their own safety, the soldiers said, that they were being sent east. Bent under the weight of their sacks, they crowded into the courtyard of the synagogue seeking food and rest.

Rivka was at the factory bringing Papa his lunch when in rode five Cossacks on stamping ponies. She nearly fainted as they made straight for her, each one a promise of harm. The lead rider dismounted, tall in his high fur hat, his bushy mustache flaked in frost, his eyes narrowed, his pantaloons billowing as he took his long, conqueror's strides. "Where is the boots man?" he bellowed.

She pointed, too terrified to speak. He ordered her to show them the way.

He was their commander, come to order a new pair of boots. Rivka watched Papa take the measure himself. The skin of Papa's hands was discolored and cracked, the joints gnarled and dark from years of working with tanned leathers, with aniline dyes and waxes. But Papa was a man of business now; he rarely ever took his place at the cobbler's bench, much less at any of the machines in his bootmaking factory.

Bowing and scraping, he inquired if they had news from the front.

"*Da*," replied the commander, tight-lipped. He lolled in Papa's office chair, his splayed legs like two heavy logs, his feet the size of jack planes, the toenails long, ragged and yellow.

Papa brought him fine leathers to choose from. "What glory," he said, "to be part of this great Russian advance that can only end in glorious victory."

"Victory!" The Cossack spat. "Victory? A million of our fine Russian lads lost. For what? To gain two million stinking Jews!"

AT THIS TIME, Mischa still had not maimed himself, and Papa redoubled his efforts to get the boy to act before the Cossacks or the army would. The men of the village could hold a boy down, he said, and do what was necessary for him afterward. Did Mischa imagine anyone liked it? But it was unavoidable for a long life, the army being anti-Semitic through and through.

Rivka believed he'd be better off going to war. There must be compensations for the hard life one would have to lead and the terrible dangers. Not every gentile could be hostile to Jews; you might find a protector and fare all right. At least you'd have all your fingers and toes and both your eyes. You could run and dance, knead bread and tie knots and gaze in wonder at the whole wide world beyond their little village.

Mischa kept promising he'd do it himself without any help, but day followed day, week followed week, and soon it was months, and still Papa was pressing Mischa to act.

"I'll take you to the zoo," Rivka offered. "We'll bribe the guard to let you stick your hand into the monkey cage."

"What good will that do?"

"The monkey will bite off your finger."

"What makes you think so?"

"I don't know. Maybe I'll put honey on it."

"Are you crazy? You've never even seen a monkey."

"So what? Neither have you."

"And you disapprove of self-mutilation."

"But Mischa, at least we'll have an adventure."

He gave her a knowing grin. "Where is this zoo with its biting monkey?"

"Never you mind. I'll find you one, even if we have to go all the way to Kiev." How fine it would be to see Kiev!

The day came when Nachum returned from war. Two men in torn and filthy uniforms trudged through the sleet, shlepping him on a litter down the same street he had marched up so bravely, so expectantly, not six months before. Mischa took one look at his childhood friend, and that very night went down to the shed where Rivka found him and the severed trigger finger from his right hand.

His *right* hand, mind you. Nobody would think to ask if he was a lefty. He was.

As for Nachum, he'd never march again, for his legs were severed below each knee. His commander had sent him out to a listening post to try to hear the enemy's plans. The air temperature dropped, the relief was delayed by a German raiding party, and he was forced to lie within a few feet of the German front line, unmoving for hours. By the time he could drag himself back and have his frozen feet attended to, it was too late. Gangrene set in, and they amputated.

"Soldiering is no occupation for a Jew," said Papa when they all paid a visit. "They'd never send their own on duty like that. That's what they use the Jews for."

But Nachum, twenty pounds thinner, his cheeks gaunt, his eyes huge in his skull, stuck up for them. "The two men with me at the post that night were goyim," he said. "They lost their legs, too."

"All three of you?" gasped Papa.

Nachum's eyes flashed. "What? You're worried about business? Six boots you won't be able to sell?"

Nachum, he was some troublemaker, even without his legs.

There was a time before the war when everyone believed Rivka was Nachum's intended. She'd known him since earliest childhood.

He was taller even than she, very skinny, and like most Jews he walked with a stoop, his shoulders hunched as if eternally expecting a blow. He had an interest in worldly ideas: Zionism, Socialism, the Jewish Question. She tried to keep up with him, to challenge his intellect as he challenged hers. He gave her pamphlets to read with difficult titles she could not understand, such as *Auto-Emancipation*. He gave her a pamphlet that said Jews could not be Jews except in their own country of Eretz Yisroel, and another that said Jews could be good Jews and also good citizens of their host countries everywhere, and a third pamphlet that said Jews ought not to be Jews at all, if Rivka undersood that one properly. She peppered her conversation with quotes from them all, and she thought Nachum favored her because of this. Mind you, nothing ardent was ever uttered, and of course it would be up to his parents to choose his intended, but his parents were willing to hear his opinion. This she knew for a fact.

A few weeks before Nachum went off to war, papers were signed betrothing him to the daughter of a wealthy grain merchant from just north of Rovno, about fifty versts distant. Rumor said she was prettier than Rivka and a good cook, with not a thought in her head. It was a marriage that was also a business deal. Nachum's father had once been a man of substance in the community, a distiller who used to pledge the largest sums in *shul* each year at *Kol Nidre*. After 1905, when the Tsar outlawed distilling to Jews, he went on making a comfortable living selling vodka clandestinely to the peasants and kosher wine openly to the Jews. With the war on, the Tsar had outlawed vodka, and Nachum's father contemplated a pauper's empty cupboards. But he was betting that the war wouldn't last long, the Germans would quickly overrun their corner of Russia, and maybe then the Jews would have a better life. Under German rule, he'd be free to distill grain alcohol, the grain coming wholesale from Nachum's father-in-law. But what was in it for the father-in-law that he should wed his daughter to a distiller's son? Maybe the same calculation.

The first Rivka knew of the betrothal was when Nachum stopped greeting her. She gave him her usual openhearted smile, but he passed by without so much as a glance or a nod. Her best friend, Rachel Aaronsohn, hissed in outrage upon hearing of it. "He was never good enough for you," she said. "Not one of these *schnorrers* is good enough."

"Easy for you to say. You're a pear. I'm a string bean. Who wants a string bean?"

"I'm a very freckled pear."

"You're round and juicy." Rivka's eyebrows bobbed up and down, and Rachel, blushing, tossed her head, auburn curls springing around her rosy face.

She said, "Listen, Rivka. Let's make a pact."

"What? Never to marry?"

Rachel grinned. "Never to marry, until…." Until they could marry two brothers: one rich, the other wealthy; one good-looking, the other handsome; one kind and the other gentle. Their houses would face each other across a broad, tree-lined boulevard, and their children would grow up to marry one another. No child of theirs would have to disappear to avoid the army, as Rachel's brothers, ages nine, ten and eleven had disappeared—gone to visit their maternal grandparents in Lithuania, it was announced, but Rachel whispered that they'd been smuggled to Antwerp and from there, God willing, to Cuba.

And so a solemn pact was sworn between them. But from the day Nachum's engagement was announced, Mama never ceased urging Papa to arrange a marriage for their daughter. Whenever Rivka said something saucy or spoke of her hunger to see the wide world beyond their doorstep, Mama cocked her chin, looked at Papa and said, "This one is itching for a match."

Again and again, Papa refused. "With the war on, who talks of marriage? Bad enough if Rivka should end up a widow, with God forbid a child and no husband to care for her. Worse yet if she should find herself burdened with a living cripple for a husband. God forbid like Nachum, who can't earn a living."

"A disabled soldier is entitled to the Tsar's pension."

"Which won't keep a cat alive."

"She needs a husband."

"Wars don't last forever. Better wait and see what Rivka's prospects will be."

Mama would quiet down. Rivka would be left to mull over her prospects. Sooner or later, Rivka would let slip a hint of her unsatisfied appetite for unheard-of, unhomelike, and possibly unJewish experiences. Then Mama would smile at Papa in their private way. "Sooner, rather than later, understand?" According to Mama, family was everything, and the center of the family was the wife. But if the teasing twinkle in her smile meant that the things done by night in the marriage bed could stop Rivka from thinking and asking questions and seeking adventure, then Rivka decided she was in no hurry to be a wife.

Papa, bless him, merely gazed at Mama and shrugged. "The war won't last forever."

II

Dudie

BY THE TIME Mischa's wound healed, it was the spring of 1915, and still no end in sight to the conflict. A long column of Polish Jews, the men in dirty caftans, some with their sidelocks shorn, one with hundreds of tiny red pinpricks forward of his ears, looking bloodied as if—*Gutt in himmel*, the sidelocks had been ripped out. Prodded by a squad of slouching, wisecracking Russian soldiers, they came shuffling through, headed eastward to God-knows-where. Papa spat in the dirt. If the Jews of Galicia were the poorest in Europe and the most backward, the Jews of Poland were little better. *Chasids*, most of them, whereas Papa if you could call him anything, you'd call him a *Misnagid*, one who embraced modernity, who dressed and acted like a Westerner, and not in the black robes and fur *shtreimels* and dangling forelocks of the Poles. Papa worried. What if the Tsar planned to force these millions of Jews permanently into the Pale of Settlement? Who would make room for them? How could they possibly be absorbed?

There were far too many refugees now for the synagogue courtyard. Only the sick went. The rest, a vast overflow, camped in the fields outside the village. Sometimes Mama brought them tea and bread. A five-minutes walk to the end of the street past sturdy wooden homes and well-tended yards had once brought her to a hillside meadow rising to birch forests beyond its crest. Now a dark morass of mud and misery rose there: hungry children, desperate parents, ragged blankets thrown across their shoulders and atop their pitiful piles of belongings. For the bit of food she gave, she got in return the most horrific stories. Some she repeated, sad-eyed, to her family. Some she would only whisper to Papa late at night after Mischa and Rivka had gone to bed. The refugees told of a rout, the Germans advancing and the Russians retreating back over the ground taken in the fall of 1914. Scrambling rearward, they brought havoc to Jewish communities all along their route. It was bedlam. As soon as the first Russian soldier was spotted near a village, all the Christians set crosses in their windows. Where no cross showed, the Russians felt free to vandalize. They began by stealing goods from Jewish stores. The pilfered cloth and pastries they sold to peasants for pennies, the jewelry they pocketed. The wine they drank. When they had made themselves sufficiently drunk, they rampaged through the streets, setting fire to synagogues and hanging men at random. All Jews were suspect as spies. It didn't matter which particular one you executed. If the brave and invincible Russian army loses territory day by day, it stands to reason—Russian reason—that Jewish treachery must be to blame.

A MAN KNOCKED at their door raising funds for the homeless refugees of Austria and Poland. Papa declined to help, in case he, too, might be accused of spying. "We don't know who these people are."

"They're Jews. They need our help."

"They're Jews. *Nu*. But are they Jews first, or are they enemies first?"

"They're people first. They got in the way of armies. That's all."

"You're naïve."

"Maybe. But I'd rather help an enemy than live with the suspicion that I let an innocent *shlemiel* go hungry." After the last Russian soldier leaves, the man said, then the Cossacks ride in.

They loot whatever the soldiers have overlooked, burn everything to the ground, and rape the women, all of the women, even grandmothers of sixty-eight, seventy years, and the girls, even as young as three years old.

"Bassia," Papa ordered Mama. "Take the children out." Later on, after the man went away, Papa stormed all about, furious that such things had been uttered in front of Mischa and Rivkeleh. "Another Jew without sensitivity, without heart and without sense."

The Russian Army kept falling back, and the German Army kept advancing. The vague, distant thunder of their guns grew louder the closer they came, all through the summer of 1915. Those who could leave had mostly already left. All of the wealthier people were gone. Even hundreds of versts eastward, rumor said, as far away as Kiev, Jews were terrified, Jews were packing up, Jews were debating what was best to do. At the market, in the street, at synagogue, the endless debate was joined.

"Go now. Yesterday would have been better. What are we waiting for? More pogroms? More expulsions?"

"Wait. Stay in place. Even if there's a pogrom, *nu*, we've been through them before. We lose some of our worldly goods? They can be replaced."

"God forbid, we'll lose some people."

"Yes, some will die, it's true. But if we go, we lose everything, except what we can carry on our backs. And how many more will die, do you suppose, of starvation or disease on the road?"

The camps of refugees in the fields beyond every town kept growing. Around Rovno, a thousand Galician Jews and peasants, maybe more, suffering from hunger, dying of cholera and typhus. No food or medical help for them, except what strangers might happen to offer. In the night, Mama told Papa a refugee's tale, unable to keep her voice to a whisper she was sobbing so hard. Rivka, wide-eyed, heard it all.

A squad of Cossacks had galloped in on their ponies. The town had a lovely central square with a broad expanse of lawn and garden in the middle, elliptical in shape. Russian soldiers had already gathered the Jews in the square, where their central synagogue was located. Eighty Torah scrolls were cradled in the arms of the men. The Cossacks circled the ellipse on their ponies, kicking up mud. The foremost rider, without losing stride, bent from his saddle and lifted a girl from the crowd, a child of eleven. The pony continued, round and round. The Cossack fumbled at his crotch, releasing an enormous, erect penis. The girl stared at it bobbing in the air. Next thing, he jammed the child onto him. She shrieked all the way around the circle, three times, four times, five times around, until he threw her like a dirty rag onto the garden bed. By then a second rider had grabbed up a child, and a third rider, and the crowd pushed all the girls behind a wall of men armed only with Torahs. The next rider grabbed a small boy of six, and when his father protested, the following rider sliced off the man's outstretched arm with one slash of his saber. Papa said he couldn't credit wild rumors, but Mama said the woman who told her the story swore it was no rumor, for she had watched it with her own eyes and seen the blood running down the legs of her own little niece.

In the morning, they heard the muttering of guns. "What shall we do," Mama ventured, "if we are told to evacuate?"

"We won't be," Papa declared.

"Says who?"

"We won't be."

Across the table, Mischa signed to his sister, the fingers of his maimed hand crossing the palm of his other. A bribe, he meant. The police would protect them. Maybe.

"There were Cossacks seen outside Tarnopol."

Rivka's spoon stopped its transit to her mouth. Tarnopol was only the other side of the old frontier. Maybe half a day's walk; by pony, much less, no time at all. What if…?

Papa said, "We'll be safe."

"What makes you think so?"

"Don't ask."

Mama cast up her hands. "Don't you care about your family?"

"*Shah!* Hush up. Don't ask questions and don't talk to anyone. I supply the army. General Brusilov himself buys his boots from me. Now, bring me a cup of tea and then go about your business."

Such a sigh she gave shuffling to the samovar.

Papa rattled his newspaper. "There's word the Grand Duke Nikolay Nikolayevich is to be replaced as head of the army."

"Is that good, Papa?" Rivka asked.

"Good," scoffed her mother. "In America the news is good. Here, such things don't exist."

Papa threw down the paper and stomped out of the room. Rivka looked to Mama, who shrugged and went back to kneading dough.

Papa had two brothers and two sisters in America, in addition to his mother. They had written telling Papa to come to Chicago. Papa sneered, claiming they only wanted him so he should contribute to his mother's upkeep. "In America the streets are paved in gold? So who is letting them pick up the pavement? Tell me, better, what are my brothers' pockets lined with?" Papa waited a beat before answering his own question. "Lint."

"There's opportunity there," Mama said.

"Fine," said Papa. "Opportunity here, too. Why do I have to travel halfway around the world when I make a good living here? You want to go? Go!"

Mama said her place is with her family.

"And as to Palestine," said Papa, though nobody had breathed a word about Palestine. "You'd leave this beautiful land for a desert? We don't work hard enough? When the Messiah comes, it will be time enough to go to Palestine. Meanwhile, I stay where God put me."

AT THE TIME of the new moon, dark outside and a late frost, a tap at the door, whispers in the blackness, a cry, quickly muffled.

The woman looked like a walking corpse, her skin gray, her bony nose jutting out between withered cheeks. At her skirt were two waifs, a girl about six years old, a boy of two or possibly three. Both sucked at their thumbs. The girl wept silently. The boy seemed to be examining his toes. Neither of them carried anything—not a toy, not a scrap of clothing. A sleeping infant was slung like a sack of flour over the woman's shoulder. With one fist she gripped its tiny feet, her forearm crossing a damp spot where her engorged breasts leaked milk onto the thin cotton blouse.

They had walked forty miles she said (that's fifty versts, Mischa whispered). They hadn't been long on the road when the soldiers took their shoes.

"Your shoes?"

She shrugged. There was nothing else left to give up.

"The children's shoes, too?" It was none too clear that the children would own shoes, poor as these people appeared. Still, for *Shabbes*.

Her head moved, the barest hint of a nod.

"Of what use, tell me, are a child's shoes to a soldier?"

The woman sighed. No one confided in her, least of all the Tsar's soldiers. "If it were me, I'd sell them to a peasant along the road. A few coins here, a few there...."

The little girl spoke up shyly. "The soldier laughed. First he looked at my feet, and then he laughed."

"*Shah*," said the woman. "Be quiet, you, and you'll learn something."

"But Mama, why did he laugh?"

"I told you why. What's the use of telling you one minute if you're only going to forget the next? He thought you'd have hoofs instead of feet. He was surprised, so he laughed."

"Jews have feet," said the little boy, emboldened by the success of the girl. "Just like people. Babies have feet, too. Mama has a baby."

It had been born along the road. She'd had trouble walking for several days and one afternoon had gone into labor. Before they could find her a barn or outbuilding, the pains had prevented her going any further. Within a matter of minutes, it seemed, the first twin had been delivered on a patch of grass by the side of the road, shielded only by a thicket of furze and gorse. A half hour or so later, the second twin had come, but it had lived only minutes. A few local women had stopped and, seeing her plight, run to the nearby village and brought a midwife, who took care of whatever needed taking care of. Then they'd given her and the children lodging overnight, but beyond that they were not prepared to do, fearing reprisals from the soldiers.

The walk to the frontier was not as long as the walk to where the babies had been born, and from there, they'd been given a ride here. It was a blessing, the help one Jew gave another. A blessing.

The woman had a brother-in-law who was first cousin to Mama's cousin far to the north in Grodno. Not exactly family, but close to it, so she could scarcely be turned away even though her husband was killed fighting for the Kaiser at Lemberg. Grodno, she reported, was in the hands of the Kaiser. "Tsar or Kaiser, either way, it's not good for the Jews," she said. "The Russians accuse us of being spies. And the Austrians coming back? They, too, will accuse us of spying—for the Russians! Any scrap that's left, they'll take."

THEY STAYED A week. On the eighth day of the infant's life, Papa organized a hasty *bris*, inviting in a handful of old men from the synagogue to welcome the child into the convenant with God. A little wine, a bit of cake, and it was over. Even the talk seemed hurried, a word about the war, a word about the refugees, who were being rounded up, sick and hale alike, and loaded onto trains to be transported east. Those who could claim relatives would be permitted to deboard in Kiev. The rest were to go on all the way to Voronezh, in Asia.

A bris should be a happy occasion, but Rivka felt bad for the poor little thing. Strangers were his godparents and a stranger his *sandek*, the one who had the honor of cradling him while the circumcision was performed. Then, the way that baby squealed! Nothing happy in that. Afterward she held him and let him suck at her finger, dipped in sweet wine.

"Can we keep him, Mama?"

"What? What do you mean can we keep him? Silly girl, Rivkeleh."

"Why not? Why can't we?"

"Because a baby goes with its family."

"But it'll die, like its twin."

"That, my child, is in God's hands, not ours."

Rivka turned angrily from Mama, fists balled, face prickly, and noticed the Galician mother peering at her from the corner, her narrowed eyes sharp and hard.

A POLICEMAN CAME to retrieve the family. The woman wept, the children wailed; the baby, wrapped up in swaddling head to toe, only the teeniest bit of dark fuzz peeking out of the blanket, mewled once and then fell silent. Rivka reached for him, one last kiss, but the mother jerked away and hurried out of the yard, not looking back, not saying goodbye, not even a thank you. "Wait, Mama!" the children called trotting after her in the dawn light. The yawning policeman brought up the rear.

Mama shook her head. "*Galitsianer,*" she said. "No class."

Later, Rivka went down to the shed to change the goat's bedding. The cat stirred when she entered, got up and came to her, meowing. She meowed back and went about her work. But the cat kept up her noise, rubbing herself against Rivka's legs, moving off, then returning, rolling herself in the new hay.

"Pest," Rivka said. "What do you want from me?"

The cat mewled, a sound so human Rivka's breath caught in her throat.

At the back of the empty stall, her kittens squirmed and shifted in their nest. A ghostly something glimmered above them, small whitish somethings snaking in the air. Rivka moved toward them. The baby lay on his back, naked in the midst of the kittens, arms and legs flailing about. He made small, barely audible noises in his throat.

What to do?

If she hurried, there might be time to get him to the train before it left. Loading the cars with hundreds of refugees takes time, and anyway the rails were full of troop transports, supply transports. It could take hours to travel only a few versts. If she hurried, she might make it. The woman must have calculated no one would visit the shed until evening, by which time the train would be far away. But Rivka had gone early to the chore to get away from Mama and the echoing house.

The child looked warm and cozy in his nest of soft fur. Rivka backed away on tiptoe. If he slept, he wouldn't cry. If he cried, she would come to him. Once the train was gone, his mother would have to keep the kitten she'd wrapped in his blanket, and they would have to keep him.

HIS NAME WAS David Yakov, and they called him Dudie for short. They hired a wet nurse, but as soon as he could sit up, Rivka had him weaned, arguing that she'd look after him better than any outsider could. When he sucked greedily at his hands, she rolled him pacifiers out of linen and soaked them in honey. Before he could crawl, she'd taught him to drink milk from a cup. He grew like a weed under her care. Soon enough, he was drawing himself up on sturdy little legs, moving about the room from one piece of furniture to the next. Rivka was afraid for him that he might pull the samovar over on himself and for some weeks would not allow it to be lit except when he slept.

Mischa, maybe a little jealous, said Rivka spoiled the child. Mama said he was too thin. Mama said Rivka should not become so attached to a scrunch-faced little monkey who was not her own. Mama might just as well have saved her breath, and Mischa, as well. Rivka knew that her Dudie was perfect. Still, she couldn't help being offended when passersby in the market merely smiled as he babbled at them—went on about their business and did not stand enthralled.

She sang as she went about her chores. When Dudie started following her into the yard, she slowed her pace to let him "help" her. Her work took hours that way, but Rivka didn't seem to mind. Mama and Papa stared open-mouthed. They had never seen Rivka so joyous. Mama had disliked the toddler stage, when one had to watch the children so closely, when the diapers stank and required endless scrubbing and boiling. Of course, Mama had had two to worry about at once, Mischa running off in one direction, Rivka in another. Only yesterday, it seemed. Now Dudie ran about, but Mama couldn't chase after. She felt stiff in the morning. She rose from her bed slowly, painfully, and shuffled about, bending and stretching her arms as she worked, trying to ease out the pain in her joints. She carried a deep sadness about with her, the sadness of old loss.

BY THE FALL of 1915, no one anymore was charging the Jews with spying. The catastrophe was just too huge. Millions of Russian soldiers lay dead. The Germans held a vast chunk of Russian land, their line running from Mitau in Lithuania south through White Russia and the Ukraine, through Pinsk, Dubno and Tarnopol to Czernowitz in Austria. "What a sad day for Mother Russia," Papa remarked, "when our glorious Russian soldiers are too demoralized to bother murdering, molesting and stealing from us Jews."

While Mischa studied, Rivka helped Mama bring food to those leftover refugees still camped in the fields. Sometimes she felt only sadness when they took the bread, tears coursing down their cheeks. Sometimes she felt apologetic at having good clothing, a stout roof over her head. What must it be like, she mused, to live in fear of the shells and, worse, to sleep under an implacable sky. Other times, Rivka wanted to kick them: the women who wheedled and whined; the children who knocked the kopeks from others' hands, all of them scrabbling in the dirt over the same coin when she gave enough for all. Then, the men with their stooped shoulders and lowered eyes. "Step on me" was written all over them, so who could blame the soldier who did, or the peasant? It was when she entertained these thoughts that Rivka felt most ashamed.

FLOUR BECAME HARDER to get in the second year of the war. Who knew the fighting would last so long? And longer yet, for the armies had dug in, and everywhere a stasis was taking hold, a paralysis. Wheat was hard to come by, and eggs, milk, everything. They were told the shortages were due to the armies in the field needing to be supplied. But close to the front as they were, word leaked back that the soldiers were not being fed well, and sometimes not at all.

Food was stolen right out of their kitchen one day while Mama was out back laundering. They assumed the culprit was one of those dog-hungry soldiers who'd come trudging through town in the morning. But war turns the world upside down, making beggars of rich men and rich men of beggars. Suspicion fell on Aaronsohn, Rachel's father, one of the intelligentsia. When Rivka used to play with Rachel, Aaronsohn would look up from his work and smile at her from his study, a small room right there in his house, with a writing desk and shelves full of books, journals and papers. He had edited one of those Yiddish newspapers, a socialist rag, Papa said, foolish nonsense from top to bottom and beginning to end. If you asked Papa, nothing in it could be trusted, not even the page numbers.

Every so often, Aaronsohn would call Rivka in and ask her questions. The first time he did this, her head barely reached the bottom corner of the lectern-like desk where he stood, a compact, mustachioed man with deep creases in his face. Did she think girls should be permitted into the *cheder*?

What did she know? She was just a child. Anyway, it was a matter of tradition and law, wasn't it?—not a matter of what she thought. Nevertheless, she began to form an opinion. And it was then that she'd asked her brother to teach her Torah, if he thought she could learn. This he did, using Mama's Yiddish *Tsenerenah.*

Early in 1915 the Tsar ordered all the Yiddish presses closed down. Within weeks, hundreds of publications across the Pale of Settlement, representing every conceivable political and spiritual platform, ceased to exist. A few went underground and kept publishing under new names. If Rachel knew that her father was involved in one of these, she didn't say. But one icy winter night, the police banged at Aaronsohn's door and took him away.

"Don't see Rachel anymore," Papa ordered.

"She's my friend, Papa."

"She's a danger."

"Who is? Little Rachel? What can she do to me?"

People who went away like Aaronsohn came back a shadow of themselves—or not at all. Aaronsohn returned from prison a broken man. The thief in Mama's kitchen turned out to be not Aaronsohn, who was probably incapable now of the energy or the courage it took to steal. No, the culprit was—Rachel.

Of all people, Rachel, reduced to petty thievery! As soon as Rivka knew this for a fact, she went in search of her friend. She looked high and low, at Aaronsohn's house, at the well, at the river, in the fields. In the cemetery she found her at last, bobbing and swaying in prayer over the grave of her grandmother.

"Rokheleh!"

The girl turned, frowned. "I don't want your pity, Rivka."

"And I don't want your baseless suppositions. I came to ask your help."

Rachel's eyes narrowed, but she said nothing.

"It's Dudie," Rivka said, taking for granted that Rachel would do anything for her darling boy. "I need help with him."

Icily, Rachel said, "You want to hire me for your dry nurse?"

They stared at one another, both shocked, each angrier than the other. For a good two minutes, neither of them moved. Then Rivka reached out her hand. "Come with me," she said. "I could use a friend to talk with while Dudie chases pigeons."

Who could resist such an offer?

Often, the girls were to be seen gabbing their way along the village streets, Dudie swinging between them from their outstretched hands. On specially fine days, you'd spot Rivka galloping, Dudie on her shoulders a-shriek with laughter and Rachel not far behind.

PAPA'S BUSINESS HAD never done better. The factory was kept open round the clock, Jews taking Shabbes off, Christians Sunday. Jews were known for making good boots. It was believed they had secret ways, arcane ways, of tanning leather and working it. The ignorant said they mastered the craft by magic in order to conceal their devil's hoofs. Papa's reputation in the art of boot-making stemmed partly from being a Jew; but also he had both the machinery to mass-produce boots for new recruits and the artisans to hand-make fine custom boots for officers. He himself made General Brusilov's boots by his own hand and brought them himself to Eighth Army Headquarters. No one else touched them. Brusilov was happy, Papa got huge contracts, and the business grew month by month until it became too big for him to handle alone, and someone in the family had to be brought in to help.

Mind you, Papa was still a member of the bootmakers' *chevrah*, who were all pledged to treat each other equally. So really, he should have asked the *chevrah* for the help he needed. Since the war, some of the other artisans had begun grumbling that he was getting too big for his britches. "Nothing's to be done," he said, throwing his hands up. He made the investment in the machinery and bore the risk, not they. Didn't he treat his workers fairly? No strikers here, no Bundists messing around. His employees put in ten-hour days, not fourteen or sixteen, like the bootworks up in Grodno (which in any case was behind enemy lines), and he paid them a decent wage, if not a lavish one.

Rivka turned out to be a capable bookkeeper. Mischa was hopeless, not from lack of ability, but from lack of interest. Papa didn't know this, though, and Mischa was careful to feign disappointment at not having inherited the head for numbers his sister had. A knack for languages was also an asset, he told Papa. Merely send him to school, let him learn foreign languages, and after the war he'd be able to help Papa expand the business to foreign lands. "Enough of the *cheder*. Enough of the *melamed*. Enough of Talmud and *pilpul*. Give me French and English and proper German, and we'll become the Rothschilds of the boot business."

Papa laughed. Papa's family had raised its share of rabbis and learned men, his own *tateh* a scholar of some renown. But Tateh died young, murdered in the upheavals of 1881-2, and Papa had refused further schooling, apprenticing himself at age ten to a bootmaker. Once, long ago, maybe he'd thought of a life of learning, but he had long since forgotten that dream. Brains were better put to use earning bread for the table and a good, solid roof over the family's head. Ideas, what were they good for, what did they bring but dissatisfaction with your lot and no way to improve it?

However, this idea of Mischa's might have some practicality in it. Papa put an ad in the newspaper offering tuition to the gymnasium to ten qualifying Christian boys, so that the quota requirements could be met. A *minyan* of *sheygitzes* stepped forward, and in the fall of 1915 Mischa was sent for secular schooling in Rovno. It was their first separation, and it would have gone hard for Rivka, left behind at home, had Dudie not been there demanding her attention with his feed me, change me, pick me up, put me down, comfort me, dress me, clean me, watch me, bathe me, talk to me, hear me, teach me, laugh with me, love me. All day, every day, his sweet imperiousness softened the blow.

That separation was followed, in the fall of 1916, by one more permanent, for Papa had ingratiated himself with Brusilov's staff. The General by then, two years into the war, headed up the entire southwestern front. So it was an easy matter to arrange the necessary bribes. Mischa was able to gain passage to Petrograd and entrance to the University, where places were more readily available because of the war. Everything these days, it seemed, was because of the war. If St. Petersburg became Petrograd, it was because of the war. If families were broken up, it was because of the war. If people got sick, it was because of the war. If they starved, it was because of the war. If they rioted and were shot, it was because of the war. And what was the war because of? Why, German-lovers. Traitors among the army's general staff. Traitors in the government. The Hunnish Tsarina herself, it was whispered, had a direct telephone line to her native land. How else could the fighting go on and on like this? How else could millions of Russian soldiers have died or been wounded, and yet still Germans were occupying Russian soil?

Their new servant girl, a Ukrainian peasant, told Rivka the war was all a plot to murder all of Russia's peasantry once and for all. "They're in on it together," she said, enumerating on her fingers. "The generals, the Duma, the nobility, the Tsarina and her lover, that mad pseudo-priest Rasputin." Only the Tsar was innocent. The Little Father was devoted to his people and would never do anything to harm them. "That is why he hasn't the heart to order the soldiers forward. That is the only reason why he hasn't driven the Germans out."

Rivka knew nothing about Rasputin. Ask anyone here, and you'd be told, "What does a Jew know about a priest?" But from Petrograd, Mischa wrote that he'd seen the mad monk, that the man was gigantic and had eyes like coals, dark and burning. That he had some sort of mysterious power over the Tsar and Tsarina. Some said it was because of the Tsarevich, who was sickly. Some said he was the Tsarina's lover. Some said he had many women among the aristocracy. Some said even filthier things, which he would not repeat.

IN DECEMBER OF 1916, Rasputin was assassinated by a group of nobles who were trying to save the monarchy from itself. The mad monk was a hard man to kill: they poisoned him, shot him, shot him again, then clubbed him before he was dead enough to be dumped into the River Neva. Through January and February, food riots and workers' strikes spread across the land. Petrograd was brought to a standstill. Marchers carrying red flags were joined there by the police detachments sent to disband them. In March of 1917, amid demonstrations so fierce and widespread that he was prevented from reaching the capital, the Tsar from his railroad car, having lost the support of his generals, abdicated his throne. Mischa sent home exclamatory letters. World-shaking things were happening. Rivka barely took note, consumed as she was with her child, let him live and be well.

With Mama's help, Rivka cleared the ground out back for a bed of vegetables. Food of any kind was so scarce. Even in the warming weather, even though you had the money to pay for it, you couldn't get what you needed for a growing boy. Rivka's periods stopped, and she worried: had she been impregnated by a dybbuk in an uneasy sleep one night? But Mama assured her that it was only the hunger, and when times became better, her monthlies would return.

Mama moaned quietly as she bent over the rows planting their precious seedlings, each one hard to come by. When she reached the end of the row and slowly straightened, a small whoosh of air escaped her, half-grunt and half-whine. She pushed her hair back, leaving a grainy streak of soil across her forehead. "I never expected to have to do this sort of thing again," she said. "I thought we were past all that, for good."

"I don't mind," Rivka said. She liked the smell of the moist, loamy earth in her nostrils. She liked the tiny, foreign world of insects one discovered beneath the surface, a world as oblivious of her as she had been of it only moments before she'd turned over the soil. She even liked the exertion of hard work, the trickle of sweat that made its way between her breasts.

"I wanted life should be different for you, Rivkeleh. I wanted—eh," she said, dismissing the thought with a swat of her hand. Wanting was a waste of time.

"You wanted?"

"That was my mistake."

"Yet you wanted *I* should want," Rivka teased.

Mama nodded. "For nothing," she said, turning the word game around. "I wanted you should want for nothing."

Rivka wanted for *something*, but what that something was she didn't know, and meanwhile she had Dudie filling her life.

ONE DAY, SHORTLY before the boy's second birthday, when Rivka and Dudie were outdoors working in the garden, Mama came to the back door, an odd look on her face. "Wash up," she said. "You and the child. And come inside. We have visitors."

Dudie wanted to stay outdoors. The sun was shining. The day was unseasonably warm. Birds were singing, all nature playing. Why should he be the only small creature required to go inside? This was the question she imagined couched behind his tragic expression as she led him, tearful, to the pump. His vocabulary was limited to the necessaries: Mama, Papa, Rivkeleh, Gitteleh, milk, bread, kasha, dog, cat, horse, soldier, more please, I want, this, that, and no. Just last Shabbes he had pointed to the slice of chicken on his plate. "Cut it," he ordered. Rivka was enchanted. Her boy's first sentence.

"Come along, Dudie," she told him now, after drying his face and smoothing down the thick hair that always stood straight up from the crown of his head.

"No," he said, but as she walked up the gentle slope to the back door he trailed after, grasping her skirt so that she pulled him with her.

The woman seated on the sofa looked familiar. A man stood behind her, one hand on her shoulder. The woman was very thin, her hands bony in her lap. Her hair had streaks of gray. The man's hair was mostly gray, what showed of it beneath his hat. His other hand held a cane. Injured, perhaps, in the war. He wore western-style clothing, old but in good condition.

The woman gave a cry when she saw the boy, and that's when Rivka recognized her. She looked older, careworn, but her clothing and hair were well ordered; and unlike the last time, she seemed to be in possession of herself and her surroundings.

"My boy," she said, spreading her arms out to him. "Come, my Yankeleh."

Yankeleh? He'd had no such name when she left him, only ten days old.

"We call him Dudie," Mama said.

The boy huddled closer to Rivka.

"That's not right," said the woman.

"Come here, Dudie," Mama said. "This is your *mameleh*. Give her a kiss, little one."

Dudie stared at her, perplexed. Mama was mama, not that other lady. And his mameleh, his little mother, could only be Rivka, whose skirts he clung to more tightly, who laid her cold palm against his cheek.

"Where are your children?" Rivka's voice a knife in the room.

"My *others*? They are well," replied the mother. "They are both waiting at the train station with their aunt, the sister of Mr. Korngold."

Mama matched her formality, her ceremoniousness. "How good to hear you are all well. It must have been a long journey."

"This is Mr. Korngold," she said, indicating him with a lift of her chin. The man nodded. "I am Mrs. Korngold now. We were wed in Voronezh, thousands of versts from here. But we are here now."

"You cannot return home to Austria, you know. You'd have to cross the line of battle."

"What battle?" scoffed Mr. Korngold. "I've heard there's no fighting anymore. All is friendship and camaraderie among the troops in the field. Only the governments continue to wage war."

"I've come to collect my Yankeleh."

Rivka sank to her knees, arms shielding the child. Collect him? Like a package?

"I can see you have taken excellent care of him," the woman went on, "for which you have my undying gratitude. If he had come with us to that far-off place, surely he'd have perished."

The boy felt Rivka's breath riffle his hair, and he squirmed. "Outside," he said.

"Shall I take you outdoors, little fellow?" said Korngold. He had a mild voice and a benign face, but his cane frightened the child. "Come," he coaxed. "I won't touch you. See if you can follow me." He meandered out of the room and zigzagged through the hall toward the front door. The boy ran after.

"Dudie," cried Rivka. And more urgently, "Dudie!"

"Let him go," Mama said.

"You've been most kind," the woman said, rising. "Someday, perhaps, I may be able to repay you."

"Nonsense," said Mama.

"Nonsense," echoed Rivka. "Pay us for what? Isn't he ours? Isn't he my son? Then why pay us? It was kind of you to visit on your way through. I'm sure it makes you content to see us so well ordered here, so jolly a little group. We're such a happy little family."

The two women stared at her.

"The boy is thriving here. We are his family. We're such a happy little family."

"Daughter," Mama's voice, low and controlled, strove against Rivka's rising hysteria. "Rivkeleh, we knew this day had to come, sooner or later. I warned you of its coming."

"No. No, no."

"Get his things."

"What are you saying?"

The woman was straightening her hat. "No need," she said. "We'll manage without them."

"He has a favorite doll," explained Mama. "A little stuffed donkey. It will comfort him."

"Really, we must be going. The train, you see. Heaven knows when another might come through."

"But he's too young. Where are you taking him? It's too dangerous. Leave him with us until you're settled," pleaded Rivka, thinking, *I'll take him somewhere with me, and you'll never find us. Never.* "The war will end soon, travel will be so much safer. After you settle in, you can come back for him." Thinking, *Papa will help me. Not even Mama will know where we are. Only Mischa. I will need Papa's help to get false papers, but only Mischa will know where we are.*

Like some gypsy fortuneteller, the woman squinted right through her, saying, "You will have children of your own someday."

Then they were gone, and Rivka was in Mama's arms, shrieking.

FOR DAYS AFTERWARD, she couldn't get out of bed. Mama brought tea and toast, which lay on the tray uneaten. Papa came in after work and sat by the bed, reciting in excruciating detail what had happened at the factory—what orders had been received and what completed, what shipments had gone out and what supplies had come in, what the workers were up to and what rumors arrived with soldiers from the front. She rolled over, giving him her back.

"*Maideleh*," he cajoled. "This is not reasonable. This is not healthy. The child is where he belongs, and you have a life yet to live."

A life without Dudie? No thanks. She wept silently, remembering the way the boy had of taking her face between his moist hands to fix her attention on him alone, the little monkey, the *vantz*. Remembering his joy when Purim came—just because of its special name, Purim—not even knowing he would be given sweets or dressed in costume. The crown they made together for his small, beautiful head: Dudie the king. Dudie her sweetest life. Dudie, who belonged with her, not with strangers. How could Papa be so cold-hearted?

None of this did she say. Papa touched her shoulder. She shrugged him off. Sighing, he heaved himself to his feet and wandered away.

A pall fell over the house, a grim, empty stillness. "After a few weeks, when Rivka has cried herself out," Papa told Mama, "you'll see how things will improve." They gave her far more time than that and more leeway than anyone advised. The neighbors advised ordering her back to work, willing or unwilling. The *rebbetzin*, who brought a pot of soup, advised turning Rivka over to her to help with charitable work among the refugees. As Papa predicted, Rivka finally cried herself out; but still she wouldn't get up. True, there was no strength in her refusal. They could easily have lifted her up and set her on her feet. She'd only have slumped to the floor.

Every few days Rachel came by with armfuls of wildflowers. The aroma of the meadows on her clothing and in her billowy red hair was a repeated invitation that was just as repeatedly refused. "Rivka, I miss you," Rachel begged, but Rivka only stared up at her, uncomprehending. Every day, Mama asked Rivka for help—in kneading the bread, say, or soaking and salting the Shabbes roast. Finally, one late-April day Mama sat down beside her and said, "You think I don't know how you feel? You think no one has ever suffered what you suffer?"

Rivka barely shrugged. It mattered little to her what Mama thought.

"Look around you, Rivkeleh. What do you see?"

She picked at her quilt, avoiding Mama's probing eyes.

"You see life, little one. You see people coming and going. Dozens of people pass our front window every day. How many of them, do you think, have never experienced any loss?

"Look at you. Never went through a pogrom, never sent your Papa to war, or your brother. You've never been alone, not even in the womb. You have people who love you, and those who don't have not invaded your house to harm you."

At this, she roused. "They have, too! They took away my baby."

"He is still alive, yes? And with people who'll care for him, is that not so?"

"What difference does it make, since I can't see him?"

Her mother's eyes flashed. "You've lived in this house fifteen years, and you ask me that? You think you're the only one? In your whole life have you ever once wondered how I felt when your two elder sisters died? Their names you asked, and what color eyes they had. And that's all. That's all you ever wanted to hear, so you don't know how sweetly they played together, laughing and running in the sunshine, some silly game about farmers and their cows. Skipping in the light one day, dead three days later, both of them, Chaya and Zipporah.

"Lost to me forever, you understand. They are not somewhere in the world, they are not with people who are caring for them. They're buried under the earth, and if I want to see them, I will have to wait for the world to come. And what if I had taken to my bed then? What if I had left your Papa high and dry, given up on life?"

She had never spoken like this to Rivka. She'd hardly breathed a word about the two girls who died of diphtheria before the twins were ever born. "I haven't given up on life, Mama."

"What, then? I certainly don't see you living it."

"I can't face the long days without Dudie."

"*Vey is mir*, I know. Don't I know? But if I had let myself give in to that, you and Mischa would never have been born. And if I could have more children, believe me, I'd have more. Two, six, ten more, and I'd love them just as if I'd never heard of diphtheria. Or typhus, or cholera, or pneumonia, or scarlet fever, or consumption. I'd love them as if I'd never heard of losing."

"Why, Mama? Why?"

"What else is there to do? Is yours a better idea?"

"With Dudie, I thought God had given me a purpose in this world."

"Perhaps he has. If so, you must go out and find it."

They came to an agreement then that Rivka would get up out of bed—though she continued to protest. After all, what was the point? There was nothing she wished to do.

"Make believe," Mama told her. "Act as if you cared about what you're doing, and maybe you will come to care."

Mama and her bromides. Mama and her *bubba mayses*. But Rivka did get herself up and go with Papa to the factory. There wasn't as much to do there as she'd been led to expect. In her absence, Papa had hired an office boy who turned out to have a head for numbers, though his bookkeeping entries looked like chicken scratches in the dirt. She didn't like this fellow, Shaul, any more than she liked his handwriting. With his matted hair and cold eyes, he reminded her of a buzzard. But the work he did was careful and accurate. In no time, Rivka had brought the books up to date. "So much for needing me," she chided Papa.

"My darling girl, I will always need you."

Watchful Shaul parroted the sentiment. "We will always need you."

A LETTER ARRIVED from Mischa. Glorious things were happening in the New Russia now that the old autocracy was gone. The world would never be the same. At last, at long last, justice and freedom and the rights of the masses would prevail over greed and pettiness and the excesses of an entrenched aristocracy. He was privileged to be at the center of everything new. He felt grateful to Papa for having arranged to send him to Petrograd to be educated. It was wrong (he knew that now) to have gotten his place at the University the way he had, by influence and bribery. No disgrace to Papa, for admittedly it had been he, Mischa, who begged and cajoled and wheedled until Papa had no choice but to get him enrolled by whatever means possible. And of course, that was according to the rule of the Old Russia. All was new now, and everything would be different under the Provisional Government. It was wonderful to be in Petrograd, where the world was being transformed.

He had seen the foremost revolutionary leaders and heard them speak. He had seen the Prime Minister of the Provisional Government, Prince Lvov, and the Minister of Justice, Alexander Kerensky. He had heard Leon Trotsky, who was a Jew, did Papa know this? And he had heard this man Lenin, who had a bold new vision for the future. When Lenin spoke, the deepest yearnings of Mischa's heart issued from the great man's lips. Last night, at the Finland Station when this prophet stepped off the train into the arms of his countrymen, what a celebration it had been, flags flying, workers and students and soldiers and sailors rejoicing together at the homecoming. If only Papa could have been there beside him to witness it.

Would Papa come? Mischa was fainting for news from home. He'd had no letter for six weeks or more. Not unusual, with the trains busy at the front. The trains were overcrowded. He'd heard of mailbags being thrown off the cars into ditches alongside the tracks to make room for soldiers, for refugees. Deserters, too, would climb aboard and pitch out the mail, hiding themselves in corners behind the other remaining sacks. Who could blame them? Why would anyone want to fight this senseless war?

Did Papa think he could come? The factory would do fine without him. The men were skilled laborers, after all, and could take responsibility for their own welfare and the interests of the business. All Papa need do was allow them to organize a committee to run things. Then he could come to Petrograd and join Mischa. Oh, the things he would see! The things Mischa could show him. The world was being made new.

Rivkeleh could work with the factory committee. He knew she would be good at that, bringing about a consensus, smoothing ruffled feathers. Rivka had always been the family's peacemaker. How he missed his sister. How he missed everyone.

The more Papa read, the darker his face became, shading from pink to red to dark purple, until Mama demanded he stop before it killed him. Papa crumpled the letter and threw it to the floor. Then he spat at it.

"In my house?" Mama shrieked. "Are you crazy?"

Without a word, Papa stalked out. Rivka, frozen, watched him go.

Mama bent painfully and picked up the crumpled letter. "Young men always want something new," she said, smoothing it out against the ample aproned shelf of her bosom. "If it's new, they think it's a virgin, all innocence and dewy eyes." Carefully she folded the letter and slipped it into her pocket. "And they're forever getting surprised when the new thing turns out to have the moral character of an old whore."

Whore! It was not a nice word she used, no euphemism but a filthy word. Rivka hadn't ever thought about Mama knowing such a word, and here she was using it in connection with Mischa. She'd begun acting queerly, too, pacing about the kitchen, clattering pots, clacking spoons. But nothing was getting cooked.

"What will Papa do?"

"Whatever he wants," Mama said. "Nothing I say will make the slightest difference now." She began scouring a pot that already gleamed.

"He'll go, then?"

Mama stared at her. "Of course not. Where is your sense? Of course he won't go."

"Then there's no cause to worry," Rivka said. Mama was silent, scouring. "Is there, Mama?"

"Fool!" Mama said. "The boy must be brought to his senses."

Rivka's heart sank. What if they tried to force Mischa's return? What if Papa stopped sending him money? Would Mischa give in? Or would he openly defy them, causing a rift in the family?

"Mama," she said. "Please don't make Mischa come home."

"It's out of my hands," Mama said, starting to weep.

"He won't do it. You understand? He'll find a way to stay in Petrograd without Papa's help." He had secured a position with Mrs. Emmeline Pankhurst. The great British feminist was on a mission to Russia, needed an interpreter, and Mischa had volunteered. But if he made the request, perhaps she would pay him, and he could support himself.

Mama nodded. "Papa knows he'll refuse. I won't be able to convince him otherwise."

Relief flooded Rivka. "Then Mischa is safe there."

Mama heaved a sigh as dark and dank as a tomb. "Which is why, Rivkeleh my daughter, he will send you there to Mischa instead."

III

Yashka

THE AIR WAS electric. The great Mariynski Theatre was filled to capacity, and the buzz of people seemed barely containable within its walls. Rivka turned her face left, right, upward at the ceiling, not knowing what to take in first: the ornate decoration; the rich draperies and upholstery that had only months ago been the trappings of the wealthy and powerful; or the people themselves, such a mix, soldiers and civilians, nobles and peasants, Bolshevists, Menshevists, and others representing dozens of splinter groups, arguing with one another, heckling. Outside, some Red Guard tried to keep people from entering. Red Guard were everywhere in Petrograd. A city of four hundred bridges, and Red Guard posted at every one of them. Sometimes a lone sentry stood watch at the foot of the bridge; sometimes a clump of them lounged in the middle of the bridge, seemingly at leisure, laughing over some remark the passerby couldn't quite catch.

At the Church on Spilled Blood some idlers had heckled Rivka and her brother. They'd been on foot crossing in front of that majestic structure erected at the very spot where in 1881 Tsar Alexander II had been assassinated. She'd stopped dead in amazement at the breathtaking sight of it, its luminous mosaics and soaring onion domes of blue and gold. Mischa immediately began explaining. One legacy of the murder, he said, had been this dazzling shrine. It was a sumptuous vision. Rivka's eyes couldn't stop feasting. The other, he said, had been a nasty wave of pogroms in which their own grandfather had perished, and a reinstatement of harsh laws against Jews. Rivka murmured, "*Farshtopt*, Mama would call this place." Cluttered.

"True, and since when is Mama a judge of architecture?"

As they laughed together, at Mama's expense, there came a taunt, "What do you think you're looking at, Jew-boy?" followed by a cuffing across Mischa's shoulder.

Five ruffians made a tight circle around the twins. "Who gave you permission to look at our church?"

Their ringleader stepped closer. He was half a head taller than Mischa and broader, though about the same age. He wore a torn and dusty infantry tunic above wide peasant trousers and felt boots, all too warm for this fine May evening. His face was flushed. Along the right side, a livid scar ran out of his scalp and down past his jawline, where it disappeared behind his collar. "Nothing to say? Go around killing saints, killing God, and nothing to say? Don't kill Germans, though, do you? No, not you. Too good for that. Stinking draft dodger and his stinking slut." His fists had begun to clench and unclench, limbering up for a fight.

Quietly, Mischa said, "Rivka, let's go." He took her arm. The ring of boys closed in.

At that moment a couple of Red Guard—just two of them, with bright new insignia and shiny new caps—called, "Halt!" in a voice so commanding that the boys dropped their fists and stiffened into an attitude of attention. Without exactly pushing the ringleader aside, the rescuers somehow managed to insinuate themselves into his circle. "There are no Jews in the New Russia. No foreign nationalities, no ethnic minorities, no invidious distinctions. We are all equal."

"We are all hungry," mimicked one of the hooligans.

"We are all poor," added a second.

"We all have an equal right to be hungry and poor."

"Because we are fighting a bourgeois war," said one of the Red Guard, while the other moved aside and allowed Mischa and Rivka to escape unharmed.

Red Guard were conspicuously absent in the audience at the Mariynski tonight. Maybe they had been prevented entrance, for fear of a brawl. Unlike the Mensheviks, who thought the first job of the new government was to rid Russia of every last German occupier, the Bolshevik Red Guard were unwilling to wait longer for the people's reforms while Russia pursued a bloodsucking imperialist war. Yet how could even they not be proud of tonight's speaker, Maria Leontievna Bochkareva, the woman known as Yashka? Whatever one's opinion about ending the war, all Russia must admire the young peasant who, in 1914, when a wave of patriotism had swept the country, asked for and obtained the Tsar's permission to join the army as a common soldier. A woman! Not possible, one would have thought, and yet she had toughed it out: trudging to the front, climbing out of the trenches and fighting alongside the other soldiers, receiving medals for bravery under fire on the battlefield. Wounded several times, she'd recovered and returned to the front, been made a corporal and earned the respect of her men. And not a word of scandal or shame ever attached to her name. A hero of Russia. A woman.

The loud buzz in the room died as a figure stepped out onto the platform, a small man of about fifty in a western-style business suit. The lighting in the hall was not gentle to his face. In fact, he resembled a corpse, drawn and pale, his eyes sunken in their sockets. One arm rested in a sling from a wound suffered on a visit to the Front. It was Alexander Fyodorovich Kerensky himself, there at the podium. A hush settled in the room, interrupted by a few catcalls and then tumultuous cheering. Kerensky, now Minister of War, had so far refused any concession to those who demanded immediate peace and immediate land reform. He spoke only briefly while Rivka marveled that he should be up there at all. A great man, and he takes the time to talk to *lemeshkes* like me. This must be what is meant when they say the government is to be of the people and responsible to the people.

His wife was introduced. She meant to raise funds for the Home for Invalids, but no sooner did she begin her tribute to the brave patriots bearing arms at the front than hecklers in the audience started in on her. She did not last long in the face of it.

And then Bochkareva appeared—tall, broad and solid, like a tree growing through the floorboards. Her uniform was spic-and-span, the medals on her breast glimmering in the light. Her dark hair was cropped short around a square face. Small, almond-shaped dark eyes looked steadily out at the crowd. Some applauded. A number of them jeered. Her chin quivered. It had a cleft in it, Rivka noticed, and it quivered. Bochkareva stepped forward, to the very edge of the stage. There was a thickness about her in movement, as if everyone else on earth might be made of Swiss cheese, she of Gouda.

"Why do you taunt me?" she cried in a voice rich as cream. "I am the same as you. I am Yashka, a mere peasant girl from a small village in the steppe. I am nothing to waste your gibes on." The vast hall went silent. "I am only here because my mother is perishing and I must save her. I must save her or die trying!" The trill in her voice ran through the crowd like an electric current. Rivka was at the edge of her seat, spellbound. "My mother is Russia. Can you not hear her in her throes? Will you abandon her? Women of Russia, tonight I speak to you, to you whose hearts are crystal, whose souls are pure and whose impulses are lofty. For three long years your men have fought valiantly in the field. They are weary and heartsick, but I have toiled at their side, shared the mud and the blood, and I know their worth. Tonight, an evil enemy occupies our land, stalks our villages and homes. Women citizens of Russia, join with me, serve with me in this grave hour. We shall have our own battalion. We shall be called the Battalion of Death. And we shall set such a noble example of self-sacrifice that our men, the indomitable armies of Russia, will rise up as one to do their duty to rid our land of this, this...." The woman faltered, passion clogging her throat. Without willing it Rivka stood, hungry for the words to roll on. All around her, people were rising to their feet. The woman gave a great wrenching sob and threw her hands up, unable to go on. The audience burst into cheers clapping their hands and stamping their feet, and Bochkareva stood like a tree before them, eyes glistening, arms stretched out toward them all.

Fifteen hundred women volunteered for enlistment that very night.

Rivka was not one of them.

"But why not?" demanded Mrs. Pankhurst at tea the following afternoon. "This will be the greatest deed in any army on any front of the greatest war in history. If anything can save Russia now, this Battalion will. And Rivka, my dear, it will strike a blow for the rights and powers of women that your daughters and granddaughters and great-granddaughters will speak of with reverence. History is being made, and you decline to go?"

Mischa put out a hand to prevent his sister from answering. "There is no point in her going, Mrs. Pankhurst, with all due respect to your mission here to keep Russia in the war for the sake of Britain and its allies. And that includes the new American allies if and when they ever get around to actually fielding an army. No, I believe the Bolshevist cause will prevail—and soon. My sister is not a reactionary warmonger and will not become one."

Mrs. Pankhurst's eyes sought Rivka's and would not let them go. Though the Englishwoman's face was faded and soft with age, the keenness of youth glittered in her eyes. Frail she might be, and seemingly harmless in her pale pink linen suit, but Mrs. Pankhurst was a force to be reckoned with. "I think," she said quietly, "that your sister will decide for herself. Won't you, my dear?"

Gruffly, grudgingly, Mischa translated. Rivka nodded, a short quick dip of her head.

"Michael, let us hear from Rivka what it is she will do in the New Russia."

"I no longer wish to translate."

"Then I shall find another to do it."

"And my sister will no longer visit. I ask you not to visit her."

Rivka observed their growing rigidity. She touched Mrs. Pankhurst's arm. "*Zhid*," she said through her teeth, choosing the word that was an epithet, not mere description.

The older woman caught the bitterness passing between them, sister and brother. "*Zhid*? She is afraid, is she, that, being Jewish, she'll not be welcomed into the Battalion? Afraid she'll be rebuffed, even mistreated?"

And that's how Rivka found herself the next morning in front of Bochkareva in an office at the Kolomensk Women's Institute, which was being transformed pell-mell into a training camp for Yashka's volunteers, whose ranks had swelled in less than twenty-four hours to two thousand women. University students, peasants, professionals, nobility—all wished to serve, wholly ignorant of what they were letting themselves in for.

They were given a physical examination. Some failed, most passed since the standards were anything but stringent. If they had the wherewithal to climb up out of a trench and advance toward the enemy, that was sufficient. Next came an interview devised to impress upon them the seriousness of the task before them, the indispensable necessity for strictest discipline, the unacceptability of any flightiness, any smallest sign of flirtatiousness that might bring down shame upon the Battalion. More failed, most passed. When Rivka arrived at eight in the morning, squads of the chosen were forming up on the grassy square of the Institute and learning to march across it.

Mischa, having forbidden Rivka to come, learned he lacked the power over her he thought he had. Now he trailed behind, staring openly at the tramping girls. One of them stopped to stare back—and was promptly dismissed, ordered by the officer in charge to pack her things and leave on the instant.

Rivka's fear melted under Bochkareva's bewitching smile. The woman's face was anything but beautiful; in repose it held all the flintiness of the Russian steppe. But the sun in her smile annihilated any least harshness. A girl could dwell in that radiance alone. Or in the mere hope of bringing it out once more.

"My first job was with a Jewess," Bochkareva told her. "A strict taskmistress. I was only a tyke, eight or nine years old, and she worked me hard. I stayed with her almost six years, until my marriage." She paused, as if bemused at having ever been fifteen years old, and a newlywed. "That woman taught me everything worthwhile I've ever learned," she said.

"That's your reason?" Mischa sneered. "A Jew befriended you? Or, pardon me, Your Excellency, was it you who befriended the Jew?"

Rivka threw him a withering look. She had once been his protector. Now he was trying to be hers. What a terrible job of it he was doing, embarrassing himself and her.

"If you only knew," said the soldier. "I was wounded a year ago fighting the Austrians at Lutsk. I was paralyzed—for months no better than a log, lying there, day after day, unable to move even my little finger or my little toe. Only my restless thoughts moved, trying to escape from the horrible unmovingness of my body. My doctor was a Jew, a man of sterling heart, an angel sent from Heaven. He saved me."

I do know, thought Rivka, for I, too, have suffered a paralyzing wound at the hand of an Austrian: the loss of my dear little boy. That horrid woman who took Dudie away from me left me in darkness, hurt and unable to move and not even hoping for an angel to save me.

Yashka drenched Rivka in her sudden smile. She said, "There are some who will tell you they have nothing against the Jews. I will tell you, I have something *for* the Jews. If you will join me, I will…." She stopped, pondered, shrugged her heavy shoulders. "I cannot promise you safety. I cannot promise you anything, except the opportunity to do something great."

Rivka glanced across the room at Emmeline Pankhurst, who nodded, though none of their conversation in Russian had been translated into English. All Rivka had ever asked from God was the opportunity to do something great. "*Da*," she said. "If you will have me, I will join."

"Rivkeleh," Mischa moaned. "Ah, Rivkeleh, you are ten times a fool."

RIVKA WAS IN paradise. What does paradise look like? In her eyes, a barracks room with narrow cots, each occupied by a new recruit who had had her hair shorn by a barber, been issued her kit and told to get some rest. Rivka laid out her kit on the cot. It consisted of two complete undergarments of coarse linen, two pairs of foot rags, one laundry bag, one pair of boots (manufacturer uncertain), one pair of khaki trousers, one belt, one regulation blouse, one pair of epaulets, one cap with insignia, two cartridge packets and a rifle.

She couldn't get any rest. None of them could. At exactly 10 PM lights went out, but the chatter went on, an exchange of nicknames, of personal and family histories, of hopes, fears, questions. To Rivka's left was a petite blond woman of twenty-eight or thirty with three moles dotting her chin. Her name was Natalia Danilova Klipatskaya.

"A lawyer? You practice law?"

"I do." Her open expression was as intelligent as it was friendly.

"Truly?"

"Why do you doubt it?"

Why, indeed. Because for a Jewish girl such an occupation was completely out of the question. The government's quota for Jewish lawyers was so small that even if the education were possible—which it wasn't, for you'd have to leave the country to get it, a maiden alone in Germany or France, or God-knows-where—even if you could get the education, when you came back with your diploma, everyone would be against you for taking a prized position from some male law student, pride of his family. And anyway, what would you do practicing law when your babies came, or your mother-in-law got old and needed care?

To her right slept a princess. Now, say it again, Rivka. Close your eyes and repeat slowly to yourself: *To my right sleeps a princess*. Her name is Tatuyeva, and she's from Tiflis, and she is sleeping in the next bed, except she's not asleep at all, no, at the moment she's perched cross-legged on her blanket swapping jokes with the girl in the bed on the far side.

Occupying the bed opposite Rivka was Olga Stepanova, a girl about sixteen, Rivka's age, a student of ballet. "Perfect turnout," she explained, demonstrating. Her feet made a single straight line, her toes pointing toward opposite walls. As a skinny child of eight, Olga had been brought to live at the Kirov. The years since were dedicated to the effort to become weightless, as light as air in the spotlight on stage, and as voiceless. Only in the last month did she learn that she'd never become a prima ballerina after all, for she'd grown too tall. Then, two nights ago, at the Mariynski—"like a bolt from the blue, Rivka,"—there stood Bochkareva, heavy-footed, throaty-voiced. Womanhood was revealed to Olga in its true beauty: not air and water, but earth and fire. "Our Yashka has waged war and survived. Our Yashka has suffered wounds and survived. Me, I've merely learned how to dance. If I'm to be part of a corps all my life, let it not be a corps de ballet. Let it be an army corps."

Thought Rivka, this is what I've been waiting for without even knowing it. This is the path my heart chose years ago, though the path seemed eternally blocked. She remembered the awful clarity of that moment when she perceived that her yearnings never could, never would be fulfilled. This was why she'd burst into tears at Mischa's Bar Mitzvah. This was why she'd fled from the synagogue and vomited into the snow: Mischa stood on the *bimah* chanting, his new *tallis* draping his thin shoulders, and she foresaw him leaving her for the world of men, leaving her behind and invisible, as if hidden from the great world by a latticed window.

Rivka found herself confiding it all in Olga, a perfect stranger until that hour. Her brother chanted his haftorah brilliantly, portraying the lives and fates of three women, Devorah, Yael and a nameless mother, using a different voice for each one of them. Without ever missing a word or mistaking a trope, Mischa unrolled the story in his clear tenor voice: how the prophetess Devorah directed the warrior Barak to attack Sisera, captain of the Canaanites; how Barak refused to move against a host of chariots without Devorah along; and how her judgment for this failure of courage came upon him in a stunning prophecy. Mischa's Devorah was solemn, strong in command, meting out justice. *The Lord will give Sisera over into the hand of a woman*, he intoned.

For the voice of Yael, Mischa sang higher, loud and sassy, mimicking Rivka's friend Rachel. Rachel was all innocence, yet flirtatious too, and that's how Mischa's Yael behaved with the enemy leader Sisera as he escaped on foot from the battlefield, the sole survivor of the rout of his army. *Turn in, my lord. Fear not,* wheedled Mischa's Yael.

Rifka's friend Rachel with her sweet, compliant nature would never do what Yael did next. All warmth and welcome, Rachel would have left Sisera in the peace of his deep sleep and sent him on his way in the morning with some apples and a loaf of warm bread wrapped up in a cloth for the road. Mischa's Yael had steel inside her, something hard and bright at the core. In the story, she brought the man warm milk, covered him with a rug, smiled and nodded when he instructed her to stand guard at the door of the tent. Then she crept up on him in the night with a tent pin in one hand and a hammer in the other.

How often Rivka had rehearsed this scene in her mind! "Imagine Yael there just beforehand," she told Olga. "She kneels above the enemy's sleeping body, she listens to his deep, steady breathing in the darkness. She wonders, can she do it? Will she do it? She mouths a little prayer for courage, sucks in her breath. And now, she pounds the tent peg home through the soft spot in Sisera's temple. Straight through his head goes the point of the pin, all the way into the ground." Rivka's arm slashed earthward. "*Yael, blessed above women*, as the reading says."

"Amen," breathed Olga.

"Not yet amen." It wasn't over, not for Sisera's mother. Mischa would have done her like an old crone, a screechy puppet in a gypsy show with a winking eye and a wart on her nose. Rivka almost wet herself laughing when he practiced it. But Mama said think of the poor woman waiting for her son to come home from war, so he softened his reading. Still, some in the congregation sniggered when he got to the part where she peered through her latticed window crying, *Why is his chariot so long in coming?*; hoping they're tarrying to divide up the spoils; waiting without end for the return that would never come. At the Bar Mitzvah, it was then that the tears welled in Rivka's eyes and the gorge rose in her throat—not for the fate of Sisera's mother, but for what she felt must be her own fate, stuck at home while Mischa moved on without her.

Rivka shuddered now at the very idea. How awful to be a helpless female waiting in vain for your man to come home.

Olga tossed her barbered head. "You and I, we're soldiers in the Russian Imperial Army, commanded by the least helpless and most magnificent of women. From Yashka we'll learn how to live and how to die."

FIVE AM ARRIVED before anyone expected it, before it had any right to come. Someone shook her roughly and moved on. Groans from nearby. She'd been dreaming of Mischa, of that long ago summer when they'd sneaked off and gone swimming together in the river in their underthings; except in her dream they were grown, and Mischa was muscled and hairy, bulging in his underthings, and at first she thought the groans must be his or hers—but then someone shook her, and she opened her eyes and sat up with a start.

It was the Princess Tatuyeva shaking her. "We're to be on the parade ground in fifteen minutes."

Not much of a parade ground, merely the garden of the Institute. They were lined up in rows and inspected, first by the men from the Volynsky Regiment who were their drill sergeants, and when those forty were satisfied, then by Bochkareva herself, who assured them they would become soldiers. Since she had, they all would, even though they felt awkward and unsure of themselves now. On *her* first morning, she said, she had donned her trousers inside out!

Tall and straight, Rivka stood rigidly at attention. Bochkareva nodded as she passed by. "Good," she said.

We Jews are a stiff-necked race, thought Rivka. Finally, that's a good thing.

The physical strain of training all day was harder on the students and professional women than on the peasant girls, but by day's end even the peasant girls were exhausted, and no one cared that they weren't allowed out in the evening. No one Rivka was aware of, anyway. Who had any energy left to venture off the grounds after marching and running and crawling and bending and lifting and scrubbing and polishing and so on and so on?

As days passed, there were whispers, of course, of this one or that one sneaking out, but only in one case was a girl sent packing for violating curfew. You could be sent packing for other such infringements, for flirting, for the slightest scent of looseness in dress or character or comportment. Nothing was minor where the honor of the Battalion was at stake. Bochkareva would tolerate none of it.

Ordinary infringements of military law might bring anything from hours of extra guard duty to a sharp slap across the cheek from Bochkareva's graceless hand. A girl from Rivka's barracks, Maria Ivanova Medzvedova, was slapped for complaining about their meager rations of kasha and milk. "At the front," Bochkareva scolded her, "men sometimes go three and four days with nothing at all to eat. Being female, you are of course weak, but you must not imagine this as a time of hardship. It is anything but." Medzvedova tried to apologize. Bochkareva silenced her. "Hardship enough will come. You will prepare yourself for it." Half-rations were the girl's lot for the next three days.

Rivka was never slapped, nor even reprimanded. She took to soldiering naturally, as did Princess Tatuyeva, who was fast becoming her best friend Tatya. "Agile" was the word she brought to Rivka's mind. Her body, compact and womanly, moved with easy grace. Her face, with its imperially prominent nose, registered every passing thought or feeling, and her mind bounced from subject to subject, nimbly forming opinions on every topic under the sun. Though Rivka was careful to conceal her Jewishness in general, she made a point of not hiding it from the princess lest she be accused of secrecy, of slyness, and punished. Tatya, though, seemed not to think much of it, one way or the other. "I am not one of those backward Romanovs," she said.

It certainly was a new Russia, Mischa was right about that.

ONE DAY, RIVKA received a summons to see the Commander. She was training out in the garden, lunging with a bayonet, when the order came. *What have I done? Am I to be sent packing?* She rubbed the sweat from her face and neck, smoothed her uniform, and with quaking knees hurried to Bochkareva's office.

Mrs. Pankhurst was visiting. They were taking tea in the English manner. As Rivka entered, Bochkareva was eating a sweetmeat with all the exaggerated delicacy of a woman unused to Sunday best: her pinkie in the air, the little morsel daintily held between thumb and forefinger, then launched with a flourish into her upturned open mouth. She sipped at her tea, a faint lapping sound as if her tongue was unsure how to do its duty without a cube of sugar between the teeth, straining the hot brew. Mrs. Pankhurst, of course, had asked how many lumps and then dropped the three directly into Bochkareva's cup. The provisions must have been Mrs. Pankhurst's.

Rivka couldn't help staring. No one in Russia had seen sugar or cakes or even tea in months, the lower classes not in years.

Taking no notice of Rivka, Bochkareva said to the Englishwoman, "I'm only a peasant girl, raised in a small village out on the Siberian steppe near Tomsk. My father was born a serf. I never went to school, and there is much I have never learned. But a hard life has schooled me, and this I do know." Her demanding eyes sought Mrs. Pankhurst's and held them. Her voice hardened. "This I do know. The common Russian soldier will fight. He will fight harder and longer and fiercer than anyone, with the fierceness of his love for Mother Russia, with the implacability of the Russian steppe, with the icy hardness of the Russian winter."

No one translated. Where was Mischa? Perhaps busy at the University, or perhaps specifically unasked for. No Mischa, only the two of them. And Rivka waiting nervously at attention just inside the door. It was unclear to her how much of Yashka's conversation the older woman understood, however intently she might be listening, her head at a tilt, her china cup set aside, her hands folded atop a green leather document case on her lap. Yashka paused, and when Mrs. Pankhurst nodded, went on to itemize exactly what matériel the Battalion lacked. Thus and so many weapons, so much ordnance, a fully stocked field kitchen and the team of animals to draw it—all detailed meticulously, all, she explained, necessary to their success.

Evidently, Mrs. Pankhurst had come prepared. Barely had Yashka finished speaking when the Englishwoman reached into the leather envelope she held and withdrew what appeared to be a bank check. "You have my support," she said in her plummy, flutey British singsong.

Before Bochkareva could become too effusive, the visitor rose and took her leave. As she passed Rivka, she inclined her head. There was no other sign of recognition.

When they were alone, the Commander said, "Sit down."

"Am I to be reprimanded?" Rivka blurted.

"Why? Have you done something that requires a reprimand?"

Oy vey. What if she had, and didn't realize? "I have tried to be a perfect soldier in all things," she said. Whining now like a child. *Gevalt.*

"And so you have been, which is why you are here. That and the fact that you can read and write. Yes?"

Rivka nodded. Thanks to Mischa, she could read Yiddish and Russian. The holy tongue he had not given her to study.

Again Yashka told the girl to take a seat. This time Rivka followed orders.

"You have known Mrs. Pankhurst long?"

"Two weeks."

The Commander looked confused. "Well. It seems she has taken a shine to you. It seems she considers you her protégée."

Rivka blushed.

"I need a clerk. Someone who can be discreet about what she hears."

"I want to fight."

"Nothing will interfere with your duty. No one, not even me, will be exempt from the trenches when the day comes."

"In that case," Rivka said, "I accept gladly."

Bochkareva, stiffly, "It is not yours to accept or decline. You have already been reassigned."

"A WHAT?" SAID Mischa. He had come during visiting hours, six to eight in the evening.

"A princess," Rivka said smugly. Top that, big brother.

"No such thing. In the New Russia we bow to no princesses. We bow to no one."

"You're impossible, you know that?"

"Your so-called princess is no better than anyone else."

"I like her. At this moment, I like her a lot better than you."

"Wake up, Rivka. The old order is gone, and a new order is on its way. You're fighting on the wrong side of history."

History was not her current interest. "At any rate, I don't wish to fight with you."

Mischa leaned back in his chair, folded his arms and studied her. All around them were small family groups seated on benches and chairs at bare tables in the huge, echoing mess hall. "So, *maideleh.* What have you written to Papa and Mama?"

She sighed. "With any luck, I'll be at the front by the time I hear back from them."

"I've written them, too."

"About me?"

"I had to. Understand?"

Oh, she understood, all right. When baby sister turns warrior you can't exactly forget to mention it. *Dear folks, how are you? I am fine. Spring has finally come to Petrograd. Rivka arrived safely, too. Nothing else is new. Except....* She began to giggle. Her laughter grew wild and wilder until she was snorting uncontrollably; until he was in stitches, too, and begging her to tell him the reason why.

"They sent me here to bring you back," she said, wiping tears from the corners of her eyes.

"Because I've been a naughty boy."

That brought on more hilarity. "They don't know naughty," she gasped. "Compared to me, you're golden."

"Abi gezunt," he said grinning. As long as you're healthy.

Later, they left the mess and wandered across the parade ground. A thin mist was rising. "Mischa," she said, "I had to do this. Don't you see that?"

He shook his head. "All I see is it's wrong."

"But it's my only chance. You, you'll have dozens of chances in your life. Whereas this might be my only adventure."

"Not if our revolution succeeds."

They'd reached the gate. She embraced him and took in the familiar dampish odor of his skin, his clothing, like the scent of rain. "Goodnight, my brother. My golden revolutionist."

He sighed. "I'd be truly golden if I could turn you around."

This Latinate pun on the meaning of revolution was lost on her. She laid a soft hand on his arm and said, "*Tateleh,* you never will."

OLGA CAME IN moments before curfew, hair mussed, eyes bright, lips puffy, the skin around them looking scuffed. Rivka was already in bed, half asleep. The next morning, after roll call, on the way to breakfast, Olga slid her arm through Rivka's and whispered, "Guess what?"

"What?"

"Have you ever been kissed?"

Rivka stopped short and Olga swung around to face her. "A real kiss," she said. "A romantic kiss. Have you?"

"Of course not! Well…once. On the hand." Nachum, the blackguard.

"On the hand doesn't count."

Truer words were never spoken. "Are you engaged?"

The girl blushed. "Not exactly."

No one buys the cow who can get the milk for free, Mama told her, told her often. *Purity in his bride is sacred to a man*, Papa told her, just once, a month or so after she'd begun having her periods. Neither of these things did she repeat to Olga. "You let a man kiss you?"

"Last night," Olga said, and added, "I kissed him back."

She shouldn't be listening to this. Yashka wouldn't like it.

They'd reached the door to the mess, where girls were streaming in and the smell of kasha hung in the air. Rivka didn't know what to say. "Let's have breakfast," she tried. "Hungry?"

"Starved," Olga grinned. "But not for food."

Always, it seemed, Rivka had wondered how she would feel to be kissed, really kissed, and caressed in the way a husband caresses his wife. Never before had there been someone to ask, who would give her the straight story. "You liked it?" she asked in spite of decency and decorum.

"Rivka, my dove, it was like I'd been living in a small room all my life. Suddenly a door swung open, and I stepped out into an unimaginable countryside. It was like being inside a kaleidoscope. Every point on my lips was alive. Not even when dancing, not even on stage have I ever felt so aware of myself. And yet…in my ecstasy I lost myself, like my patron saint Olga, conjoining with the Great Father of us all."

More awed than scandalized, Rivka said, "It was a religious experience?"

"It was, yes. An ecstasy. Like Saint Olga."

More like Eve, Rivka thought. One moment the apple at her lips, all innocence. A single bite, and the blinders dropped from her eyes. Might it be worth it, then, to suffer the consequences, be expelled from Eden? For surely, when Yashka found out, Olga would be sent packing.

Yashka didn't find out. This one was expelled, and that one reprimanded, and no one seemed immune from Yashka's discipline, Yashka's rage. But Olga remained such a sweet-tempered creature and so anxious to please, so eager to follow directions and so adept at all physical tasks that she rarely was called out for anything but praise. If the Battalion could be said to have a mascot, she was it, universally loved and petted. How she managed to sneak out and see her beau and get back undetected Rivka never learned. Few noticed she was gone. Even fewer knew the reason why.

THINGS WERE NOT going well at the front, but General Brusilov had just been named Commander in Chief of the armies, and Rivka had confidence in his leadership. For one thing, he was Papa's patron. For another, his offensive of 1916 had been highly successful. And for a third, Yashka liked him. Yashka's opinion was Rivka's benchmark in all things.

Every afternoon now, Rivka took up her clerical duties in Yashka's office. If the work was light, she was able to coax the Commander into conversation. Usually, the work was not light, and she worked straight through until supper, sometimes going back after supper to finish up. In the barracks, a rumor flew that Yashka had joined up for the purpose of replacing her beloved husband, killed in action in the first days of the war. Rivka was proud to know different, for Yashka had confided, "Whether the drunken bastard died in the war or still lives I know not. I was lucky to escape from his tortures years ago."

Mornings, Rivka trained with the other girls. They were driven hard in hasty preparation for the great work ahead. Rivka often went to her desk with muscles sore from exertion. One day, as she massaged her cramped calf, Yashka told her that compared to the training the men got, this was slapdash. Their mission, after all, was not to make war, but to inspire the men to action by climbing out of the trenches and moving forward. They were to win men's hearts. Any ground the Battalion gained in their fighting would merely be gravy. The Natchalnik offered one of her infrequent smiles. Her teeth were misaligned, Rivka noticed. Maybe it was to hide the flaw that Yashka barely moved her lips when speaking.

Often, Yashka required "her girl" to attend her on military and political visits so that Rivka could take notes immediately following the meetings. Rivka was terrified of the dignitaries and intimidated by their surroundings, which only months before had been the exclusive precincts of the Tsar. Try as she might, she could not help gawking at everything in the Winter Palace: its airiness, the paintings on its walls, the gilt, the magnificent furnishings of exotic woods and silks and marbles and precious inlays, the splendor of its floors and ceilings.

They were in a carriage returning from there to the Institute. Yashka had come away fuming from her meeting with Kerensky. Ostensibly, she'd been summoned to report on the progress of her recruits, but she'd told Rivka she suspected something else on the agenda. After all, a progress report could be done by memo. A progress report could be followed up by telephone. She was right. As it turned out, the meeting was a ruse, an opportunity to call her on the carpet for disciplining her recruits by slapping them across the face.

"We do not do that in the New Russia," she was told.

"You will not tell me how to discipline my own soldiers," she screamed. Outside in the waiting room Rivka could hear her, despite the closed doors. "I will have a free hand with my troops. They are women and must follow strictest discipline lest they become a Battalion of Shame. This was your agreement with me. If you are going to renege on it at every petty instance of discipline, I will resign immediately." Rivka could imagine her clutching the stripes on her sleeve, fully prepared to rip them off.

In the anteroom, Rivka listened to the murmur of him placating her.

Bochkareva's voice, gravelly in anger, would vibrate like the strings of a viola when she was moved. Now, in the carriage, she warbled her indignation. "What does he know of military training? Who is Kerensky to tell me how to discipline my own soldiers?"

"Minister of War," Rivka said.

"Minister, shminister," she responded, and the girl smiled at the Yiddishism. Yashka, noting her amusement, said, "We are not so different, little footsoldier, you and I."

But Rivka feared otherwise. "I would never have the toughness to affront Kerensky."

"Pah! After you've been through the mud and the blood, petty men like Kerensky don't faze you."

Rivka's smile was rueful. "But I never would have enlisted in the Tsar's army as you did. What even made you think such a thing was possible?"

"A peasant doesn't think, merely acts. It was the autumn of 1914. I was dreadfully unhappy. I had run away from my husband. At my father's house it was not an easy place for me anymore. So I didn't think, I just walked into the recruiting office and offered myself. Everyone was infected with war fever at that time."

"And? They said yes? Just like that?"

"They said no. They laughed in my face, told me I could become a nurse. Can you imagine me a nurse? I explained how I had toiled with my husband alongside the roughest of men, doing the meanest of labors, laying concrete in the frozen steppe. If I could do that, surely I could fight the invaders of my country." Yashka paused, staring pensively out at the passing avenue, perhaps brooding upon the invaders, who still, almost three years later, occupied her country. As the carriage turned a corner, it was nearly swamped by a clutch of veterans carrying signs that demanded peace and bread. Neither woman acknowledged them. The Commander, roused, went on with her story. "Those recruitment officers reacted just as you'd expect—'Whoever heard of a *baba* in uniform?'—plus some lewd remarks about camp followers."

"I'd have taken to my heels," Rivka said.

Not Yashka. She demanded there and then to see the Commandant, who also refused her, saying it would be against the law to make her a soldier.

"Who can controvert this law?" she demanded.

The Commandant shrugged. "The Tsar." Then he offered to help her telegraph the Tsar seeking permission for her to enter the Imperial Army as a common soldier. Why the Commandant was willing to do this extraordinary thing Yashka said she didn't understand, then or now. But Rivka was perfectly sure of the reason: it was because of Yashka herself, the force of her personality, the drive that made you help her go wherever she wanted to go and do whatever she intended to do, believing implicitly, fervently, in the rightness of her goal.

But not everyone had Rivka's faith. One evening, when the Natchalnik was away, a stranger dressed in grease-stained worker's clothing with a cloth cap on his shaggy head managed to talk his way in through the gate and began speechifying. Why hadn't they formed a governing committee, he asked one of the girls. This was the wave of the future. Why did they continue the backward practice of obedience to the whims of an officer class, he asked another. They were no better off than under the Tsar. They might as well be serving the Tsar, since they acceded to corporal punishments.

The fact that he was young and handsome, with a flashing white smile, didn't do his chances any harm. A crowd gathered. Some argued with him that discipline was essential because of the speed of the training and because of the great work they'd signed on to do. But he belittled this mission of theirs, since it was designed to prolong the war, and what was the war but an imperialist folly? Wasn't peace what they all wanted, and an equal say in their country's destiny? They were free citizens now, each and every one of them, so why were they willing to slave under the rule of their reactionary Natchalnik, this freak of nature, Maria Bochkareva?

The girls argued among themselves, but the more they contended the more they convinced themselves of their right to liberty and self-governance. The man was gone by eight o'clock, the close of visiting hours, yet the barracks were still in an uproar well after midnight. Rivka waited up to warn Yashka, who, without hesitation, ordered her soldiers out to form ranks. They did so, with many a grumble and snide remark and flippant—or nervous—laughter.

"Those who want a committee move over to the right," ordered Yashka. "Those against it, go left." There was a pause, and then a jostling, some elbowing and shoving, and when it was done, more than a thousand women stood on the right, and only about three hundred on the left.

"So much for your pledges of absolute obedience," Yashka scolded.

"So much for your autocracy," called out one of the mutinous, a recruit who'd been disciplined numerous times and slapped once for her impudence. "We are not serfs, but free women."

"You? You are not worth the uniforms you wear."

"And who are you, please, to judge us? We no longer recognize your authority. Come girls, we'll elect a new Natchalnik!"

A cheer went up. Olga, though she had stepped to the left alongside Rivka, cheered too, and began inching toward the majority. One of that crowd beckoned with open arms to embrace her.

Yashka's tight lips twisted bitterly. "Did I organize this Battalion to be ineffective and demoralized like the rest of the army? I told you at the beginning that I would be strict, that I would shout and punish. We were to serve as an example. This place," stamping her foot, "this was to be a hallowed place. You were to go to the front as saintly women—for I hoped, with God's help, that the enemy's bullets would never touch you. Had I known what cheap stuff you are made of, I would never have come within a thousand miles of you."

A howl went up from both sides. Yashka turned on her heel and left them.

Rivka raced after. "But what if they try to leave?"

"Let them."

"In their uniforms?"

"As they choose."

THE BARRACKS WAS in an uproar, some girls reasoning, arguing, some screaming, hurling curses and epithets, some weeping. Klipatskaya, at the thick of things, pleaded in her lawerly way for the women to stand firm and not abandon their commitments. "This is our chance to show the world what women are capable of. Do you want to end it with stupid quarreling before it's even rightly begun? We have an enemy to fight. The enemy is not our Natchalnik."

Tatya, off by herself, stood watching. "Nothing will happen tonight," she told Rivka. "No minds will be changed. This thing must run its course."

"But what is its course?"

Tatya could only shrug.

It must have been close to three in the morning when Rivka, sick to her stomach with exhaustion, crawled into bed. Across from her, three of the mutineers were trying to convince one of the faithful that the committee system was the thing of the future, which the whole army must embrace, including their Battalion. The holdout, a big, stolid peasant woman of forty, merely frowned and shook her head. In the corner behind them, with her back turned to the rest, Olga obsessively went through her pliés, first position, second, third, fourth and fifth, bending and stretching with circled arms.

Seven hundred girls were missing at the morning roll call. Hundreds more failed to report for parade after breakfast.

"I've come to say goodbye," said Olga. "I'm leaving."

"You can't," Rivka said.

"But the others want me with them."

"That's politics. What do you care about politics?"

"I care about my freedom. *They* care about my freedom."

Rivka took her fluttery hands and held them. "Remember what you told me on our first night here, how Yashka showed you what it is to be strong? Yashka saved you."

The girl hung her head.

"Now, when Yashka needs you, you cannot desert her. Your place is here."

Olga's damp eyes lifted and met Rivka's. "Are you sure?" she pleaded.

"I'm sure."

YASHKA WAS GONE all day, meeting with her superiors, being coaxed and cajoled and then ordered and finally browbeaten to let the girls form a committee. Nothing worked. She held her ground. She would disband the Battalion before she would allow a committee. She would go home and live in peace in her village on the steppe.

She returned to the near-empty Institute, visibly demoralized and upset. The remnant of her Battalion was called to order in the garden. "I have just come from Minister Kerensky," she announced. "I'm going home. You are disbanded." A cry went up, quickly silenced. "No, there is nothing more to be said. I hoped to make this Battalion an example that would shine forever in the history of our country. I hoped to show that where men failed women could succeed. This is war, and in war there should be no talk, but action. A committee means nothing but talk and talk. Committees have destroyed our army."

"But not us!" grunted the faithful peasant woman who, through the long hours and against all arguments, had stuck to Yashka.

A chorus of other voices called out, begging Yashka not to abandon the Battalion. "We'll stand by you," they chanted.

"The prospect of discipline doesn't daunt you? Nor of sacrifice?"

"Punish us all you want," called Medzvedova, the girl who was the first of them all to be slapped, and was then put on half-rations for three days.

Yashka rested a grateful hand on the girl's scrawny shoulder. "For you alone I wish I could stay," she said, "but my orders are to form a committee, like the rest of the army, or disband the Battalion. I leave tomorrow."

GENERAL POLOVTZEV, THE Commander of the Military District, was at dinner that evening when he was told of an angry mob demanding to meet him. He wiped his lips, put down his napkin and went outside to see what the uproar was about. Yashka's loyal three hundred, bristling with rifles, awaited him, Rivka at their head, along with Tatya and Klipatskaya.

"What have you done to our Natchalnik?" demanded Klipatskaya.

The General, astounded, tried to calm them. "Girls, girls," he said. "I haven't done anything to her."

"We are not girls. We are soldiers. And we want our Natchalnik."

"You'll form a committee, and you'll have your Natchalnik. And I," he said, desperately trying to inject a note of levity—"I shall have my dinner."

"We will not form any committee," said Rivka sourly. "We want strict discipline in accordance with our pledges to Yashka." The business end of a hundred rifles backed her up.

The General sighed. "I'll come to your barracks tomorrow morning. Oh nine hundred hours. We'll work this out then."

The rifles didn't move.

"You will not disband the Battalion?"

"I won't. No."

Had they prevailed? They weren't sure. Tomorrow would tell the tale. Rivka hurried to inform Yashka, who had gone to spend the night at the home of one of her supporters, a feminist of the Russian nobility. The house, situated along the River Neva, had an immense courtyard and a grand staircase leading up to an imposing front door. As she stood just outside the wall summoning the courage to go in, her neck was gripped by the hand of some fellow passing behind her. She swung around, ready to fight the man, who was smaller and slighter, no match for her.

"Whoa, Rivka."

"Mischa! What are you doing here?" She peered through the gloom at her pale, curly-dark-mopped brother.

"Come with me."

"Are you crazy?"

"We need to talk, Rivka. Right away."

"What's wrong? Who's ill? Is it Mama?"

"No, no. *Keinahoreh* they're fine. So far as I've heard."

He was trying to steer her away from the house, away from this avenue of palaces. She'd gone a few steps with him, but now stood firm, refusing to go further despite her watering eyes. "I'm on a mission, or I wouldn't be out at this hour."

"I know that."

"Wait for me. As soon as I've delivered my message and been dismissed, I'll return here. Whatever you need, my brother—food, money—I'll see that you get it." She moved to go, and this time when he gripped her shoulder, she cried out.

"Rivka, what do think you're doing? This is a monarchist you're supporting. A tsarist."

"Who? Yashka? Don't be silly. Yashka is no more for the Tsar than—than God is."

"Anyone with a brain in her head has walked out on Bochkareva. Who is left there, Rivka? Only a handful of sheep. You follow her around in a flock because you don't know what else to do with yourselves."

"Where have you heard this?" Her tears spilled over now, not the cold tears of fear, but the hot ones of anger. "Who sent you?"

"You think she is Mother Russia?"

Rivka flushed crimson. This was tantamount to calling her an idolatress. Once, back in September of 1914, when the war was new, Rivka had said, "When Mother Russia calls us, shouldn't we answer?"

Papa snorted, "Russia is no Jew's mother."

"What then? What is a Jew's mother, Papa?"

She'd watched her father's mouth working. How he'd have loved to retort unblinkingly, his rough hand stroking his beard, one finger in the air: *Torah! Torah is the Jewish home, the only mother a Jew needs.* Trouble was, Papa, though he would not defy tradition, had little use himself for Torah and less for God. So with Rivka prodding him, demanding, "What, Papa? What is a Jew's rightful mother," Papa pointed to Mama chopping onions at the sink and shouted, "There is *your* mother. Of what other mama have you a need?"

Mischa's caustic reminder of this now pained Rivka, left her momentarily speechless and sputtering. Her brother leapt upon the advantage.

"The committee system is the only democratic way to run the military," he said. "The entire army uses committees. But not your

Bochkareva. If your Bochkareva had her way, she'd not only slap you all around, she'd bring back capital punishment."

"You're the one who took me to hear her speak."

"My mistake. I thought you had more sense."

"What do you know about the army anyway? You're just a student." Such a curl-lipped sneer she gave, anyone would have thought the word "student" was synonymous with "worm."

He withdrew his hold on her. "I don't recognize you anymore, Rivka. I don't know who you are."

"Fine with me," she said. "When we meet again, we'll be no more to each other than strangers." She turned, and strutting with more than her usual military bearing, head, neck and back stretched to their utmost, she left him in the street.

IN THE MORNING, the General came as promised, with a retinue consisting of Kerensky's adjutant and several female patrons of the Battalion, including Mrs. Pankhurst. Yashka instructed Rivka to join them and take minutes of the meeting. Rivka ran to get her pen and paper, and, when she returned with them, found the General already berating Yashka. "You are a soldier, why don't you obey orders?"

Without hesitation, Yashka retorted, "Because they are against the interests of the country. The committees are a plague. They have destroyed our army."

"It is the law of our country. Are you above the law?"

She shook her head. "It is a ruinous law, designed to disrupt the front in wartime. The Germans work all day while our boys talk."

"Then do it as a matter of form," he said. "Your girls are so devoted to you that a committee elected by them would never seriously bother you."

One of her patrons, a duchess, urged, "Do it, Yashka. Think of the trouble you would save." Others joined in, though not

Mrs. Pankhurst, Rivka noticed. The more they tried to convince her, the more agitated Yashka became. Rivka could see trouble coming, if they could not. Rivka could see it in Yashka's stiffening shoulders and working jaw. Rivka feared the Duchess would soon be slapped. She reached out a steadying hand, and maybe it prevented something worse from happening.

The Natchalnik began shrieking, "Get out of here. Get out of here, all of you. You want to destroy the country."

The General was on his feet in an instant. "Shut up, you! How dare you shout like that? How dare you insult this uniform?"

"I'll do more than insult it," she thundered, stepping forward, fists raised.

"And I'll kill you for it!"

"Go ahead, then. Do it," she bawled, tearing open her tunic and pointing to her thinly covered breast. "Kill me this instant!"

The patrons shrank back, knocking over chairs, mewling. *What is happening here?* cried a voice in Rivka's head.

The General threw up his hands, palms out, and took a step backward, muttering, "What the hell? What the hell?" He told Yashka she was a demon, no woman at all. "I can do nothing with you," and he stalked out, followed by the others.

"Don't despair," Mrs. Pankhurst whispered to Rivka before withdrawing with the rest.

It was hard not to despair. Everything was upside down. There was no work to do. Some girls went out on the parade ground and drilled each other. Others wandered aimlessly, not knowing what to do with themselves. They thought Rivka might tell them something. Rivka couldn't even darn her own tunic. She sat on her cot, needle in one hand, tunic in the other, biting her lip and waiting, like everyone else. Yashka stayed mute behind a closed door.

Later came a telegram notifying Yashka officially that the Battalion would be allowed to continue, with her at its head and without a committee. Oh, such hugging and cheering! There was a quickly thrown together celebration, Yashka allowing the girls a thimbleful of vodka and a bit of cake scrounged from who-knows-where. "Speech, speech," they cried, and Yashka, up on a bench, said, "It was a hard fight for me, but there is no retreating when I know I'm right."

"We fought, too," Olga called out exultantly. "We fought hard for you."

"Of course you did," said Yashka. "Aren't you my girls?"

Indeed they were. But they were no longer two thousand strong.

PETROGRAD'S WHITE NIGHTS upset Rivka. They made it hard for her to watch the moon's progress. She'd come to Petrograd right after the full moon of Pesach. She hadn't noted the days since then, hadn't thought about the Omer being counted or the weeks flying by. But with the moon waning to darkness, it seemed to her that the time of Shavuos must be near. Heaven forbid the holiday had passed without her even doing…what? Well, without her even making a nod in its direction, setting aside time to say a prayer of thanks to God for giving his chosen people the Law at Mount Sinai. Without eating dairy, as was traditional. Dairy, though, was almost impossible to find. What wouldn't she give for a nice helping of borscht with sour cream? Or sour cream with blintzes, half of them cheese, the other half blueberry. Or just a bowl of sour cream alone, and maybe a little fresh radish and cucumber to top it. A little bowl. A ladleful. Even a spoon. Was that so much to ask?

And someone with whom to share the holiday. There wasn't a Jew here that Rivka knew except Mischa, and they hadn't spoken since the night of their argument—their "spat," Rivka dubbed it so as to think of it as something insignificant and temporary. After all, what was it about? Only politics.

Mischa, no doubt, had plenty of Jews with whom to celebrate. Among the Bolshevists were Jews by the carload, it was said. One of the drillmasters, not realizing to whom he spoke, had told Rivka that the Tauride Palace, where the Bolshevists met, needed to be fumigated once a week, it smelled so badly of Jews. Among the Bolshevists, no one practiced their religion, it was said. Rivka watched for the thin crescent moon to rise over the city and wondered about Mischa.

IV

The Front

ON JUNE 24, 1917, after six weeks of training, the Battalion of Death left the grounds of the Institute and marched up the Nevsky Prospekt to Kazan Cathedral. Though a cold, fine rain was falling, crowds of well-wishers with flowers in their arms and cheers on their lips lined their way. By then, just three hundred of the girls remained, their ranks thinned partly by illness, injury and dismissal, but mostly by Yashka's uncompromising stand on the committee issue. As they approached the cathedral, Rivka felt giddy with dread. War she was prepared for, but an expedition to the heart of the *goyish* world, never. Hundreds of thousands, maybe millions of Jews had died because of the teachings that issued from churches. *In every generation,* as the Passover Haggadah taught. She would never come out of this alive. Either she would drop dead of her skipping heart, or else something would identify her as a Jew even midst the sameness of the military, and they'd murder her on the spot.

The great colonnaded arms fronting the cathedral seemed to reach out and pull her in, then closed inexorably behind her. She froze, as though she'd turned to salt. She must not keep marching. She was shoved from behind, Tatuyeva hissing in her ear, prodding her forward. No, no, she must run away! "Step, step, step!" ordered Tatya. She heard a creak, surely not that huge oaken door on its hinges, surely the bones of all her ancestors rolling over in their graves.

And suddenly she was inside the very belly of the beast. Marble columns rose upward forever and forever in all directions. Gold everywhere, and icons floating on a silver wall. They must be saints crowding one atop another all up and down the wall. She was about to faint from a tortured vision of a gory man on a cross. Nothing, not even combat, could be worse than this moment: the Archbishop praying over them, chanting and swaying in his long robes; Bochkareva kneeling before him; the women making the sign of a cross upon themselves. She squeezed her eyes shut. *Sh'ma Yisroel* she mouthed to herself over and over again.

Damp breeze and faltering sunshine: outside again, not remembering how she got here. She gulped air. It seemed she must not have been breathing in there. The Battalion moved away from the church, marching smartly toward the Warsaw terminal, until a knot of Bolshevik toughs blocked the way. They threatened violence. Yashka treated them like the insects they were. "You must be afraid of us," she bellowed, "since you bother to interfere with our going to the front." The toughs growled insults at her, but all the same they dispersed.

THE BATTALION REACHED the front, east of Vilna, after two nights and the better part of two tiresome days on the train, in windowless boxcars furnished only with double-decker bunks and a pail. Their meals were provided at predetermined stations, where supportive crowds hailed them and ovations were made in their honor—though at the perimeters, never absent, were bands of troublemakers demonstrating against them and against the war.

A sea of men was solidly massed on both sides of the tracks when they deboarded at Molodechno, headquarters of the Tenth Army. From a distance came the vague boom of cannon, nearly drowned by the deep muttering of a thousand male voices. "The whole army has come to meet us," Olga said, blinking in the sudden light. The men did not seem hostile, merely curious, laughing and pointing and performing acrobatic antics to catch the girls' attention. Yashka, her voice like a bullhorn, ordered them to make way. Still elbowing each other and joking, they stood aside, and she marched the girls two versts under the hot sun to their temporary quarters.

Inside the long wooden building with its steep roof and deep dormer windows they found nothing but two long wooden platforms running the length of the walls. The air was stifling. As soon as they'd dumped their packs, their guns, ammunition belts, gas masks, pup tents, trench spades and food pails, the women began unrolling their overcoats and spreading them out over the rough boards. It was then that Yashka briskly announced, "Come, girls, we're going swimming!—Why do you stand there staring like idiots? Fall in!"

A party of men trailed them across the fields and through a small wood. The girls kept their good order, and they carried their rifles. The men badgered them, but kept well back. Just before a small railroad bridge, Yashka ordered them like hounds to stay, and they obeyed. The girls crossed the bridge, beyond which was a sheltered cove fringed by willows that secured them from lustful eyes. The eddying water had a tinge of pure emerald and was so clear that the pebbled bottom was plainly visible. Those girls who were observing their time of the month stood sentry, while the rest stripped and, shrieking, plunged into the ice-cold river. The water was delicious, the freedom even better.

Yashka stood on the riverbank looking pleased with herself. She had trained them, she had gotten them to the front. The men here were curious, they were interested, they seemed ready to follow wherever the women would lead. Who else but Yashka could have achieved all this, and in so short a time? If she was *kvelling*, she had reason to.

OVERNIGHT THE MOOD turned ugly. Some of the other Molodechno barracks held deserters and Bolshevik agitators. Near midnight, they came knocking at the walls, shouting insults and curses. Those who tried to enter were met with the muzzles of rifles. Furious, they hurled stones at the windows and thrust their hands through the shattered panes, shouting, "Baba, baba, come out baba. Come out and play." One grubby paw caught Klipatskaya by the hair. When she screamed, the brute pulled all the harder until Tatya poked at him through the broken window with the tip of her bayonet.

"One thing on their minds," said Rivka to Yashka.

"Two. That, of course. And drink."

All night long, the rude noises, the catcalls and stone-throwing continued. No one slept. Except when they took sentry duty at the entrances, the girls huddled together in the center of the room. By the time the early summer dawn came, a mob of at least a hundred had gathered outside. "In the old days," Yashka muttered, "it would have been sufficient to execute a couple of them, and the rest would be transformed into respectable, obedient human beings." Now, she went out to confront them. "You villains," she shouted. "Rogues! Do you not know what shame is? Leave us alone. Let us rest before going to the lines. If you have questions I will answer them, but leave my girls alone."

One of them stepped forward. He was tall, gaunt, with narrow eyes and a three-day growth of whiskers bristling from prominent cheekbones. His hands had brown spots on them like a piece of fruit going soft. "Why do you fight for the bourgeoisie?" he said. "You shed the people's blood, and for what? For the rich, for the exploiters?"

"What is it you want?" she said.

"We want peace."

"How will you have peace?"

"By leaving the front and going home."

"And hand Russia over to the Kaiser! If we all go home, Germans will walk right over our defenses. Do you know what will happen then?"

From somewhere in the back, a man called out, "You'll lose your job, Madame Officer." The men howled with laughter. Rivka, listening behind the door, shuddered. Were these the heroes of 1914, the victors of Lemberg?

"Here is what will happen," Yashka said, starting out quietly, almost as if musing to herself, and increasing in volume until she was shouting. "*Here* is what will happen: they will crush the people and your new freedom. Do you understand? There will be no peace until we conquer the Germans."

The men shifted and muttered. Again, the tall one spoke for them. "The Germans are not our enemy. They are tired of the war, too."

"Shoot them, kill them, saber them, but do not fraternize with the foes of our beloved Russia."

"They fraternize with us!"

"They fraternize here but send soldiers to fight our brave and noble allies on the Western Front."

"What allies are they if they want no peace?"

And so on in endless circles, arguing and deriding while a hot July sun climbed the sky. At last thoroughly incensed, Bochkareva threw herself at them. "Go! Get out of here. Now, you fools!" she shrieked, hurtling among them. "You hear me? You are fools. Get away from me—or else kill me." A wild woman, she struck her breast, daring them, while Rivka held her breath. "Kill me this instant!" Cowed by Yashka's fury, they kept backing away from her, one by one. In small, sullen groups, they wandered off, grumbling.

AFTER A HASTY BREAKFAST, the Battalion marched, each girl carrying a pack that weighed sixty-five pounds. From Molodechno they marched thirty versts past fields and woods to Redki, from Redki six versts to Beloye, the sunny sky turning to clouds, the clouds to rain. Wherever they stopped to rest, men gathered and stared. Babas in breeches!

Traffic along the road increased, supply trucks heading west toward the lines, ambulances east away from them. Shrieks of pain could be heard from inside, every time an ambulance bounced on the rough and broken road. Hearing them, one of the girls faltered and fell to her knees.

As they neared the battle lines, a soldier, pointing at Rivka, called out, "Virgin." Rivka froze.

Klipatskaya, marching alongside, shifted her rifle, aiming for the man's privates. "I should hope so," she countered.

"*Nyet!*" gesturing up at the sky overhead, where shells were flying westward, softening up the enemy, breaking apart the barbed wire that shielded their trenches. "Virgin," he repeated.

Klipatskaya laughed, nodding, and Rivka let out the breath she'd been holding. All he meant was that it was her first time at the front, first time going up the line. She'd peer out into no-man's-land for the first time and for the first time meet her enemy. But what then? She'd frozen up at the merest hint of violation. How would she conduct herself in the face of a trench bristling with bayonets and machine guns?

On July 6, they reached the forward lines and waited behind the communication trenches for the order to advance. The ground shook beneath them as Russian artillery bombarded the Germans all that day and through the night and all the next day. The din was terrible, drowning out everything. The earth seemed to be burning, and the sky. Surely nothing could live out there, no leaf, no bird, no enemy.

IT WAS DUSK ON the second night when finally they entered the communication trenches and began moving up the line. The closer they got, the more squalid became the trenches, wet, crumbling, rat-infested, reeking of blood and feces. Rivka was able to brave the filth without recoiling. She was only a tremulous girl, it was true, and one of only three hundred at that, but Yashka had buoyed them all up, gathering them at the mouth of the trench and broadly mapping out her plan: how together they would put steel back in the spine of the common Russian soldier; how as they rose up out of the ground, hearts would be set ablaze from one end of the Eastern Front to the other; how all Russia would rise to follow them until not a single German boot was left on Russian soil.

No sooner had Yashka stepped down off the speaker's stool than seventy-five male officers presented themselves. She'd inspired them, and they were volunteering to die along with the Battalion. Yashka's narrowed eyes probed their motivations and their fitness. When they neither bridled nor quailed under her brash scrutiny, she permitted them to join in the advance. During that short summer night, as they arranged themselves along the first-line trench, as vodka was passed from hand to hand and bursting shells sucked the breath from their lungs, the waiting soldiers, men and women alike, seemed to withdraw into themselves. It was a grave and glorious hour.

Rivka's mind filled with the faces of her family. History, once of no concern to her, was about to be made. She was among those making it. If only she could share this time with Papa, Mama and Mischa. Not Dudie; Dudie she banished immediately, he should never have to witness such things. But the others, she hoped they had her in mind now. Most of all Mischa, who despised Yashka's plan. Let it happen, just as Yashka said it would. Mischa would have to eat his scorn. Let it happen, and when it was over, peace would come, not a coward's peace, but the rightful peace Yashka demanded. Then all the unbelievers would be forced to eat their odious words. Particularly those nearby, those smart alecks among the common ranks who, even in this last hour, with the sky lightening, were calling out ugly taunts. No officer would climb over the top, they jeered, much less a woman. And if by mistake any should find themselves up there, why, you'd see them turn and hightail it double-quick back to safety. Quadruple-quick—they'd run so fast their boots would be left empty behind them. A ruse was in the making, a black charade to trick the unwary and the gullible out onto the battlefield. Catch us falling for it? Ha!

Rivka shivered, despite the warm night.

"Ignore them. You'll do fine," whispered Gennady Fyodorovich Filippov, first cousin of the adjutant Lieutenant Leonid Gregorievich Filippov. Because the two Filippovs were inseparable, Rivka thought of this one as Filippov Too. He had the high cheekbones and almond eyes of a Tatar, separated by a high-bridged, curving nose. His head was small, his face narrow, and the grand architecture of his nose made him appear cross-eyed. Put a Bukharan yarmulke on him, he'd look like the Asian third or fourth cousin of just about anybody in her shul—which is why she felt inclined to believe him. "You'll do fine," he repeated, awkwardly patting her shoulder.

WHISTLES SHRILL: THE great moment is here! For Rivka now, each second stretches out forever, each encapsulating a separate act, like the small book of photographs Uncle Shmuel sent from Chicago, that, when the pages were flipped quickly enough, became a moving picture of a streetcar proceeding along an avenue and stopping to let off a fine lady in a heavy woolen suit and wide-brimmed hat, carrying a furled umbrella over her arm.

First she observes her booted foot climbing the fire step, then her hands gripping the edge of the trench, the soil coming apart in her fingers and streamlets of it running down the cuffs and arms of her tunic. Now she's pressing with her knees against the embankment, and next to her Filippov Too, sliding, is trying to secure his hold. She panics: *what if we're left behind?* But now she's over the top, and the air behaves differently up here, it breathes, it moves against her skin. She pushes into it, crouching as she's been taught to do, and running full out, or trying to, over uneven ground. One foot trips in a rut, and she saves herself from falling with the other, which then collapses against the broken earth, and she's saving herself again, and that, she learns, is what's called running here in no-man's-land. Things zing past her ear—*bullets?* The pandemonium is such that she can't tell whether she's shrieking or someone else is, or maybe a shell is falling out of the sky. Yet she can sense the merest whishing of the wind past her ears, and her heart thuds like the roar of a thousand guns. Through the smoke and the fog she can see no one else, yet she's never been less alone, an essential corpuscle of some grand, straining organism, no thought, just running. Nothing is clear anymore, nothing stretching outward in all directions, everything flying past, everything blurred, and Rivka sprinting hard; suddenly she finds herself cresting the lip of the enemy trench. Shouts and the popping of rifles retreating, and now a handlebar moustache swims up in front of her. His eyes widen in a surprised face, and when she forces her bayonet into him, he gurgles. How can she be hearing him gurgle in the midst of this hubbub? The bayonet has not gone in easily, and it will not come out easily. But that man gives up his life easily. She is sure she would not give up hers so easily.

Death is not what she had expected or been led to believe. But already she has forgotten her expectation in the actuality of the bayonet slicing into the man not at all cleanly, the jolt traveling up her arms and assaulting her shoulders. She hears a moan, harsh as stone rasping against stone, "*Sh'ma Yisroel.*" In horror she thinks, "I've killed a fellow Jew." But the man hasn't spoken. The man is dead, with unblinking eyes and a trickle of blood still dribbling on his chin. It is she who screamed and whose scream became a moan and whose moan became a prayer.

Adjutant Filippov appears next to her. Grabbing her rifle, he leans his back against the trench wall and kicks at the Austrian's torso, releasing the bayonet. The Austrian slides away. Rivka, seeing him fall, bends double and retches. How could she have transformed a living being into this corpse?

Her first kill is the one that will haunt her memory even if worse are to come. Waiting by her side while she vomits, Filippov does his best to be encouraging. "Don't worry," he says, "it will get easier." Lieutenant Leonid Gregorievich Filippov has narrow shoulders and sad-looking blue eyes. He's an old soldier, though still a young man. He has been in the fight since the beginning, wounded four times, one of them seriously. Long ago he gave up hope of surviving combat until the coming of peace.

THE REST OF that day, Rivka cannot be sure whom she kills or does not kill. She fires her rifle repeatedly, but there is no more hand-to-hand combat. In good time, the Battalion gains the enemy's second line, and Russian soldiers behind them swarm into the trench. *Gutt in himmel!* It's happening just as Yashka predicted! A handful of women have led the way, and the entire army is following them to victory. In the face of this onslaught, the Germans bolt like deer, like rabbits, like mice. They take to their heels like they'll never stop 'til they get to Berlin.

Except what is the small, terribly effective weapon they've left behind to explode in the midst of their enemy? Vodka, a load of it. And beer. As the women begin advancing toward the third line of trenches, the men in great guzzling numbers barely glance their way. Enough war for today. Time to get soused.

The women press the attack, shooting, yelling, slashing, the cost to them ever greater as alone they plunge onward. Comrades fall away. Klipatskaya, blown off her feet, whispers to Rivka, "*Milaya, nitchevo*"—my dear, it's nothing—while she drowns in a pool of her own blood.

The German third-line trench is flabbergastingly neat and well appointed compared with the mud hole the Russians customarily put up with. Rivka slumps onto the duckboards and sits there. She is not doing anything, not feeling anything, not thinking anything, just staring up at the blank sky overhead for a long stretch of time. Eventually Tatya finds her there. "The Natchalnik wants you," she says.

Bochkareva has sent back a messenger with a request for troops to relieve them. Lips compressed, she hands the written response to Rivka. Already she has scented out the answer before it is read to her. "We are deliberating," it says.

"Deliberating? Deliberating! An army that does not take orders is not an army."

Nonetheless, the Ninth Corps of the Third Army is deliberating what to do about the relief order. Comply? Or not comply? Obeying isn't even on the table. Obeying as a concept no longer exists. And neither, evidently, does haste. The summer sun is sinking in the sky by the time the follow-up message arrives.

"The Ninth Corps has decided it will make no move to attack. If the Germans attack, we will of course defend the Motherland. But we will not go forward in search of a fight."

Yashka's face turns beetish, a plate of fresh borscht. "The Germans are *in* Mother Russia. Our land! Occupied! Who will fight for it?" She spits in the dirt and dictates a message so full of curses and imprecations it will get them all killed. Rivka, taking it down, urges a milder tone, and Rivka prevails.

But the position they've won at much cost—nearly a third of their strength—is now untenable. They wait until dark and then retreat, returning the way they've come, over ground littered with corpses and body parts, with ammunition belts, gas masks, food pails, the motley detritus of war. They're harried all the way back by German raiding parties. Exhausted, floundering in the blackness, the girls cannot contain the fear they've held at bay all day long. They run flat out for the last couple of versts with enemy snipers firing on them. One of the bullets finds Yashka. She is carried back unconscious by Filippov, aided by Rivka when he falters short of the Russian line.

YASHKA'S WOUND PROVED not to be serious, except that her hearing had been affected, temporarily God willing. While she recuperated, Filippov was put in charge. The women did not like this, but they followed his orders, going out on patrol because it was what the Natchalnik would want, and they earnestly wished the Natchalnik to be proud of them.

"Bring me good news," she begged Rivka each time Rivka visited the hospital. There was no good news to bring. Except for the Battalion, no one was waging war. An informal truce of sorts had been called by the men, who were thoroughly weary of fighting. Up and down the sector, under cover of darkness, enemies exchanged food, tobacco and memorabilia. Their tunic buttons had become the currency of trade.

One bleak night, Rivka led a raiding party into no-man's-land. From a shell hole, she watched grimly as a half-dozen young Germans passed silently by in the blackness. Possibly they were on their way to raid the Russian lines. More likely, they had fraternizing in mind. Their purpose made no difference to Rivka. “Fire,” she roared. Rifles flashed, and the men went down.

Filippov had been partially right about the killing getting easier. She gave the order, watched the men fall, and none of it touched her like her first kill had—not even when she had to cut the throat of one of them who had not died but lay wounded and was screaming in German, possibly calling out their position to his fellows in the trenches. It had gotten easier, just as Filippov had predicted, and for that very reason, it was immeasurably harder. For who was this monster who could slit a man’s throat, have his hot blood spurt all over her hands and feel nothing but relief that the job was done? Who would recognize in Rivka now the gentle girl she had once been? Would Papa know her, would Mama trust her, would Mischa forgive her, would even Dudie, if she could find him, come running to her with a kiss?

IN A MATTER OF weeks Bochkareva recovered her hearing. As soon as she could travel, she went alone to Petrograd to meet with Kerensky, who was now Prime Minister, and General Kornilov, the latest Supreme Commander in Chief of the armies, replacing Brusilov. Brusilov was a good man, a good commander, according to Papa. What was happening back there in Petrograd? How Rivka wished she could talk to Mischa. Mischa might be able to explain things to her. Brusilov had been Supreme Commander only six weeks, and already he’d been replaced! Where was the sense in that? Rivka had seen Lavr Kornilov once or twice in Petrograd, a wily man with a long, thin face, Vandyke beard, straight nose and piercing dark eyes. He was said to be as committed as Kerensky to continuing the war. Yashka declared her confidence that he would support her position on restoring military discipline in the ranks. But for how long would he be permitted to serve?

In Yashka's absence, a sharpshooter's bullet creased Rivka's shoulder. It happened just after midday, a blow as though somebody had punched her arm very hard just below the shoulder. She spun around to see who, not connecting the single shot she heard with the jolt she felt. There was no skirmish in progress, so it must have been a sniper, though where an enemy sniper could hide himself at midday was a mystery. She wanted to hunt for him, but the wound was gushing blood, and she felt dizzy trying to inspect it, and Olga was pulling at her other arm, insisting she get it looked at.

The nearest first aid station had no medical personnel. Whoever had once manned the post had vanished, leaving a fly-covered mound of amputated limbs and a meager cache of bandages behind a splintered wall. Olga searched, but there were no other supplies. A passing stretcher bearer helped her uncover and clean the wound as best they could. Rivka bit into her lip while they probed.

"Be brave," Olga said.

Sweat beaded on her forehead, yet Rivka welcomed the pain, the nausea. It was the price you paid, the price of adventure, of becoming a seasoned warrior like Filippov, like Yashka. A small price, it did not requite the damage she'd inflicted on the bodies of others. Nor did it cover up the pain of losing Klipatskaya.

"Flesh wound," the stretcher bearer said. "You're lucky."

"From a stray bullet," Olga conjectured, and Rivka nodded woozily. Neither of them thought it had come on purpose out of a Russian rifle. But that possibility was no longer unthinkable.

BY THE TIME Yashka returned in late August, the situation at the front between the so-called combatants had degenerated beyond stasis, beyond live-and-let-live into out-and-out fraternization. In broad daylight, in no-man's-land, Russians were gladhanding Germans, standing about arguing which side really meant war, which peace; whose government was betraying the common man and why. Stationed in their trench, the girls of the Battalion scowled in contempt. Their obvious disdain was generally ignored, though on occasion men of their own side leered at them and called out insults. *Slut, Kornilovist.* These were wearisome, but not as hard to bear as their day-in, day-out inactivity.

One hot afternoon, in a sudden sunshower, a beautiful young German boy, hatless, blond, with the lithe body of a gymnast, came sauntering across the field, hands in his pockets, whistling. In one swift action, Bochkareva grabbed the rifle out of Rivka's hands, sighted and shot him in both knees. Above his puttees, blood bloomed like fresh roses. The boy dropped to the ground yowling. A few of his mates rushed to his aid. The other Germans who'd been gadding about in no-man's-land retired helter-skelter to their trenches and began firing. Before the smoke had cleared away from the rifle in Yashka's hands, the whole sector was in an uproar.

"Are you nuts?" yelled Filippov Too, running at her.

"He was coming to flirt with my girls. Didn't you hear the song he whistled? It was a courting song!"

"Are you nuts?" he repeated, and now it was unclear whether he meant Yashka or the troops of the Ninth Corps. Those men had swung their weapons around and were training them not on the enemy, but on the girls of the Battalion of Death, who quickly took cover around the nearest zigzag in the trench wall, dragging Bochkareva into a half-destroyed dugout.

Yashka shrieked, "They dare to draw arms against me? Our own troops?"

They dared do more than that. They dared attack the dugout, shouting, "Kill the Kornilovist."

Maria Ivanova Medzvedova guarded the entrance to the dugout—the same Medzvedova whom Yashka had put on half-rations when they were all green recruits. "Step away," the men yelled. Medzvedova was only five feet, one inch tall. She held her ground, a slip of a girl in a uniform too large for her. Their rain-spotted rifles drew closer. "It's not you we want. It's that witch inside. Step away."

She wouldn't budge. And they shot her through the heart for it.

Rivka, standing just behind, caught her crumpling body. Splashed red, Rivka neither spoke nor raised a rifle against them. They might easily have shot her, as well. But the men, perhaps befuddled at having killed a mere kid with an overbite, acne across her forehead and great staring brown eyes—the men shuffled backward and then drifted away. Enemy fire, too, fell silent.

Briskly, Bochkareva emerged and slapped her hands together, as if dusting off a bit of soot. "Back to your posts," she ordered, and the girls went without a word. The rain had stopped. Everything would go on as before. Except that a boy Rivka didn't know was crippled for life, and a girl she did know was dead. Woodenly, Rivka collected the things from Medzvedova's pockets.

Worse even than the mutinous assault was the confusion she felt in the wake of it, confusion about Yashka. Never had Rivka known the Natchalnik to doubt the rightness of her beliefs. Never had the Natchalnik been less than ruthless in carrying them out. It was clear she would say and do whatever it took to accomplish whatever she deemed necessary—and never so much as a moment spent recriminating herself on behalf of those who suffered for it or died for it. The Natchalnik is a great woman, thought Rivka, no question about that, but a perplexing one all the same.

Rivka loved her. All the girls did, for she was as loyal to each and every one of them as to herself—and utterly selfless in Russia's cause. For proof, look at the way she talked about her life. It was not personal at all; it was the story of the Russian Peasant, the soul of Mother Russia. Or, brooded Rivka, does Yashka imagine that Mother Russia is *her* identity, and is that why she and only she must show the army the way to victory?

Her loyalty to all of them was surely the generous, unstudied outpouring of an instinctively great soul. Or was it only a sign that none of them existed in her mind except as addenda to herself? Rivka was honored to be close to her, and charmed with her humanity, her love of the Russian masses. But oh, how brutal Yashka could be, uttering whatever entered her mind and never apologizing. One time, Rivka had worried aloud whether the Tsar's children were being mistreated in their imprisonment. "Never in my life have I heard anything so weak and lily-livered," Yashka had said. "You are the mealiest gob of pudding I've ever come across."

Deeply offended, Rivka risked objecting. Yashka must take it back, for she couldn't mean it. It wasn't true.

Yashka had retorted that Rivka's bruised ego was only further proof of her weakness. Not surprising in a woman. All women were weak by nature, said Yashka then.

All women except Yashka, thought Rivka bitterly now.

The girls at their posts nervously glanced to left and right and behind them. The least of threats seemed to them to come from the front. Filippov crouched near the mouth of the dugout, a lit cigarette cupped in his hand. He watched the ash grow. He watched the smoke rise.

"What now?" Rivka said.

He shrugged, watching the ash, not looking up at her.

We'll see who's weak, Rivka resolved, and ducked into the dugout. Yashka was bent over the table, studying a tattered piece of map by the light of a guttering candle. Rivka clamped her fingers over the flame, extinguishing it. "Enough," she said. "It's over."

The sting of a slap across her cheek, her neck snapping to the right with the force of the blow. Bochkareva's spittle on her face,

Bochkareva's distended mouth screaming, "Never! Never over. Order them forward."

"But why?"

"Order! Them! Forward!"

"None of the men will follow."

"Then we will rid this land of the enemy by ourselves."

"Two hundred girls? Alone?"

"Give the order."

Rivka gave the order. They clambered out of the trench. Ahead, a small wood. It bristled with rifles. Fifty girls went down, cries and screams everywhere. The enemy, though superior in number, withdrew, for what was the point of losing anyone over a useless bit of shrubbery? Tree by tree, the girls took the land. Yashka was sunny, moving from unit to unit congratulating the girls.

"Rivka," she called. "I need you."

Rivka followed. A message, she was sure, to be written to Kornilov. *We can still fight*, it would say, *We can still win*. They passed through a small glade, beyond which the land dipped. Two steps further, and they were upon the couple. A man underneath. On top, Olga. The round white curve of her naked buttocks was like a moon that had fallen from the sky and having hit the earth was now bouncing up and down. The man grunted. Rivka, never having seen the sexual act in progress, tried hard not to see it now, tried instead to make out the man's nationality from his muddy crumpled trousers and mud-caked boots and the filthy cuffs of his tunic at the edges of the hands on the girl's hips. A snap, sudden sound of a bayonet being fixed in its slot, and now Yashka was barreling at them, Olga half-turning and raising her arm against the onslaught, Yashka lunging, the bayonet finding its home in the girl's soft heart.

A howl rose in Rivka's throat and died there. Without a word, silently she watched the boy, a Russian, roll out from under, jump to his feet and stumble off, pulling up his pants as he ran.

"But she loved you!" Rivka said, an accusation, a challenge.

"On the field of battle, to be rutting like pigs? It's an outrage."

"You didn't have to kill her."

"What would you have done? Tell me."

"Not with a bayonet."

"Yes, with a bayonet. There and then. Nothing else would have been adequate."

"Ah, but she loved you so."

"Evidently, I was not her only love," Yashka said, not dryly, not at all dryly, but angrily.

Later, a burial detail was ordered.

"See what the world has come to?" Yashka preached. In unison, her soldiers nodded. Rivka scanned their weary, earth-stained faces, perplexed. Her friend Klipatskaya—smart, competent Klipatskaya—was dead at the hand of the enemy; and her friend Olga—amiable, generous Olga—dead, horrifically, at Yashka's hand. Of the good friends Rivka had made in Petrograd, only Tatya remained. Of their original three hundred, only a bit more than half were left. With dead eyes Rivka watched her comrades-at-arms giving their assent to Yashka's words—*See what the world has come to?*—and she wondered what it was they thought they could see.

FILIPPOV TOO HAD drawn a portrait of Yashka and sent it to the papers. It was published, with a brief article focusing on Yashka's peasant roots. When it reached her at the front, Yashka called him to her dugout. "Gennady Fyodorovich…" she began.

"You must call me Gena, since I call you Yashka."

"Everyone calls me Yashka. I will address you according to my own standard, not yours."

"I meant no offense."

"Nor did I take any. I am very pleased with your attitude toward my girls. You are respectful of them, besides being a good fellow to have by one's side in a fight."

Gennady accepted the compliment with a nod, at the same time shooting Rivka a puzzled frown. What was this all about?

Rivka shrugged. Yashka would come to the point in her own time.

"It seems the *St. Petersburg Gazeta-Kopeika* likes your artwork."

Gena flushed. "It's your work that's important here, Yashka. I'm only a vehicle for getting it noticed."

She grunted. "When the distance is long, a vehicle is everything."

"If I've been of service to the Battalion, I'm glad of it. I would do a great deal more to drive the Germans out of Russia."

"Good! Do more. From today forward, you may have all the access you want to my girls. Make likenesses of them as they go about their duties. Show them just as they are."

"In between my own duties—"

"You have no other duties. Your Lieutenant Colonel releases you for this purpose. Something good will come of it, mark my words."

"I am to report directly to you?"

"You are to bring me drawings. And Gena," she added, "just drawing. There is to be no flirting. You know that, don't you?"

"Natchalnik, I certainly do."

BY SEPTEMBER, THE army was crumbling to pieces. Men dropped their weapons and walked away. The ones who didn't desert outright went instead to the German trenches at nightfall. Mornings, they stumbled back drunk and arguing fiercely among themselves. "What orientation do you take?" one challenged another. It seemed there were as many orientations, platforms, parties, stances as there were men still in the trenches. Cadets,

Narodniks, Social Democrats, Trudoviks, Bolsheviks, Menshevik Internationalists, Menshevik Defensists, Anarcho-Communists, Social Revolutionary Maximalists, Right Socialist Revolutionaries, Left Socialist Revolutionaries…every last one of them claiming to have the sole key to Russia's destiny. Sheer madness, judged Rivka. A man would more readily fight his neighbor over an almighty -ism than fight the enemy over mere land. And to think it was only half a year since the Tsar was overthrown!

One evening, the corps to the Battalion's right in the front line was scheduled to be relieved at seven. Rivka was at command headquarters with Yashka when the report came in that the corps in reserve was refusing to move up. The Commandant, a potbellied, red-faced man of the old school, ordered, "Shoot a few of them. They'll come around fast enough." But as soon as word of his order got out, what "came around" was a mob a thousand strong shouting, "Shoot *him*, that bastard, that Tsarist shit!"

Colonel Belonogov and several others volunteered to speak to them. Belonogov was well liked among the men, for he made sure that even the lowliest footsoldier was fed on schedule and wore boots in good repair and went regularly to the baths every two weeks. Because of his popularity, he was the one selected to go out and calm the men. He stepped out onto the porch, hands raised, palms open, a smile creasing his cheeks. "There'll be no shooting, boys," they heard him say inside as they shut and barred the door behind him. Boys was the last word they heard from him. There were shouts of threatened executions, there was a scuffling, the harsh crack of wood hitting bone, and a sudden bleating. Then no sound you'd identify remotely as human: barks and grunts and a hideous bellowing roar. A dozen audacious hands hoisted the peacemaker off his feet and flung him to the crowd. A hundred swarming feet improvised. Within minutes they'd trampled him to death, but hundreds more kept on kicking at his body.

Inside, the Commandant was slumped in his chair, head in his hands. The rest of his coterie stood about stunned and useless. The terrible thudding of boots went on and on. Rivka crept close to Yashka. An ancient, hopeless, inbred panic was rising inside her, kindled by centuries of pogroms, burning away everything but her helplessness. "Don't go," she whimpered. "Please, don't leave me here alone. There is the back door. We can escape together."

Yashka's lips curled. Here was a creature so chickenhearted it didn't even merit the dignity of a slap across the face. She shouldered Rivka aside and demanded of the room, "What would you have me do? Shall I cower in a corner while mutiny runs wild through the lines?" Rivka's shame was complete.

Crossing herself, Yashka threw open the door. A devil's chorus of insults greeted her. The colonel's broken body lay bloodied and filthy at the bottom of the steps. Men milled about it, baring their teeth like ravenous dogs. "This is Belonogov," she cried. "Wasn't he always good to you? Didn't you boast of him that he was good to you?"

One or two of the men nodded. Dozens more shook their fists at her. "Look at this bird!"

"Why did you murder him? Tell me."

A chorus of answers came at her.

"Because he was one of the exploiting class."

"They all suck our blood."

"We've bled enough."

"We'll kill you, too. Your Excellency."

Yashka nodded. "I am no 'Your Excellency,' but plain Yashka. You can kill me right away or five, ten minutes from now. Yashka will not be afraid. But I must speak my mind."

"Who is she to question us?" somebody shouted. "Why let her talk?"

"Don't you know me? Don't you know that I am one of you, a peasant soldier fighting to free the land? Who was it suffered and fought with you, if not I? Who saved your lives under fire, if not Yashka?"

"True, it's true," said one to another. Yashka was working her magic.

But another shouted, "Bourgeois. Murderer. Kill her!"

"Scoundrel, I am at your mercy, and I came out to be slain. You will kill me yet. But tell me, suppose you were in the Commander's place, elected by your own rank and file. Tell me, what would you do in his place?"

"Ha, I would see once I got there, baba."

"That's no answer. You are a plain soldier of the people. Say, then, what you would do if our corps were in the trenches and another refused to relieve it." She cocked her head, waiting. The fellow merely gaped.

The crowd muttered, shifting and jostling. "What would you men do?" she demanded of them. "Would you hold the trenches indefinitely or would you leave? Answer me that."

"Leave," several of them called out.

"We would leave anyhow," said one of those who'd threatened to kill her.

"But what are you here for? To hold the trenches or not?"

"To hold."

"Then how could you leave them? That would be treason to Free Russia!"

Rivka, huddled inside, listened to Yashka countering their angry accusations, lobbing question after question at them, gradually persuading them that they had been wrong, and what they were about to do was wrong.

At last Yashka pointed to the heap that was Belonogov's broken body. "Why did you kill this noble soul? What did he want you to do but hold the trenches?"

"He wanted to shoot us," ventured one sullen voice.

"Nothing of the sort. Never was there a commander who took better care of his men, like a father his children. Wasn't it only a month ago he was to be transferred, and you implored him to stay? No no, it is you who did the killing. You are given freedom, and what do you do with it? You act like common cutthroats."

The men were silent, all of them. Many bowed their heads. Yashka allowed the moment to lengthen before going on. Finally, she said, with brisk efficiency, "We must have a coffin made. Who will do it?"

One or two volunteered to get the timber. A few more to do the carpentry.

"How about a grave? We must bury your beloved Commander with full military honors." Several gravediggers came forward.

Someone went to look for a priest, others to gather the makings for a wreath.

"Now," she said, turning to the rest. "Your weary comrades-at-arms are waiting to be relieved. Will you go to the trenches?"

Subdued and contrite, the silenced men went to their posts.

Belonogov's funeral was held later that afternoon. The coffin, an oblong box of raw boards, had been draped inside and out with a white sheet. The general's body had been cleansed, but was so disfigured as to be unrecognizable. Yashka herself wrapped him in canvas and placed him inside. Four green wreaths—three more than was customary—had been made and set atop for the procession. The priest had tears running down his face. The General and his staff, carrying candles, were sobbing, too. Behind them marched all of the corps who were not on duty, their lamentations so loud it was said they could be heard across no-man's-land by the enemy.

When the body was laid to rest, thousands passed by to drop handfuls of sand into the grave. Rivka watched their lips moving in prayer. How docile each one looked shuffling by, how humble and sincere in grief. But she had seen the hellhound they became thronged together, each one a fiendish particle of the savage will. How much longer, she worried, can Yashka's magic quell their brute fury?

LATER THAT SEPTEMBER, Bochkareva returned tight-lipped from another brief trip to Petrograd. Only to Rivka would she confide her despair at what occurred there: Kerensky dismissed General Kornilov and imprisoned him far to the south of the capital, at Bykhov. His reason for this? Kornilov had marched his troops on Petrograd attempting, Kerensky now claimed, to impose a military dictatorship. Kornilov, for his part, maintained that Kerensky had ordered him to Petrograd, which was every day being torn asunder by workers' strikes. It was now Kornilov's widely quoted opinion that Kerensky must have been co-opted by the Bolshevik rabble into playing him false; that the country was sliding into chaos, and that all loyal Russians must unite behind him and his army to save their dying land.

"It can't be true," Rivka said.

"Do you doubt me?"

"People are falling out with each other over nothing."

"Nothing, you say?" muttered Yashka, and she handed Rivka a letter from Mischa. It was scribbled on a half-sheet of wrinkled paper. The words were stiff, as if written by a stranger to a stranger: he is well. Conditions in Petrograd are hard. Food is scarce. Deserters everywhere. He has marched in the demonstrations of the workers and sailors. He is thinking of joining the Red Guard. He's heard nothing from home. Has she?

Perhaps he didn't know that she'd had not a word from her parents since joining the army. She'd written, but there was no response. It was possible, of course, that none of her letters—or theirs—had gotten through. Deserters were known to throw sacks of mail off the trains to make room for themselves in the cars. But it was now six months since she'd left home. Surely one letter at least would have gotten through, if they'd written to her, if they hadn't turned their backs on her. In older times, Jewish parents sat *shivah* for their children who went to war, knowing they'd never return. For a week they stayed in the house, slumped on low stools, shuffling about in felt slippers, offering up psalms, the mirror covered, their clothing rent. Neighbors visited bringing food and comfort. The child was lost—if not taken by death, then inescapably converted by force or bribery to the Tsar's faith. Lost and gone, never to be reunited with family. And Rivka, was she now dead to Mama? To Papa? Was she dead to everyone and everything she had known?

A THIN RIME OF autumn frost covered the ground on the morning the Battalion was moved forward again into the front lines. No soldier laughed anymore at the babas in breeches. If not for them, the sector would be utterly quiet and hazardless. With less than two hundred girls still at arms, Yashka continued ordering forays into no-man's-land. The women reconnoitered at observation posts and in scouting parties. Any hint of enemy movement prompted rifle shots, the sweep of their machine gun. For a while the enemy tolerated this, expecting their enthusiasm to abate after a day or two. When the fighting continued, the Germans sent over a heavy barrage of artillery. The Battalion sustained four dead and fifteen wounded. One of the fallen had been standing beside Rivka, and Rivka's tunic was soaked with her blood. Men of the corps to the left and right of them in the lines had also been killed or wounded because of "Yashka's War." Two committee delegates came to confront her. They were slope-shouldered, heavy-footed men with grizzled faces and smoldering eyes. "We have freedom now," they said. "You cannot make us fight."

"I won't ask you to fight," Yashka retorted. "Don't ask me to fraternize." Rivka watched, gore-drenched and numb, as Yashka struck her own breast in emphasis. "Let me fight the enemy alone. Let the enemy fight only the Battalion. If, as you say, I have freedom, it is my freedom to get killed if I want to."

And indeed, the Battalion were at their posts firing at the enemy when word came that the Bolveshiks had overthrown Kerensky and seized power in Petrograd. A roar moved across the landscape with the spreading news. "Peace!" the men shouted. Hurrahs went up for Lenin, for Trotsky. Caps were thrown in the air, and men danced on the lips of the trenches. "Peace! Land! Freedom!" A woman of the Battalion threw down her gun and joined them. Another. Briefly, it was all celebration, all joy, all camaraderie.

Then, without warning, everything changed. "Down with the bourgeoisie!" footsoldiers bellowed. "Kill them. Kill every last one of them." All along the line, officers scurried for their lives. On Yashka's orders, the Battalion were rounded up and then force-marched back to Molodechno. The two Filippovs were still with them, along with a handful of other male officers who had remained loyal, as well as the men who drove their supply wagons, the barrel-chested cook and his beanpole of an assistant. Twenty girls were missing. They'd been separated from the Battalion in the rear lines when the slaughter began and were caught finishing up a minor bit of work on the supporting trenches. They hadn't a chance: lynched, left hanging all in a row.

For a few tense hours overnight, the Battalion were made safe in the barracks of Molodechno. This night, everyone herded together seeking consolation, including the men, who had always before kept their distance from the women. Yashka looked on and said nothing. She made no reprimand to the cook who, in the absence of provisions, was swapping recipes with anyone calm enough to share in the game. Nor to Leonid, who was bravely failing to lighten the mood with his stale jokes. Nor to Gennady, an inch-long stick of charcoal in his fingers, who was sketching portraits of the girls on scraps of paper. It had long been whispered in the Battalion that Gennady Fyodorovich Filippov was sweet on Rivka, and therefore so was Leonid Gregorievich Filippov, for they did everything together. This was nonsense, as stupid as the nonsense others stuck to that Rivka was sweet on Yashka and vice versa—an opinion which, when it reached Rivka's ears gave her cause to observe with a faint, sad smile, "There's not half a kopek's worth of sweetness left in me."

Filippov Too reached into his pocket, pulled out a crust of bread and shared it with Rivka. They'd had nothing to eat since morning. Chewing at this small bit did more to whet her appetite than to calm it. "In 1915, when I was shot," said Gennady Fyodorovich, touching his chest, site of the old wound, "I could have gone home and been a pensioned hero. I guess I've been a fool."

"Isn't being a fool what life is about?" said Rivka with false cheer.

"So it would seem," he murmured, his eyes wide as a child's. "I never thought of it that way."

"Why, how old are you?"

"Twenty-one."

"Not many years older than me, after all."

"So what was the point of living another forty or fifty years if I violated my own code of ethics and walked away from a fight? I had to be able to sleep at night, you know."

She smothered a yelp of laughter, for this was absurd, given the time of night and their circumstances. "You're a decent man, Lieutenant. I hope you make it home in one piece."

At dawn, an ugly crowd milled outside their barracks, drinking, shooting off rifles into the air, demanding the Battalion surrender to them. Yashka stepped outside.

"Why do you threaten me? I am only a peasant like you."

"We are comrades. You are an officer. You mistreat the soldiers in your command by maintaining the discipline of the old regime."

She made her usual argument, that her discipline, admittedly harsh, was necessary lest her women become a battalion of shame. "Women are not like men. Is it customary for them to fight? What would become of a few hundred girls among thousands of men let loose without supervision and restraint?"

The mob was having none of it. The Battalion must disband without delay. "Three minutes. You have three minutes to surrender your weapons."

Three minutes was more than the girls needed. A long row of them filed out of the barracks shouldering their weapons, the men of the Battalion interspersed among them. The crowd smirked and catcalled and made lewd gestures. One of the ringleaders stood there, watch in hand, calling out the shrinking moments in intervals of fifteen seconds.

What would Yashka do? Rivka knew she would sooner take on the entire German army than surrender to this Bolshevik rabble. But the game was up. Peace, some said, had already been declared, and in any case, the war was over in Russia. Would Yashka fire on her own countrymen? Rivka's eyes scanned the men massed together. Most of them had come out unarmed. Would she obey Yashka's order to fire, if given?

"Time's up!" shouted the timekeeper.

A silence, in which hundreds of hearts throbbed in unison.

"Shoot!" Yashka commanded, and blindly Rivka squeezed the trigger. All up and down the line, girls were firing, some into the air, some point-blank into the crowd. Amid the roar of guns came screams and cries, men dropping or falling to the ground, others pushing themselves backward away from the acrid air, the smoke and the danger. Hundreds of men with one thought: to die on this of all days would be ludicrous.

"Go!" Filippov yelled. The women began escaping, out through the rear of the barracks to the wood beyond, while Filippov and the others kept shooting, covering their flight.

Already the mobbers were re-forming, bringing up guns and ammunition. Ten minutes and they'd be at full strength. "Harridans, mad bitches, we'll tear you all to pieces!"

Rivka, at Filippov's elbow, wavered. "Now!" he ordered. She ran with the others, ran full out: arms and legs pumping, lungs screaming for air, seven versts without letup through dense undergrowth, brambles tearing at her clothing, briars flaying the skin of her hands and face, thorned branches jabbing at her eyes.

A small clearing, the murky heart of the wood. A hundred and fifty terrified girls came plunging in, stumbling in, limping in. They huddled together, clung to each other, waiting for the marauders, for the rampage that would spell their doom.

The Battalion's wagons had headed off in a clatter for the village of Krasnoye. This had been Filippov's idea, a decoy. The plan was that after holding off the mob as long as possible, the men would outrace those hotheads to Krasnoye in the supply wagons and then melt into the fields and woods, stripping themselves of all signs of rank and becoming just more worn-out soldiers on their way home. All that night, Rivka lay awake in the darkness, listening to far-off shots. Flames flared in the sky and screams were carried on the breeze. Every rustle of the woods turned them all to stone.

Early the next morning, there came a low whistle, repeated three times. It was the cook's assistant, who had managed to infiltrate the mob and gone chasing up the road with them after the wagons. Every nook and cranny of the village was searched, but of course no sign of the women was found. "That Yashka, she must be a witch," they said to each other over swigs of the potato vodka they blundered onto in a cellar. When they were dead drunk, the cook's assistant had managed to slip away. The countryside was crawling with crazed soldiers, peasants and workmen hunting bloodsuckers and exploiters under every bush. They hunted phantoms, but they murdered flesh and blood. At last he came to the obvious truth: the Battalion must disband.

Yashka was slow to respond. "What have I not hoped from this Battalion," she said. "Everyone, Brusilov and Kerensky included, believed our self-sacrifice would shame the men. But the tide of ignorance has swamped all that was good and noble in Russia. The men know no shame. A pitiful finale for Russian womanhood, is it not?" She blinked strangely at the assistant. His eyes sought the ground. "One does not want to live," she sighed.

They hid another long day beneath thickets of gaily colored leaves. The women shivered. Autumn woods are dank and chilly when one hasn't eaten, and they had no supplies. No orders were given. Their Natchalnik was uncommonly silent and withdrawn. Rivka sat with Tatya, the last of her companions still alive.

"Come to Tiflis with me," said Tatya. As if Tiflis were around the corner instead of thousands of versts to the southeast, beyond the crests of the Caucusus Mountains.

Rivka shook her head. "I must go home." As if home were a hop, skip and jump rather than a week's unimpeded walk southward into the Ukraine. Not that unimpeded was something she could expect.

"It's unsafe, your village. It's so near to the frontier. The Germans—"

Tatya didn't know the half of it. If the Germans were a peril, so were pillaging Cossacks, anti-Semitic Ukrainian nationalists, and hotheaded Jewish Bolshevists. Any of them posed a danger. Yet her biggest fear was that her own family would turn their backs on her. And with good reason. For hadn't she turned her back on them? If not by intention, then by what she had become, the taste for war in her mouth, the smell of war on her skin? "Still," she said, "I must try to go my own way home."

Tatya took Rivka's scraped and oozing hands in hers. "If ever you change your mind, the invitation remains open."

Rivka's eyes filled. "And they say you're not a princess. They should only see you now."

It was the afternoon of the third day when they began dispersing. Every quarter hour, a handful of women went off to one of the villages or train stations scattered across the countryside. A kiss, a blessing, a quick exchange of hugs, and they slipped away into the world. By five o'clock, the Battalion of Death was no more.

V

Mischa

FOR WEEKS RIVKA walked. Having been taught to maim and kill, having been put in a trench and handed a rifle, having been expected to make war, she had now been put back in a skirt. She was now expected to go back and make beds, make bread, make Shabbes, make babies. The skirt felt loose around her legs. Underneath it, she felt lawless. She wondered as she walked what the biblical Yael must have done after pounding the tent peg through Sisera's forehead. On that part of the story, the holy text was silent. Rivka knew full well now how the slaying itself went—the resistance to the sharpened point of the man's flesh, muscle and bone, and then a sudden surrender, the shaft sliding slickly through his clotted brain. How Yael's hand must have jerked back so as not to foul itself with the gore bubbling out; and how she forced her attention outward to the tent's perimeter so as not to witness the man's body clutching, its stiffening and release, the nose-piercing reek of feces. Rivka had imagined her war would be, like Yael's, an opportunity for valor. Instead, it turned out, like everything else in her life, to mix high and low moments willy-nilly, without simplicity and without clarity. Amid the smoke and the noise, you couldn't make out what was actually happening, so how could you be sure which were your good actions and which your bad? Maybe, thought Rivka, it would have been better, after all, to wait behind a shuttered window for the return of your warrior, either carrying his shield or laid upon it. Too late for such thoughts: she had seen what she had seen, and the shutters could not be put back. It seemed in her life there was always too much of one thing, not enough of another. Too much peace until it was monotony. Too much adventure until it was chaos. Too much truth until it was horror.

Bochkareva could not be left alone to fend for herself. Rivka located a synagogue, where she organized clothing for them and wigs to cover their shorn heads. Yashka was like a dazed child, saying little, passively obeying Rivka's instructions. It was terrible to see her unnerved like this, worse than when she had strutted and slapped and ordered girls around. The Natchalnik, for the moment, was a beaten woman. Even at the front, where maintaining cleanliness was impossible, Yashka had meticulously brushed out her uniform every morning herself. Now, she could only by repeated reminders be cajoled into washing the dirt from her hands and face.

They trudged southward, avoiding marauders on the roads, moving at night and hiding out during the days. The countryside was in anarchy. Corpses lay unburied on the roadsides and in the woods: men, women and children, many stripped of their clothing, bony if death had come by starvation, gory if by violence, black-faced if by cholera. She thought she had been inured in her time at the front to all the horrors that humans could inflict upon one another. But that had been at the front amid the clamor and noisesomeness of battle, the filth of the trenches, the stench of no-man's-land, and the torn, charred, unearthly landscape of the war. The horrors she witnessed along the route where no enemy boot had yet trodden were something else again.

These things she could not forget: a gray old woman squatting by the side of the road, her naked frame wrapped only in a ragged blanket. A large brick house with a fine courtyard, at its center a marble statue of a winged sea monster rising from the roiling waves. The front door of the house was gone, and broken shutters lay about on the ground, along with the shattered innards of a gutted piano. Ringed about the base of the statue were the corpses of the family who'd lived there—a man, his wife, and four children, their heads hammered to pulp. At the center of a clearing, a stiff and frozen soldier, his officer stripes torn away, eyes open, lips retracted as if snarling, and on his chest, a brown dump of coiled excrement still steaming.

The children were the hardest to bear. By the efflorescence of the fires that bloomed every night, Rivka examined the face of each small corpse they came upon, swatting away vermin, praying not to uncover a shock of black hair, two eyes like olives and a sweet bow mouth. One day when they ventured into a market for food, she knelt down beside a child of about two. He looked so much like Dudie her heart stopped. He stared at her, thumb in his mouth.

"Dudie," she whispered. Then, correcting herself, "Yankeleh—it's your Rivkeleh."

The child's chin quivered.

Immediately, his mother scooped him up. She gave Rivka a long, suspicious stare.

Rivka turned away. This was not her boy. Her boy would be older now. Almost four. Maybe he wouldn't know her anymore. Maybe she wouldn't know him, and he'd pass right by. Could that be? Would it be him, and she'd see just another refugee like the scrappy little, filthy little ragamuffin she'd caught trying to filch her boots while she slept in the woods their first night out on their own?

After many nights of steady trudging, they reached the city of Rovno, which festered like a boil: swollen with people who had nowhere to go and inflamed with madmen of every stripe, who argued passionately on street corners, whose fights pulled in bystanders, spilling into the streets, stopping traffic. Everyone who was not elated with the recent turn of events was angry—and everyone, elated or angry, wanted what he could grab. Men boasted openly of dragging landowners out of their homes and murdering them. Hearing this, Yashka sank down weeping in the dust. "Ah, that such a day has come," she wailed, "when Russians are content to show the enemy a white flag, taking up arms instead against their own countrymen." A knot of toughs began eyeing her and edging nearer. Rivka grabbed Yashka's arm and dragged her away. It was typical that Yashka's first coherent thought since leaving the front had to be shushed lest they both find themselves dead at the side of the road. Her protests rang as Rivka hurried her out of there.

Below Rovno the countryside looked peaceful, unaffected by the war. The Germans were sure to come, though. Nothing was stopping them, unless it was their own shortness of supplies and troops. The air was crisp with a fragrance of apples. How could that be, with frost everywhere and winter setting in? Yet it seemed to Rivka that the air smelled of apples, sweet and tart together. She felt revived by it. Yashka, too, seemed to find some healing power in it. Gradually her shoulders squared themselves, and a spring returned to her step. They were on the move all night, following the railway south. Soon it would be dawn, but with the smell of home urging her forward, Rivka pushed on. Then, in the semidarkness a greasy odor of ash reached them. Yashka sniffed at the breeze and scowled.

It was an hour or so after sundown the next night when they crept behind walls and over fences into the village. From the little Rivka could see, the streets looked run-down, ramshackle. Shutters hung loose from shops that looked abandoned. A door here and there stood wide open. She'd grown up in this village expecting nothing ever to change. And now—in the blink of an eye, it seemed—everything had. She couldn't even be sure of the simplest welcome. Why would anyone want to know her when she'd been disobedient, willful, unwomanly?

In her parents' back yard, the shed was empty, the garden a tangle of weeds. The back door to the house swung open. Instinctively, the two seasoned soldiers dropped to the ground and took cover. A man—too short to be her father—stepped out and pissed, right there from the doorstep. Rivka bit down on her hand to muffle her squeal. With the light behind him, she couldn't make out his face, but she could hear him grunting in satisfaction as he folded himself into his trousers and went back inside, leaving the door ajar. A woman closed it, not Rivka's mother. "I don't know these people," she moaned. Although something about the woman was familiar.

"I'll go," whispered Yashka.

"Wait."

"Please. Let me do this."

Rivka stared. Never before had she heard the Natchalnik use the word please.

Bochkareva walked up the slope and around the house to the front. The man answered her knock.

"Where are the family who lived here?" she asked in a wild peasant Russian redolent of the steppes. Rivka, concealed nearby, smiled in relief. The old Yashka, working her magic.

"Who wants to know?"

"I come from Petrograd."

"And I'm the fallen Tsar. You're an imposter from some rat hole in Asia. Don't think you can fool me."

Yashka bowed, assuring him she had no intention of playing with the comrade. "Since the war I have been a laundress in Petrograd. Comrade Lenin—I do his shirts."

It was plain his first impulse was to smack her. His arm came up, palm open, but the story was so preposterous he burst out laughing instead. "Let me see your hands," he commanded. They were filthy and calloused. He sneered. "Where are your burns, then, laundress?"

She drew up her sleeves and showed him scars on her knuckles and forearms. Plausibly they were the work of boiled water and hot flatirons. She pointed to one. "On the very day of our Glorious Revolution, I was ironing a shirt of purest linen and white as snow—"

He cut her off, snarling, "And what brings the woman who cleans off Lenin's shit marks to stand at my door this morning?"

"A message from Comrade Mikhail Lefkovits."

From somewhere behind him came a woman's cry. "*Mischa?*"

His head swiveled. He barked an order of silence.

"Nobody here by that name," he told Yashka.

"Of course not. He is in Petrograd. I have a word from him for his family."

"I've already told you," he said. "Lefkovits doesn't live here. I do. Now, on your way, before I get the police after you."

"Please, a bit of bread—"

He slammed the door in her face. But Rivka, hidden at the side of the house, could hear, through the window, Rachel's voice pleading with him. "Was it Rivka at the door? Tell me, Shaul." And then a bleat, and the thud of her body hitting the wall.

Her best friend Rachel. Beaten by her father's unctuous office boy. In her father's house. What on earth was going on here? Who could she trust? Who might betray them? If the village was loyal to the Provisional Government, they could be accused of desertion; if to the Bolsheviks, then of counterrevolution. The fame of the Battalion had spread far and wide; surely, in her own village, Rivka would be recognized, her allegiance known. Until Mama and Papa could be found, until she knew how that toady Shaul had invaded her home, she must not show her face.

OF ALL PEOPLE, it was Nachum, her once-almost-betrothed, who told her. Two more nights in the gathering cold convinced her she had to take the chance that he would still be there and that he would be sympathetic. She rapped at Nachum's door, which was answered by a haggard-looking woman barely resembling the pretty young Miriam he'd married. Without a thought, she threw her arms around Rivka, catching them both by surprise. Nachum, too, was overjoyed to see her. So much had changed in so short a time that nothing of the old woes mattered anymore. To the contrary, meeting again, recalling what went on between them in their innocence—each grief, grudge, quarrel, heartache—was now a kind of pleasure. Especially in the face of what Nachum had to relate. They were sitting together over cups of a steaming brew so thin it might just as well be called water. "What do you know of my parents?" said Rivka. Nachum cleared his throat. Twice.

"The bootmakers *chevrah* took control of the boot factory, forcing your father out," he said. "But it was not they who murdered him."

She blanched. Murdered him?

Nachum's words kept coming, a swarm, an ambush. "It was the Bolsheviki, celebrating their takeover. They set fire to the factory, and when your father, bullheaded man that he was, tried to stop it, they strung him up and left him for the birds to devour. No one dared touch him for fear of suffering the same fate."

She found that Miriam was squeezing her hand. Dread begged Rivka not to ask, but of course she must: "And my mother?"

"Gone," said Nachum.

"Dead?"

"God forbid, Rivka, no. She couldn't continue on alone. Her arthritis was worse, she could hardly move. She has cousins, she said, up north in Grodno."

Rivka nodded. Cousins they barely ever saw.

"Two fellows from the Jewish relief agency said they could get her through the lines. She went north with them in a horse cart."

"—leaving word behind for you and Mischa," added Miriam. "She said to tell you this: 'Don't follow me. Follow your future.'"

Rivka wept without voice, without tears. At length, she asked, "And our home?"

"Seized by Shaul. He says he owns it, because of what your father properly owed him for his work at the factory. Rachel lives there with him."

"She's his wife?"

He shrugged.

"But why?

"What else was she to do? They're destitute, her family."

HALF THE WORLD, it seemed, was on the move. The two women blended in with refugees, returnees, displaced persons of every kind crossing the vast land by whatever means came to hand. Telegraph lines were cut, railroad lines were cut. Revolutionary gangs wearing red armbands roamed the roads with murder in their eyes.

Before leaving the village, Rivka had found a moment alone with Rachel and begged her to go with them. Rachel refused. It was too late for her, she said. She was too afraid. Besides, her mother counted on her. Rivka had never paid any attention at all to Rachel's mother, a drab creature always in the background who, after her sons left, seemed to fade entirely. Rachel, now, was washing out in the same way. Her parents would starve if she went away, she told Rivka. "Shaul gets Mama food. Papa is too frail to do it. No one will do it if I leave."

Rivka and Yashka traveled by train when they could. Otherwise, by peasant cart, telling trumped-up stories that were scarcely believable. On the last leg of their journey, Yashka—in a babushka and covered with a grimy cloak they'd found on the roadside—played the role of Rivka's ancient, sick mother, moaning and choking and calling upon God to take her soon. The peasant, who had lost one eye and three fingers of his right hand, took them all the way to Petrograd, never dreaming that Yashka was only twenty-eight years old.

The city was a shambles: shops closed, banks shuttered, food scarce, electricity uncertain, everyone on strike. Rain fell nearly every day, which didn't stop the crowds parading through the muddy squares waving revolutionary banners. *Long Live the Union of the Revolutionary and Toiling Masses!* Proclamations and decrees plastered the walls, covering fading posters that advertised long-closed theatrical pieces, opera, a concert by Chaliapin. Class warfare was out in the open. Its leadership and most of its followers believed this was only the prelude to a European-wide upheaval. The Winter Palace had been looted, its furnishings torn to pieces or carried off, its provisions plundered. Artillery surrounded the palace now: sailors from the Baltic Fleet preventing further raids on the Tsar's capacious wine cellars. Supreme Commander Kornilov was in prison, having been put there by Kerensky, who'd accused him of attempting a coup d'etat. Kerensky, too, was said by some to be in custody, though by others to have gone into hiding. The rest of the Provisional Government had fled or turned Bolshevik. Rumors choked the air. Most of them Rivka dismissed, but she could not rid her mind of the one she overheard about women soldiers who'd been raped and then tossed alive out of the upper-storey windows in the Winter Palace.

They couldn't get to Mischa's street because of an armed skirmish between the Reds and a band of holdouts opposing the Bolshevik takeover. Two days they waited to reach his shabby room, and then two more fruitless days hoping Mischa would show up. Rivka tried the University, then the Tauride Palace, where the Workers and Soldiers Council met. She took to scouring the streets, even asking complete strangers about her brother. Mischa was gone, and no one could tell her where. He'd evaporated like a ghost into thin air. The only evidence he'd ever been there at all was a torn and yellowing remnant of *Pravda* that she found between his mattress and the wall. *What is Kerensky?* it said. *A usurper, whose place is in prison with Kornilov. A criminal and a traitor to the workers, soldiers, and peasants, who believed in him. Kerensky? A murderer of soldiers! Kerensky? A public executioner of peasants! Kerensky? A strangler of workers! Such is the second Kornilov who now wants to butcher liberty!*

ONE DAY, YASHKA was "invited" by a Red Guard and a private with a naked sword to the Smolny Institute to pay a call on Lenin and Trotsky. She went willingly enough, never doubting that her influence and her view of affairs would be of value to them. She expected to return that evening, and before leaving promised Rivka to ask about Mischa. She was held two days in the dank cellar of the building. Rivka brought food and left messages begging her not to forget Mischa.

Upon her release, Yashka announced that the Bolsheviks had invited her to join them at the highest level of government. "Naturally, I refused their blandishments." Naturally, she instructed Lenin and Trotsky on the cruel but absolute necessity of pursuing the war against the Germans, whose grip upon Russian lands was every day becoming tighter. They treated her like an illiterate peasant (which, admittedly, she was), one who knew nothing of politics, of war, or of the world. "Rogues and fools, one or the other," she ranted. "All of them."

"Of Mischa? What did you find out about my brother?"

She stared at Rivka, frowning. "Don't you be a fool."

If ever Rivka came close to slapping Yashka, it was that moment. The blow was right there, incipient at the end of her arm, sweating in the fastness of Rivka's fist. But despite all the failings Rivka had witnessed in her, Yashka was still formidable: madly capable, had she fathomed Rivka's fury, of baring her breast and shrieking, "Beat me! Kill me!" In such a case, what could Rivka have done but fall to her knees weeping and begging for Yashka to come to her senses? So all in all, it was better that Yashka happened at that hot moment to turn away from her—stepping to the window to view a demonstration pass by in the street below—and the occasion for slapping was lost to time.

As far as Yashka was concerned, Mischa was never the issue. Whether or not she had learned that Mischa was on his way south with the Red Guard, Yashka told Rivka nothing about it. Of what use to her were his orders to destroy counterrevolutionary activity? Or the fact that he obeyed orders scrupulously because of his passion for the cause of Bolshevism? No one could have predicted he'd turn out to be such an excellent soldier, that men would trust him as their leader because he was capable of calculating his chances, and he never took chances except when they were necessary. For Yashka, politics were the issue. War was the issue. Russian fate was the issue. Would Rivka never understand this?

THE LAST TATTERED remnant of the Battalion of Death was ripping in two. General Kornilov had escaped from prison and made his way south below Kiev to the Don region. Yashka was for following him there: the General would rally loyal troops around him and crush this plague of Red Guard spreading across the land. With Kornilov, they could continue the valiant struggle to redeem Mother Russia. Rivka argued that all of the Ukraine would soon be in German hands. She was not ready to surrender to foreign rule, but neither would she fight the Bolsheviks. She was for heading into Georgia if the roads weren't blocked. Tatya would take them in—if she still lived, if she had made it all the way home—and then Rivka could try to rescue her mother from German hands and bring her to Tiflis.

"Traitor! Go, then."

"With pleasure!"

But she didn't go. Neither one of them left the other. Together, they drifted south, disputing, quarreling, angling off to east or west, then wandering back in the opposite direction, each one threatening daily, sometimes hourly, to abandon the other. Meanwhile, the Germans nibbled at the land, and the Red Guard went on building their blockades. The two women made a wide berth around Kiev, which was said to be in Bolshevik hands. So, too, if you could trust what people reported, were Poltava, Kharkov, Ekaterinoslav, Odessa, Nikolaev.

Rivka remembered the day early in the war when Mama asked Papa, "What will we do if the Germans come?" Papa gave a shrug and said, "We can learn German." It so happened Rivka understood a few words of German, a few sayings and proverbs. She'd been with Papa several times on his trips into Galicia. Their business was conducted in the shtetls, but to get there they had to pass through an Austrian town, peasant boys taunting them all the way. "*Alle Juden stinken,*" the children shrieked, lobbing stones, laughing. This was all of that language Rivka felt she needed to know. In Bolshevik Russia there would be no more Jew-baiting, no pogroms. Jews were to be equal citizens, as good as anyone else, comrades all.

Yet these same comrades had murdered Papa. So what was Rivka to do, and where was she to go? To Mama—and the usurping

Germans? With Yashka—to shed more blood under the command of counterrevolutionary Kornilov? Back to Mischa's Petrograd, insurrectionist and brawling? All the way to Princess Tatya—on the chance she still lived and had made it home into Georgia? West or south or north or east, nowhere made good sense. Thus Rivka fretted, her mind spinning itself in endless tangles of doubt.

It snowed in the night, wet and heavy, blanketing the piney wood where they slept. They had built a rough shelter and were huddled together sleeping by a guttering fire. They never heard any footfalls until the squad of local milita was upon them demanding to see their papers.

"What do you want with us?" Yashka mewled. "A couple of harmless babas?"

They didn't even bother to smirk, just tied the women's hands and prodded them forward, stumbling, out to the road. It was a trudge of about seven versts to the squadron's headquarters. By the time they reached there, Rivka was soaked through and exhausted.

A man was brought in. He walked with a limp. His clothing was threadbare. Dark eyes glistened in his weathered face as he studied them. "It's her," he said, pointing. "Bochkareva."

"How—"

The squadron leader held up his hand to silence her. "You are the woman known as Yashka."

"I have never seen that man before in my life. How dare he claim to know me?"

"A mere formality," he said. "The whole world knows you, Yashka."

A sudden gleam of satisfaction brightened the Natchalnik's face.

"And in any case," the officer continued. "You were traveling the road toward the counterrevolutionary terrorists and their useless efforts. That itself is cause enough to execute you both."

"Not so," bluffed Rivka. "We are making a visit to our friend in Georgia. We've lost our way. We have an invitation. If you'll free my hands, I'll be able to show you her letter." There was no letter, but with hands free....

He was too young, this fellow, to wear such a hard face, such empty eyes. He smiled his handsome, monstrous smile in her face. His rank breath whiffled her hair. "Why waste my time with a forgery?" he said. He turned to his men, made a quick slice of his thumb across his throat, and left the room.

Rifles poking their spines, the women were prodded back out onto the road. The snow had stopped. "Boys, I am one of you. I am only a peasant." Yashka's voice rich and plummy.

"Shut up, whore," ordered her captor, slamming the butt of his weapon against her ear.

They were herded to a ditch by the roadside and instructed to kneel. Rivka fought down the bile rising into her throat. This, then, was to be her fate. To die for nothing, to lie unburied in an unconsecrated piece of gravelly mire at the back end of nowhere. Her muscles had turned to water, but she willed herself as she sank down in the mud not to soil her name. Let the end of her life be brave.

The men joined a knot of Red Guard waiting at a roadblock just ahead. The officer in charge was not a large man, but his dominance over the others was patent, even though his back was turned to them while he studied some document in his hand.

"Be content," Yashka whispered. "You have done well and honorably."

Coming from Yashka, these words of praise meant everything to Rivka. Yashka had seen her at her worst. "I hope so," she said unsteadily.

"In this life it's the best one can hope for. The rest is of no consequence."

Now, the officer turned and strode their way, the sun behind him in the clearing sky. The skirts of his heavy woolen coat swung across his boots as he approached them. His gait was so familiar that even with the sun watering her eyes Rivka knew him.

She did not cry out, nor did Yashka.

He cupped her chin in his right hand, the one with a missing forefinger. Among his men it was gospel that this lost digit had been eaten off by rats while he lay insensible in a dungeon. Mikhail Iakovich, it was widely believed, had spent years as a political prisoner at the Tsar's infamous Shlisselburg Prison, where he'd been beaten and tortured and left for dead on the cramped and slimy floor of his cell. Some fellows claimed to have been there themselves, in such-and-such a month, in such-and-such a year, and with their own eyes to have seen the comrade caged up. The bolder among them claimed to have exchanged a word with him.

There was little time, Mischa murmured, and very little he could do for Bochkareva. He would get her to the nearest train station. From there, she was on her own. He recommended going east. Germans were flooding in from the west and would soon take Kiev. The Bolshevik Red Guard were coming in force from the north, killing landowners, counterrevolutionaries, anyone whose sympathies did not match their own.

"But you're one of them," said Rivka.

"I do what I can to rein them in. Someone has to."

"Even though they murdered your father," said Bochkareva.

Papa dead? He hadn't known. He swung away from them into the trees, his shoulders slumped, arms limp at his sides. Papa, the strongest influence of his life, gone. Mischa had disagreed with nearly everything Papa taught him about business and politics, about learning and the way to live. He felt he'd failed his father by not being the right kind of son. Yet he had loved Papa and knew that Papa loved him. They'd shared something, a belief in ethical behavior, for lack of a better term. The expression of this belief was as different as each from the other, but the ethic was the same. For Papa, it was to be found in the development of a thriving enterprise, one that treated workers fairly and produced goods one could be proud of. Ah, Papa, so proud. From nothing he had built something that supported men and their families and enabled his customers to tread firmly upon the earth. Papa preferred to see the fairness in this. Mischa saw the unfairness. Not that Mischa minimized Papa's accomplishment, far from it. Surely, Papa had been heroic, but Mischa believed in a better way: one in which workers would not be obliged to rely upon the ethical heroism of employers who were rarely like his father. One in which the means of production would be owned by everyone, and everyone would share fairly in what was produced. Everyone would know the pride in production. Everyone would be rewarded with the fruits of labor. No one would live off the work of others. No one would suffer from want.

Through the trees, Mischa could see the men under his command becoming uneasy in his absence. At the roadblock, they shifted their weight and muttered as they kept watch. Several had their weapons trained on the women. Yashka seemed on the point of addressing them until a stiff frown from Rivka quelled her. Every time these comrades of his committed an act of barbarity, it horrified him. Now, barbarity had struck home in his own family: a senseless leftover from the old regime, an act of wantonness carried out by a populace not yet attuned to the values of the new. *Papa*, his heart cried—half prayer, half promise—the new will come, though progress is necessarily slow. First, the revolution must be secured from those who oppose it. Then the world will see something unprecedented—a polity based on the welfare of the masses, not just a favored few. To bring this just society into being, Mischa stood prepared to give up his own life. In such a time as this, the value of any man's existence meant something different from what it had ever meant before. He grieved for Papa very deeply and sincerely—but that was personal. Poor Papa, who'd never understood.

Mischa squared his shoulders and came back through the trees. Rivka, sorrowing with him, but reliant on him, was relieved to see his control regained. It was none too soon for that trigger-happy squad of his.

He helped the two women to their feet, untying the cords that bound their wrists. "Get out of the country," he told Rivka. "Get out if you can. Come back when this madness is over."

"You will see to Mama?"

"I'll see to her."

"She's in Grodno with Cousin Chana."

"Then she's safe. For now."

"And you?"

"I'll be fine."

"Mischa, come with us."

"Impossible," he said. "That I cannot do. My place is here in Russia."

"How did this happen, that we two should choose opposite sides?"

He shook his head. There was no answer, of course. Just the question.

"You're staying because of that man. It's him, Lenin."

Fiercely, he said, "It's anyone who would bring this new world into being."

"He's not a god." To hold herself back from embracing him, Rivka rubbed at the rope burns on her wrists. "Don't think him a god, Mischa. He'll break your heart."

"Go," he said. "We are on the right side of history. They—you—are on the wrong side."

No, she was not. But she had no comeback, no truth to fling in the face of events. And even if she possessed the truth and the means to articulate it—this hour was not ripe for it. People weren't ready to hear, not even Mischa. Fight for this truth, and you would lose. You might lose everything. But bide your time, waiting for the right moment, and in the meanwhile you'd have to make yourself complicit in the atrocities of the hour. There was no good course of action if she stayed.

"Get to America if you can. Go to Uncle Shmuel in Chicago. The war can't go on forever. Write to me when mail service is restored. Send me word through Mama."

"One thing you must do for me."

"Name it."

"Find Dudie. Take him under your protection." When his face clouded, she added, "If you can."

He promised.

"I will always love you Rivkeleh, my little sister."

She smiled down at him. "And I you, my big brother."

AND SO SHE slipped eastward into Asia with Yashka, using papers from Mischa that gave them safe passage thousands of versts across the vast steppe to Vladivostok. The train was filthy, crowded and dangerous. It crawled across the flat, empty land while they leaned against a wall or crouched on their haunches. Men poked and prodded them, pretending to stumble into them when the train lurched, grabbing their breasts as if unwittingly. Everywhere, strife, starvation and disease. Countrymen raised fists, or shovels, or rifles against one another. Every so often, the train stopped, and soldiers of the Red Army climbed aboard. Yashka never referred to them as an army, always in public as the Red Guard, in private as rogues and scoundrels. Mischa's papers were good, never questioned except by one fox-faced member of the local soviet in a small village several hundred versts beyond Cheliabinsk, gateway to the Urals.

The fellow couldn't have been older than twenty-five, though he strutted about as if the whole world ought to fall on its knees before his magnificence. He had them hauled from the train under guard and made them stand shivering in the freezing wind while he examined them, enthroned in a sleigh. Gently he stroked the gray head of a hound wrapped up with him in the thick carriage robes. He asked impertinent questions suggesting first, that the papers were forgeries, and poorly executed ones at that; second, that the women had procured said forgeries by performing hideous sexual acts with the gang who faked the documents; and third, that they were conspiring to overthrow the great Bolshevik revolution all by themselves, two pathetic clumps of rag who could hardly aspire to the status of womanhood—a theory which produced such gales of laughter from the wastrels hanging around that he sent the women back to the train, sent them in much the same way as he would kick his dog into the corner when he tired of it.

For her own protection, of course, Yashka was out of her uniform, wearing a wide peasant skirt with blouse and shawl, but she frequently ordered men about, raising their ire and their suspicion. Fortunately, she kept mostly to herself. When they pulled into a station, Rivka was sent out to buy bread and tea. But money was worthless in the new Russia, and anyway, no bread was to be had.

Where the Bolsheviks held sway, the peasants were told to trade their grain for goods at much less than the grain was worth. Field after field burned, destroyed by the farmer's own hand. Or else the grain was loaded into private boxcars and sent eastward out of Asia toward the great cities of Russia, snarling traffic on the rails, the cars stoutly defended by armed men who had returned from the front with their guns and a determination to get a decent return on the work of their hands. At one stop, a skeletal man with a bush of coal black hair had been hanged in the middle of the village square. His crime? Stealing a three-month-old out of its cradle. His purpose? To prepare and then eat the infant. After seeing this, Rivka refused to leave the train again until Tomsk. But fear stalked the train, too, and no one was safe.

Cadres of Czecho-slavics, who had yesterday been Russia's prisoners of war, were today forming into units and fighting pitched battles with Reds along the railway. Add to them the packs of just plain bandits who might attack the train and steal whatever you had—Rivka's coat was taken at gunpoint, along with Yashka's flag of the Battalion, kept hidden all this time; add the lice who made a vast picnic of the throng of crushed-together humanity; add the cold, the dampness, the malodorous clothing of travelers who'd spent too many nights in waterlogged trenches or moldy prison cells or smoky peasant huts, and you had a journey that, like the war, combined long hours of discomfort and boredom with brief but all-consuming moments of terror.

AT TOMSK, IN Asian Russia, they left the train and walked most of the way to their destination in the village of Tutalsk. Yashka's family home there was a mean little shack, low-ceilinged, dirt-floored. Yashka's father smelled rankly of drink and sweat. He said little and was gruff when he did speak. Her mother was overjoyed to take them in. She served them platters piled high with cabbage and pig parts that glistened in their own fat. Her withered face, too, shined with grease. She stood back, arms folded across shrunken breasts, watching them chew. Such a feast, who knew what it had cost her? Rivka did her best to avoid the disgusting meat, stomach lurching with every careful bite of cabbage.

There was a sister, Nadia, to whom Rivka took an instant and deepening dislike. What it was about her that Rivka found so repellent she couldn't say. The girl was decent enough, if a little mulish. Her mannerisms were much like Yashka's: the way she smiled, tight-lipped; the way she had of grasping a glass of tea from above; the way she had of scratching at the corner of her mouth when deep in thought; the way she tossed her head in anger. Rivka had thought Yashka an original, yet now here was another like her. Rivka felt obscurely cheated.

Yashka herself was exuberant, full of girlish energy, glad to be Maria, Marushka, Manya, Manka, once again.

After a few days, her mother begged, "Stay with us, both of you. You'll be safe here." Rivka would rather have died than live in that hut and eat that food. As it turned out, she didn't need to say so, for Yashka was equally bent on leaving. Yashka had a mission to carry out. And as usual, she had the ability to surprise Rivka with it. Having failed to ignite the hearts of fourteen million Russian soldiers, who were wrongheaded, of course, she said, but even now coming to their senses—she would now embark on a new and vital quest to ensure that the Allies of Western Europe and America would not abandon them.

"The peasants are almost to a man against the Bolsheviks," she claimed. "They need only a leader to inspire and unite them."

Rivka, keeping her reservations to herself, wondered aloud where such a leader might be found.

Yashka said, "They know me. I am of the people."

Behold Russia's savior. "To do what?"

"Restore the front," she said.

"A yor mit a mitwoch," muttered Rivka.

Yashka threw back her head and laughed, surprising Rivka, who thought she wouldn't understand the Yiddish—"in a year and a Wednesday"—meaning, roughly, it'll never happen.

"Little footsoldier," she said, "I will do it. You will see."

"How?"

"I will go to America and ask for their help."

"How will you survive in America? Do you have family there?"

"I have no intention of staying long."

"What then?"

"I shall tell our story to all who will listen." Her eyes grew bright. "I shall travel from the west to the east of that great land, to the capital, Washington, D.C."

"Where you will graciously deign to meet with the President, I suppose," said Rivka, no longer bothering to hide her sarcasm.

Yashka seemed not to notice. "I shall fall on my knees in front of Mr. Wilson and beg him to send troops and arms and food for our forsaken land. I shall offer to lead."

Gutt in himmel, she was in earnest.

"From there, I'll sail to England and call on King George."

"What makes you think the monarch of the British Empire will be waiting to see you?"

"What makes you think he won't?"

That was Yashka for you.

"From there, I'll return to Russia to continue the fight."

"The fight is over," Rivka said.

Maria Leontievna Bochkareva shook her head. "Never over."

WHEN THEY BOARDED the train again they were met with the news that a peace treaty had been signed giving up all of White Russia and the Ukraine to the Germans. The capital was being moved from Petrograd east to Moscow, a safe distance from the new German border. It was March of 1918. Mama's crocuses would be coming up, yellow and white against the black Ukrainian earth. Rivka hoped they'd give Rachel pleasure even for a moment.

Gray uniforms might at this moment be marching along the streets of their village. She prayed life would be easier for her *landsleit* under German rule. She knew it would not. The Germans needed the harvest to feed their armies, who were being starved out behind a British blockade. They would strip the country bare. The peasants would find a way to blame the Jews. They always did, whenever food became scarce. Pogroms were bound to erupt, and would the Germans lift a finger to stop them? Probably not. Why should they? Especially since Jews were known to be prominent among the Bolshevist leaders. She said a prayer for Rachel and for her neighbors and all the people of the village. Including Shaul? No. She knew she ought to, but she could not include Shaul in her prayers.

Interlude

Yashka's Version

THE GREAT JEWISH writer S. Ansky describes Russia at this time as having two regimes, each ignoring the other. Think of it, its dual realities. Then think of this: that as with the public, political history, so it was with private, personal histories. Rivka had one story, but it was not the same one Yashka told. Two realities, neither ignorant of the other, yet each ignoring the other. In Russia at the time, this too was possible. So now, here is Bochkareva's version, as she told it:

When the Bolsheviks took power in the fall of 1917, Rivka left the front on her own, like the rest of my girls. Where she was headed, I knew not. Rivka is a good girl, and she is dear to me. I do not say that she lies, only that she has been led astray by her own dream of what ought to be. I did not go south into the Ukraine with her. Though I was still being hunted, I would not hear of shedding my uniform. By dint of luck, I managed to get myself smuggled away from the front in a motorcar, crouching on the floor in back so as to stay hidden from guards at the checkpoint. It was a harrowing few moments that seemed to stretch out forever. Fortunately, they did not search the car, else I'd have been dragged out and shot. Mine was the narrowest of escapes, and only the first of them.

I made my way by rail to Petrograd. Upon deboarding, I was politely arrested by a Red Guard Commissar accompanied by a private with a naked sword. They took me to the Smolny Institute, headquarters of the Bolshevik Government. There, I was forcibly separated from my pistol and sword and sequestered overnight in a dark cellar without food, water or sanitary facilities. In the morning, I was brought before Lenin and Trotsky. Picture them triumphant before me: Lenin looking like the typical Russian, Trotsky like the Jew he is, and me disarranged after days on the run and a night in their cellar. Nonetheless, they greeted me courteously with praises for my service and my courage. Soon enough, they came to the point, which was to invite my participation in their Bolshevist party!

Not for the world would I join them. They pretended not to understand why. I knew the uselessness of arguing with them, but even so, I tried to convince them of the necessity of prosecuting the war against Germany. "Take the soldiers away from the front, and the Germans will come and seize upon everything they can lay hands on," I said. "This is war. Why did you take it upon yourselves to rule the country? You will ruin it!"

They laughed in my face. Who was I? Only an illiterate peasant woman.

After I'd argued all I could, I asked, "Am I free to go?" I was not at all sure of my release. When they rang for a Red Guard, I feared he might take me straight to prison. He escorted me from the room—and gave me a passport and free passage to my home near Tomsk.

For a week I traveled unnoticed, confined in a train compartment. How did I eat, you may ask. It was awkward, but not impossible. I arranged for a sympathetic passenger to buy me food at the stations. Then, on the eighth day, when the train slowed nearing Cheliabinsk, I took the chance of leaving the compartment and stepping out onto the gangway to stretch my legs in the fresh air. Bad luck: a knot of soldiers recognized me and immediately began harassing me. I was a harlot, they said. I ought to be killed. "You fools," I said in turn. "What harm have I done you?" Fools they certainly were, but strong and quick, too. Instantly I was picked up and thrown from the moving train. I'd have been killed had I not landed in a bank of snow piled along the railway. Though badly injured, I was able to continue the journey.

Four days, four agonizing days, my right knee dislocated, my leg badly swollen, heavy as a log. When, after four more days, I reached home, my sisters, mother and father were all waiting for me at the door of the coach, crying and sobbing. My impending arrival and invalid condition had been telegraphed to them, and they had taken it into their heads that I was coming home to die. I was a month recuperating under their care, passing Christmas and meeting the New Year in bed. As I began to heal, I took short walks into the village. At the post office I found a letter from my adjutant Princess Tatuyeva, telling me of her safe arrival in Tiflis. Then a telegram arrived from General Anosov in Petrograd: *Come. You are needed.* I did not falter. I left immediately.

It was January 1918, and the Germans had begun their lightning advance into the heart of Russia. The mood in the trains was transformed. "We're being sold out!" could be heard, along with other outbursts of doubt and confusion and even rancor against the Bolshevik government. "We were told that the Germans would not advance if we left the front."

Reds on the train were careful to explain that it was only the German bourgeoisie who were pursuing the war, that the great revolution would soon spread to Germany. "Any day now," they said.

"Hmmmm," came the response. "Unless Lenin and Trotsky have also been delivered into the hands of the accursed Germans."

The awakening of the masses, I felt, could not be long postponed.

IN PETROGRAD, THE river was so full of the corpses of slain officers you could have leapfrogged across it on their backs. Terror ruled the city, and everywhere people hid, starving. At a secret meeting of officers and other anti-Bolsheviks, I was asked to go south and establish a link with General Kornilov, who was thought to be operating with the remnants of a loyal army somewhere in the Don region. "I will not draw arms against my own people," I warned. "Every Russian is dear to my heart, even those who, for the moment, are misguided." However, I did agree to seek out Kornilov, report the support he had in Petrograd, and open communication between us.

I traveled south by train costumed in the white wimple and dark habit of a Sister of Mercy. Only my eyes, nose, mouth and cheeks were visible. Men spoke to me on the journey, as men feel free to do. Without recognizing me they griped unanimously about "that she-devil Bochkareva." One man, filthy and ill-favored, barked, "She ought to be executed by firing squad. No trial. Why waste the time?" Oh, how he detested Bochkareva—but he was much taken with me as the Sister of Mercy, and before the trip was over, he proposed marriage! I put him off by promising to wed as soon as my journey was over and I could return to him. He gave me his address, and I pledged to write to him. Perhaps he is still waiting for my letter.

After several days, we reached a point thirty versts north of Zverevo, where all passenger trains had to be switched to other tracks going east or west. Only military transport was permitted to proceed further, since the front began thirty versts directly south at Zverevo. The front at Zverevo, I had learned from my suitor, was not a continuous line, but a series of posts maintained on one side by the Reds and on the other by the Kornilovists.

Still habited and wimpled, my uniform tucked underneath, my feet in army boots, I left the train and approached the Commandant of the station. I was a penniless Sister of Mercy, I claimed. I had to return homeward immediately by direct route through Zverevo. It was urgent that I reach my sick mother at Kislovodsk, the famous spa resort in the northern Caucusus Mountains. "Private passengers are not permitted," he said. To bolster my sob story, I showed him three things: a false passport, a ticket direct to Kislovodsk, and a face filled with tragedy. The Commandant made an exception for me and cleared me straight through.

Of course, I did not go on to Kislovodsk. At Zverevo, I disembarked and walked until I found an old peasant chopping wood outside his hut.

"Good day, grandfather."

"Good day, little sister."

"Would you drive me to the city?"

"Which city?"

"The one where my sick mother is waiting." I named the place of Kornilov's headquarters.

The old man smacked his forehead. "Great God! How is it possible? The Bolsheviks don't let anybody pass."

"But people do go sometimes."

"Sometimes they do."

"I will give you fifty rubles for getting me through."

He scratched his neck and considered the matter further. Then he harnessed his horse.

WRAPPED IN A peasant shawl and the old man's shapeless overcoat, I sat like a heap in the cart. "What shall I tell the sentries?" whined the old man.

"Tell them you are carrying your sick baba to a hospital in the city. Say she is suffering from a high fever." He was sitting on a pelt, and I had him cover me with it, so that my skin would become hot to the touch.

We approached the sentries, my heart pounding. I began to moan as if in pain. The horse stopped, and a voice asked sharply, "Where are you going?"

"To a hospital in the city."

"What have you got there?"

"My baba. She is dying."

Here I groaned louder. There was a pause, some muffled conversation among the guards. I could not see what was happening. Then the horse started up again. Without uncovering my face, they had let us through.

SOME LITTLE TIME later, I heard a harsh cry, "Halt!" We had reached Kornilov's lines, and my driver began to repeat our story. Imagine his surprise when I threw off my coverings, paid the man his fifty rubles and jumped down from his cart! I would not need him anymore. The faces of astonished men surrounded me, and I was laughing so hard I could not explain myself.

"Who are you?" said an officer.

"A Sister of Mercy going to see General Kornilov."

"The devil you will. You're arrested."

This sent me into new peals of laughter. I threw off my headdress. "It's Bochkareva!"

That's how I reached Kornilov. He greeted me jovially, "How do you do, little sister?" It was February of 1918.

What did we talk of, me and the "renegade" General? Of the heavy darkness settling on Russia. Of the need to enlighten the masses. Of the great cause lost, unless the Allies could be persuaded to aid in both reconciling with the soldiery and reestablishing the fight against the encroaching Germans. On all this we agreed. With no money, no food, and a force of only three thousand, Kornilov's condition was precarious. But when the General asked me to join him, I had to decline once again to fight against my own countrymen. "The Russian soldier is dear to me, although led astray for the present," I told him.

I parted from Kornilov the next day. My mission there had all gone so easily that I had determined to return across the lines by myself. I was cautious, crawling much of the way on all fours. I had made a couple of versts through the war zone when I had the misfortune to be sighted by a Red patrol. Shouting, "A spy! A spy!" the men chased me into a wood and sent a stream of bullets my way. Once I was among the trees, it was not hard to evade them, and I was soon able to go on my way, but I knew my costume would no longer protect me. Much as I had savored the disguise, I had to bid the Sister of Mercy a sad farewell. Deep in the forest, I took off and buried the dress and wimple and the false papers that went with them.

I came out of the trees in uniform and made my way back to the train station at Zverevo, where I turned myself in to the Acting Commandant, one Ivan Ivanovich Petrukhin. Petrukhin reminded me of Rivka's brother, a young man with an open face and thoughtful eyes. "I am on my way to Kislovodsk," I told him, "to seek care at the mineral springs for the unhealed battle wounds to my spine." I showed him my ticket and my letter from Tatuyeva. I could see he was disposed to believe me and let me go. But at that moment, in came the ruthless brute Pugachov, assistant to the Commmander of the Bolshevik Army. Puffing and perspiring, he rubbed his hands together and boasted of having just gouged out the eyes of five Kornilovist officers. His hideous cackle sent shudders up my spine.

This Pugachov was hot for executing me immediately. "I wouldn't even waste bullets on her. I'll call the men, and they'll make a fine kasha of her!"

Petrukhin, however, insisted on summoning ten members of the Investigation Committee to consider my case. The Investigation Committee were all common soldiers. I felt nothing could be expected from them, certainly not mercy or reason—and meanwhile Pugachov ordered me brought to a railway car where forty imprisoned men awaited execution. "You will not be released alive," he told me. No matter what the committee's decision, Pugachov vowed to kill me.

This was no idle threat. A killing ground only a few hundred feet away was littered with bloated, half-naked corpses heaped everywhere. A doomed prisoner could not avoid tripping over the rotting bodies as he was led in horror to the place of his own execution. Cooped up in the poisonous air of the car, with nothing to do but contemplate my end, I wept and fell to my knees and demanded of God why I, of all people, deserved such a death.

The door to the railroad car opened. "Bochkareva!"

Somehow my heart leaped with joy. "I am here," I answered, believing my prayers had been heard, and I was to be released.

"Take off your clothes!"

What did this mean?

An old general's name was called, and then a number of other prisoners' names were read out, all officers, all ordered to strip. It was a call for execution. The Bolsheviks needed all the uniforms they could get, and this was the inexpensive way of obtaining them.

We were led from the car, twenty of us in our underwear, to a slight elevation of ground. We were placed in a line with our backs to a hill. There were corpses behind us, in front of us, to our left, to our right, under our very feet, at least a thousand of them. We waited. Two other members of the Investigation Committee had to come, since all twelve were needed for the execution. The two were on their way. The wait was agonizing, and tears streamed down my cheeks. "Don't grieve," urged the old general, putting a fatherly arm around my shoulder. "We will die together." He was a good man, and his strength gave me courage.

Acting Commandant Petrukhin, meanwhile, had been working in my favor, using the time to angle for further delay. He'd applied to the Commander in Chief and obtained an order to keep me under guard, but unharmed. When all were assembled on the killing grounds—Petrukhin; Pugachov; the full committee of twelve; a firing squad numbering a hundred soldiers, sailors and Red Guard; plus we hapless victims shivering in our underwear—Petrukhin presented the Commander's signed order. My heart was in my throat.

"Too late!" roared the ruthless Pugachov. "It's enough of talking." He lifted his arm. The executioners raised their rifles. The order to shoot was on his eager lips when one of the newly arrived committeemen stepped forward, blocking the line of fire.

"Are you Yashka?" he said, peering intently at me.

"How do you know me?"

"Remember how you saved my life in that March offensive? I was wounded in the leg and you dragged me under fire out of the mud. I would have perished there, in the water, and many others like me, if not for you." He craned his neck, a painful expression on his face. "Why do they want to shoot you?"

"Because I am an officer."

"I won't allow it!" he cried. My God-appointed savior pulled me out of line and occupied my place himself. "Before you execute this woman, you will shoot me first!"

Commotion. The hundred soldiers and sailors of the firing squad began arguing among themselves, deliberating my fate. They were hopelessly divided. Five minutes, ten minutes, my life hanging in the balance, my nineteen compatriots waiting stoically in that cold desolation. For them, there would be no reprieve from death. Finally, the Investigation Committee put their heads together and took charge of the melee. "We have an order from the Commander in Chief to keep Bochkareva under guard," they declared. "It shall be obeyed."

That brute Pugachov was in a white rage. The committee members closed about me, and we marched off the field. Behind me, I heard Pugachov raving like a madman. "Fire at their knees." A volley of shots split the air. Cries and groans roared in my ears. I turned and saw a hundred bloodthirsty savages rushing upon the heaped-up victims, their bayonets thrusting, their boot heels stomping out the last flickering bits of life. It was more than I could bear. I staggered and fell to the ground in a swoon.

BY ORDER OF the Commander in Chief, I was transported under guard to Moscow to await trial by a military tribunal. The journey by train took three days. Upon my arrival, I was locked in a cell that already held a score of other prisoners. The cell was small, crowded, airless, no toilet. Imagine the stench, you cannot. No food was provided, nor water either.

After a few days, one of my fellow prisoners—who'd been caught cursing Bolshevism while drunk—was set free. Through him I sent word of my plight to friends in Moscow, who brought me sustenance. The generosity of this act was no small thing. The quarter pound of bread and quarter pound of butter they provided represented two-thirds of their bread ration and all of their butter for a week. I was by then unable to walk by myself and needed to be supported by the guard, who virtually carried me to the little room where we were allowed to meet for a quarter hour. No less than the food and water, the encouragement my friends gave me saved my life.

When finally I was brought before the tribunal, I clung to my story. They were six young men, all common soldiers, seated at a long table covered with a green cloth in the middle of a large, richly decorated hall. I told them of a wound in my spine, the surgery needed to extract a piece of shrapnel, the advice of a Petrograd physician to seek relief in the springs of Kislovodsk, my total ignorance of the front at Zverevo, my illiteracy, my ignorance of politics. The six judges, not one of them over thirty years of age, heard me out and then promised a ruling within the week. I was taken to yet another military guardhouse to await sentencing, this time in the company of drunken sailors and Red Guard.

Shut up in the narrow cell with ten lawless males, I was the object of constant and escalating abuse. By the prisoners, I was threatened with rape and torture. By my jailers, with execution. The week ended, and no decision came. I was driven near to insanity, every day a torment, every hour a struggle, every minute an agony. Two and a half weeks I lived in that inferno, seventeen days without a night's sleep.

And then to my utter surprise, I was released. One morning the warden opened the door and called, "Bochkareva, you are free." I could not believe him. I thought it was a trick to torture me. But he handed me a document stating that I'd been found innocent and that, as I was ill, I was to be allowed freedom of movement in the country. Just like that, I was at liberty. I went at once to my friends in Moscow, knowing, however, that I could not stay long, for the short rations made me a burden on them. The family of three received a pound and a half of meat weekly.

As soon as I felt strong enough, I took a walk to the House of Invalids, where some maimed girls from the Battalion of Death had been sent to live. Can you imagine, I found them in the street! The government, it seemed, needed the building, so along with all the other convalescents, they had been turned out to fend for themselves. A crowd of fellow soldiers had gathered in protest. Their mood was mutinous, their talk a revelation to me. They muttered against Lenin, against the Bolshevists and the Red Guard, calling them criminals and drunkards.

Said one, "Here they are evicting and arresting our own people! The Germans are moving nearer and nearer. Why don't they send the Red Guard to resist our real enemies?"

"We have been sold out," said another. "The Germans are taking away all our bread, occupying our land, destroying our country."

"A fine end we have come to. We believed that by overthrowing our officers and the wealthy class, we would have plenty of bread and land. But now the factories are demolished and there is no work."

"That's right, and if we demand justice we are shot down."

Silently, I thanked God for the awakening of the Russian people. With the soldiers coming to their senses, I knew Russia could yet be saved. However, they had no leaders. Let some appear, let some call on the people, and they could make short work of the Bolsheviks and drive the Germans out.

"What if I became your leader?" I ventured to ask.

"It's Bochkareva!" they cried. "Yes, yes, we could trust you."

The people were groping for the light, and I would take any steps necessary to help them. Right there and then, standing in that woeful street among the outcast invalids and disillusioned soldiers, I conceived the idea of seeking aid from the Allies in support of the true Russian cause. First things first, though. I knew I must see to the care of my girls. I was directed to a wealthy woman named Vera Mikhailovna. Her house—a palace—stood in a gracious park surrounded by fine old trees. Such was her kindness that Vera Mikhailovna had opened her door to many of my girls and offered them a home in the most beautiful of surroundings. The eighteenth-century stones were painted yellow and white, and inside, pale yellow silk covered the windows. A broad, black-and-white marble entry hall opened out into drawing room after drawing room, each with its own beautifully wrought ceramic stove in the corner, each furnished in its own suite of silk-covered sofas and chairs, each with its own individually patterned inlaid wood floor and Persian rugs. Fine paintings covered the walls. The grand staircase to the second floor was bedecked with gilt statuary. But Vera Mikhailovna's house, too, was being requisitioned by the Bolsheviks for government purposes. Notice had been given. Vera Mikhailovna was not free to sell any possessions, which were no longer hers, but the people's.

It was in the marbled front hall, before I even had time to remove my cap, that Rivka appeared again in my life, joyously throwing her arms around me. "The Natchalnik! The Natchalnik!" Rivka cried, kissing and hugging me and begging me never to leave her again. She was in a broken state, close to hysterical, her beloved father dead, her mother behind enemy lines, her brother estranged, gone over to the Bolshevik cause. She had no one left but me.

How could I abandon her, or the thirty other girls who were doomed to live from hand to mouth here and elsewhere in Moscow? I went to the office of the British Consul, though I'd been told he was impossible to see. Many people were waiting. I gave my name to his secretary, explained my circumstances and said I wished to go to London to see Mrs. Pankhurst. I asked for aid on the ground of my sacrifices for the cause of Russia and the Allies. Almost immediately, the Consul received me. He provided money and the papers needed. With this help I got all of the girls on the train to my mother's home in Tutalsk. I myself was determined to go on through Vladivostok to America and then to Britain to report the mood of the masses.

Of the vast distance we crossed by rail I will not speak here. Rivka has already done so with accuracy. To the soldiery on the trains and in the stations along the route, I said, "If I should get through and come back with an allied force, would you come to aid me in saving Russia?"

Vast crowds thundered, "Yes! We will! Yes, yes!"

Thirty girls I left at my mother's in Tutalsk, with one thousand rubles provided by Vera Mikhailovna for their support. But Rivka would not stay behind with the others. On the long, slow train across Asia, Rivka had come to herself. It was she who assisted me while I addressed throngs of Russian soldiers, she who kept a sharp eye out watching for any sign of trouble. When asked, I identified Rivka as my sister Nadia.

This is how I arrived together with Rivka in Vladivostok, a city with its back to the steppe and its eye on the sea. April of 1918, and me with five rubles and seventy kopeks in my pocket.

This is the truth.

Part II

Into the Hand of a Woman

And [Devorah] said: 'I will surely go with thee; notwithstanding the journey that thou takest shall not be for thy honor; for the Lord will give Sisera over into the hand of a woman.'

Judges IV, 9

VI

Filippov

YOU COULD FEEL the tension as soon as you disembarked from the train and started down the muddy streets of the squalid little city of Vladivostok. Today, the Bolsheviks were in control. Tomorrow? Who knew. The Bolshevist hold on the city was weakening, and talk of an Allied "intervention" was everywhere. It was said that in North Russia the British and French had already intervened through Murmansk and Archangel. Or were at the very moment intervening. Or would soon intervene.

But for what was the intervention, and against whom were they fighting? Some said against Germany, since Germany was still the Allies' enemy in the Great War, whereas Russia was now a neutral. Fat chance, said most others. It was an intervention against Russia's own rightful government. Russia's former allies, they said, were stalking the old Romanov empire, clawing at its edges.

Occasionally, some individual had the moxie to pose the question, "What is so rightful about this government of Russia's?"

Inevitably, someone else would quash him. "You have another to suggest? One that can rally the masses, have their support, organize services? One that, in any sense of the word, would have the power to govern?"

It must be acknowledged, though, that many fewer people seemed to be involved in these debates. Most were too busy finding the means to live another day. Disease stalked the city: diseases of upheaval and squalor, opportunistic diseases, death's major generals, cholera, typhus, influenza.

Tomorrow or the next day or the one after that, British forces would take the city. Americans were sure to follow, along with the French, perhaps, and certainly the Japanese, who'd been salivating over this foothold on the mainland since…well, since forever. The Czecho-slavics were trickling in, too. Originally enemy soldiers who had fought in the Austrian Army, then prisoners of war, they had now thrown in their lot with the Allies, angling for a country of their own upon the hoped-for collapse of the Hapsburg Empire. Their forces had been gathering—sixty thousand in all. Gradually they were commandeering first this terminus and then that along the Trans-Siberian Railway. Ineluctably they would swallow all forty-seven-some-odd thousand versts of it as it snaked from Cheliabinsk in the Urals all the way to Vladivostok on the Pacific.

In such a place, at such a time, if you didn't assume spies to be lurking everywhere, you were impossibly naïve. Many Bolshevists had already scurried north into the frozen Siberian wasteland. Yet there were still streets in the city where you didn't want to walk alone if you were anti-Bolshevik.

No sooner had the two women arrived in the city than the local soviet took their papers. And held onto them. Yashka sought out the British consul, who asked the soviet for passports allowing them to visit Mrs. Pankhurst in London, by way of America. The passports were denied. The soviet was suspicious, and the Red Guard dogged the women's every step. Things looked grim. Sooner or later, some Red out to make a name for himself would come gunning for Yashka, or else the soviet would take matters into its own hands, give her a hasty trial and execute her.

Rivka's connection to Yashka and the Battalion made her a target, too. In her favor, she was the sister of a widely known and highly regarded Bolshevist. For as long as the Bolshevists prevailed here, so long might she be safe. *Might* be, unless some nudnik got it into his head to assassinate her as a "convenience" to her brother, in order to keep his loyalty unquestioned. Back in Moscow, having a sister who'd been labeled a counterrevolutionary could be a fatal liability.

With time running out, they made a last-ditch attempt at the British consulate.

The office was not one to inspire Rivka's confidence. At the top of a rickety staircase, a few lackluster rooms were furnished meagerly with battered desks, half a dozen mismatched and uncomfortable chairs, and a row of heavy oaken file cabinets. The windows and floors were bare. It looked temporary, though for all she knew it might have been here, just this way, for decades. The man was as lackluster as the place. He listened, then sat back in his chair, fixed them with pouchy, mournful eyes, and said he could do no more for them.

They left the consulate in despair. For what had they come thousands of versts to the very edge of the continent? For what had they beaten the worst odds of death through war and revolution? Survived while starvation and disease killed millions? To discover themselves held captive in this port city? To await their fate like helpless kittens in a sack while some clotbrain of a peasant makes up his mind whether to drown them or let them go? Yashka said, "It cannot end like this. It won't." The heels of her boots rang against the cobblestones. If only her words had rung, too. If only they'd not been as strained and fretful as the glances she kept throwing behind them.

As they turned the corner into the gloomy byway where they had a room, Yashka halted and reached for Rivka's hand. The street went silent. Rivka's heart hammered in her ears. Down at the end, in front of their boarding house, loitered two men. They were dressed in tattered workmen's overalls and workmen's caps that hid their faces. One wore a khaki field jacket. It hung open and was torn at the shoulder. The other had on a woolen sweater that had seen better days. They lounged just beside the door smoking cigarettes, heads bent together in low conversation.

Rivka uttered a small cry. It was the way the slope-shouldered one, half a head shorter than the other, had raised his cigarette to his mouth, his palm cupping it, his chin dipping and curling. She knew these fellows, knew every line of their bodies, every habitual tic and shrug. "Filippov!" she cried, running toward them. Sharply, both men looked up. They were worn and gaunt, their beards unshaven, their eyes haggard, their bodies taut in readiness to pounce or to run. "What are you doing here?"

"Where else should we be?" Gennady asked, his palms raised in an elegant shrug that reminded her of her father.

She laughed. "You answer a question with a question? I think you must be Jewish."

He frowned, thick eyebrows converging above his beaklike nose. Fear stabbed her: she'd insulted him. Then he, too, burst out laughing. "If I were a Jew, I'd know better than to spend my days soldiering for someone else's gain."

Rivka's hand went reflexively to her hair and began smoothing it into place. Was that a compliment to her people, or its opposite? But these men were her friends. They knew Rivka, knew her well beneath her roughened cheeks and broken fingernails. Why worry now when it was so good to see them again? Their dear faces brought her such comfort. It was almost like being safe.

Yashka became hearty, inviting the two into the deserted sitting room of the seedy little boarding house, then calling for the landlady to bring them mead to drink. The old woman eyed the men and sniffed her disapproval. It was a full ten minutes before she appeared with a half-pint of the sweet, beery drink.

They were by then perched on antiquated divans. The upholstery was faded from red to a mottled salmon-brown. The walls had irregular splotches of the same color. No matter. The room was made sunny with their chatter.

The men had been on the move for weeks, they said, traveling together with other officers. It had been their hope to join the British Army in Vladivostok and be transported to France to continue the fight against Germany. If they could bring Germany to her knees, they could win back Russia's land for Russia.

Yashka grunted her approval.

But the Allies would not hear of it, and now the men were left with the unhappy choice of either returning the way they had come to Bolshevist European Russia or somehow trying to make good an escape to the United States or Canada.

Rivka sat wringing her hands. "What will become of us?"

"What the hell," said Gena. "We may as well eat." A feast emerged from his pockets: a few potatoes, some hunks of bread, a sack of cheese curds and a flask of vodka.

"You're *sure* you're not Jewish?" teased Rivka. He grinned and threw her a kiss.

They ate and drank until they were full, a rare luxury. Joy bubbled to their lips, made them feel young and devil-may-care. Surrounded by admirers, Yashka shone, recounting adventures from her days as a footsoldier at the front. "I was captured late in 1916 on the banks of the Styr, an early-morning attack in winter. The cold was intense, and the Germans were hard-pressed to guard us while still defending their position against a counterattack. Meanwhile, we were brought one by one before the German staff for questioning. They threatened and tormented us in order to extract from us whatever useful military information we might possess.

"Well, when it came my turn, I announced, 'I am a woman, not a soldier.'

"'Are you of noble blood?' demanded my interrogator.

"'I am a Red Cross nurse.'

"'Where is your uniform, nurse?'

"'I dressed in a man's uniform in order to visit my husband, an officer in the front lines.'"

Yashka repeated her words as a captive in such a pitiful, reedy little voice that she had the three others in stitches, gasping for breath as she went on. "'How many women have you fighting in the ranks?'

"'I don't know. I told you, I'm not a soldier.'

"'Why did you shoot, then? The soldiers tell me that you shot at them.'

"'What would you do if you saw enemy soldiers attacking you with guns and grenades? You would defend yourself. As did I, even though I am only a Red Cross nurse from a rear hospital who was only in the front lines on a visit.'"

And this simperer, this venomless rag doll was the same implacable Yashka who hauled off and slapped her soldiers, who lobbied incessantly for the return of capital punishment in the army! Leonid asked, "How long were you held captive?"

"Eight hours in all. That afternoon, our soldiers went over the top and started for the German positions. The Germans were nervous. Their expected reserves had not materialized, and the Commander decided to retreat to the second-line trenches. When they rounded us captives up, we threw ourselves, five hundred strong, against them."

"Hurrah," cheered the two Filippovs.

"The hand-to-hand combat was ferocious. We wrested away many of their rifles and bayonets. When our men rushed through the torn wire entanglements into their trenches, believe me, it was a bloodbath. Our entire line advanced across the river and took the German first-line trenches. By the end of the day, both banks of the Styr were in our hands."

"Hurrah, hurrah," they all cheered, toasting with their last drops of vodka to the great victory on the Styr. How lighthearted they felt seeing Yashka happy. All might be lost, but still they had this hour, this day. They spilled out of the house for a breath of sea air at the port, only a few blocks away. The weather had turned bright, and they were like yearlings let out to pasture. To think that after everything they'd seen, and in the midst of peril, they still remembered how to romp and frolic!

The harbor sparkled in the light. It was filled with watercraft, small fishing boats zig-zagging their way around Allied ships that stood huge and sentinel-like against the sky. Rivka extended her arm, stretching out her fingers as if by willing it she could touch them. Not until the sun lowered to the horizon did the men walk the women back to their lodgings. A message was waiting there, addressed to Yashka. From the British Consul. An American transport was due in, he said. He would try to convince the captain to take her, but the chances were slim.

BY THE TIME the American transport steamship *Sheridan* arrived two days later, the four old soldiers had mapped out and then abandoned several faulty plans for getting them all aboard without attracting any notice. Most promising were the shipping baskets that Leonid managed to organize. Even Yashka, with her size and bulk, was successful in folding herself inside. But she was loath to smuggle herself aboard this way. Any delay in loading and she might be smothered. They all might.

A costume was rounded up, featuring a hat with a thick, dark veil such as an Englishwoman in mourning might wear. It suited

Yashka. She could go aboard as a foreigner who spoke no Russian. Leonid promised to find suitable garb for the rest of them to accompany her.

Gena took Rivka aside. "I'm not going," he said.

"But what will you do?"

"I'm joining a group of Czecho-slavics. Soon we'll head back to fight the Bolsheviks."

"Mischa was in the south when I saw him."

"We're going west to Cheliabinsk, a thousand versts distant from him."

"And I'm thousands of versts from where I started." Rivka turned away. What more was there to say? Don't kill my brother.

RIVKA'S HEADACHE CAME on suddenly, then the chills. At first they thought it was flu. She began to cough. Yashka put on a gauze mask. That night, and for several days and nights afterward, Rivka had terrible dreams. Corpses rose up out of the ground and came after her, blood streaming from their bulging eyes, their glistening entrails held in their rotting hands. Behind one of them, on stringy ropes of gristle, trailed its heart, lungs, liver. In the black cavity of its empty chest, she caught a glimpse of Dudie, screaming in terror.

The dreams came and went, and she couldn't make out what was real, what illusion. Yashka grinned at her like a wildcat with menacing teeth. Mama wept over her, hot tears falling on her forehead, her cheeks. Rachel crawled into her arms, shells whistling around them. "My dear, it's nothing," she whispered in Russian, Klipatskaya's voice, but Rachel dying in her arms.

By the time the rash came out, spreading rapidly over her chest and belly, her back, arms and legs, Yashka was gone, along with Leonid. Gena was on his own to deal with the typhus. He arranged to have a washerwoman come and take away all her clothes and bedding. She dressed Rivka in ragged, but flea-free clothing and laid her down on a clean, if thin, pallet. When the chamber had been thoroughly washed down, he came back in. The woman had covered the window because Rivka was complaining of the light hurting her eyes. It was dim and cold in the room. Heat radiated off of Rivka as if from a stove.

That night, she moaned and thrashed about and cried out in her sleep. The next day, she rolled back and forth in a stupor, neither recognizing him nor responding to anything he said. Delirious, she tried to rise from the bed, and he had to hold her down while she wailed incoherently. About noon, she fell asleep.

He was heartened momentarily when she woke some hours later and asked for water. He supported her back, and she gulped almost half a glass.

"How's your headache?" he asked.

She stared at him, empty-eyed, tender and confused.

"Are you Death?" she said. "I'm to meet him here. I haven't missed him, have I?"

"No," he said. "Don't worry, you haven't."

He helped her lie down. "Rest now," he said. "Death isn't coming, after all. Your appointment was cancelled."

"No, no."

"Another time. Another place."

"Who told you so?"

He nodded. "You'll meet another time."

"Another place," she murmured, drifting off.

There was a time of pain, pain everywhere, inside and out, she herself the essence of pain, creating pain, excreting it through her pores, flooding the world with it, no way to tell where pain ended and she began, for she was the pain.

There was a time of blackness. It was during this blank, lost time that she was moved from her room. She awoke to find herself bundled in blankets in a narrow, dim space surrounded by packing cases. For the first time since she could remember, her eyes didn't hurt. She was neither sweating nor shaking. She felt limp. She didn't know where she was. She felt grateful to sink back into sleep.

HE'D BROUGHT HER aboard the Japanese ship as a drunken soldier in an oversize, mismatched uniform. Her hair had once again been shorn—this time to rid her of lice. They shared a space below decks with a small and motley assortment of nationalities and languages. Officially, the ship was convoying Anzac soldiers to Malta. On the way it would stop at Colombo, Basra and Port Said. He'd been lucky to get them aboard.

Remember, he had pledged himself to fight the Bolsheviks. When he refused to go, in order to help Rivka, the Czecho-slavics came gunning for him, believing him to be a double agent. She was still running a fever. He couldn't leave her, and he couldn't stay in Vladivostok. He'd fallen between two stools.

His grandfather's enamelled initial ring had paid the bribe. Coupled with his fervent entreaties, it had gotten them aboard just in time.

She spent most of the voyage belowdecks, sleeping. She'd lose track of time and ask Gena what day it was, what week, what month. Then she'd sleep and forget and ask again. Wednesday, is it? Thursday? The fifteenth? The twentieth?

He brought her food. Rice. Beans, tiny and red. Vegetables she'd never seen before cooked in broths with unfamiliar fragrances. She ate whatever was put before her, not caring what it was or where it came from. She ate and she slept, and the possibility of an enemy torpedo from an enemy submarine, if it crossed her mind at all, was of no concern to her.

As she improved she was told, and could retain the knowledge, that Bochkareva had left for America accompanied by Leonid. Rivka was desolate. She had expected more of Yashka. She had expected loyalty. Was this unreasonable after what they'd been through together? Rivka would have stood by Yashka no matter what.

Yashka, in her own defense, would surely have argued her higher calling, a purpose beyond the personal. Rivka's life against the millions of suffering Russian peasants, the millions who had already died and the millions more who would die if this debacle continued. Who was Rivka to expect loyalty from Bochkareva? Besides, Yashka hadn't left Rivka in the lurch. Gena was loyal. He stood by her, when he'd have preferred to be fighting with the Czecho-slavics.

And if Gena hadn't been there to stand in? What then? If he hadn't been there—Rivka understood this for a certainty—Bochkareva would have abandoned her anyway. Would Rivka really have desired otherwise, desired Yashka to stay behind in Russia when the *Sheridan* sailed, risking the chance that her important message to the Allies might never be delivered? Could Rivka wish Bochkareva to sacrifice her news of Russian support for the cause of freedom, all because of the fate of one ailing girl?

Yes, in point of fact. Rivka did wish it with all her heart.

THERE WAS A stopover at Ceylon to let off soldiers and take on others, to unload supplies and take on other supplies. By then, Rivka was feeling like herself again. She went on deck in the bright, hot sunlight, her eyes hungry. She watched small boats cut through the blue-green water, a hue she'd never known water could be. Palm trees rose up out of the sand, tall, straight, branched only at the top, where their arms swung idly. She had thought the stifling atmosphere belowdecks was due to poor ventilation, but even here, in the open, the heat was a thick, enveloping presence. Open your mouth, and you could chew it.

When they got underway again, Gena seemed different. Before, he'd been her attentive companion, sketching patiently at her side while she slept, bringing her food, helping her to the toilet, telling her (when she wasn't too groggy) stories of his boyhood in Novgorod, how he and his sisters used to hitch the roan pony to a dogcart and wander the countryside seeking adventure, finding mishap. His steadfast right arm, thrice broken, always starred in the tales. She felt she could draw a map of the area, each farm and cherry orchard, each stream, almost each hayrick. When she said so, he'd laughed and offered her his pencil and sketchpad. Then he'd happily drawn for her a picture of the house and garden where he'd grown up, and his family ranged all in a row under a vine-shrouded arbor.

Now that she was better, now that she walked the decks in the coolness of evening, her strength regained, now that she could swap stories and would have welcomed a friend to chatter with—now he'd become standoffish. She'd see his comfortable frame outlined against the sky—slope-shouldered, somewhat baggy, with a loping, loose-limbed gait—and she'd race up to meet him, curling her arm through his. Instead of his familiar smile, he'd go wintry, stiffening and pulling away. Not rudely, mind you. Resolute, as if disengaging himself ever so delicately from an encumbrance. It was awful. Once or twice, she knew he'd caught a glimpse of her starting toward him and turned on his heel and hurried away.

She was alone. The Japanese sailors never met her eye, never spoke to her, behaved as if she didn't exist. The Anzacs made wisecracks she didn't understand and didn't like. The lowlife belowdecks had been warned off by Gena.

Alone, and utterly free. No Papa, no Mama, no Mischa, no Yashka telling her her duty. And now, apparently, no Gena to remain loyal to. She need consult no one's preferences but her own. She had no possessions to guard, no home to keep. She could stay or go anywhere she pleased.

She belonged nowhere.

THERE WAS A moon the last night before Port Said in an Egyptian sky brilliant with stars. She was to debark the next morning. He'd go on to Malta to join the Allied force there. She stood on deck, watching the sky and wondering what in the world she would do with herself in Cairo. She'd be safe there with the British, according to Gena, since their hold on this land was secure. In Rivka's opinion, she'd be safe only when she reached America. By her, Egypt was not a place of safety, but a place of slavery from which her ancestors had escaped. Slavery was never a small thing, and never would she submit herself to it, no more in Egypt than in Russia, where every party had a different definition of who was slave and who master. It seemed to her things had been less complicated back in the time of Moses. Though maybe thousands of years from now, all this confusion might appear to have been simple, too. From those stars twinkling so brightly overhead, even this terrible war might be only a rumpus in an anthill.

While she mulled over these thoughts, Gena came quietly up beside her, so quietly that only gradually did she become aware of his presence. She waited for him to speak. When he said nothing, she turned to him. "What have I done?"

"You? Nothing.... Everything."

"I never meant to offend you."

"How could you offend me?"

"Ah, my friend. Hundreds of ways, I'm sure." She was picking her words so, so carefully. They came out halting and stiff, as though they didn't belong to her at all: an actress at her first rehearsal and not sure yet of her lines. "I've given you cause for anger."

He was silent again. Was she so bad, then, that he couldn't bring himself to tell her the truth about herself? In perfect dread, she waited.

"I've been avoiding this," he said finally. "Avoiding you."

Such a sad nod she gave acknowledging this.

"While you were ill, I felt free to do whatever I could, damn the niceties, damn the consequences. Just get you through it." He heaved a great sigh. "You're well now, and safe."

"Which I owe to you. If it had been up to Yashka I'd be in a hole in the frozen Siberian ground."

"You owe me nothing."

"Except my life, little value as that may have."

Gena said, "I don't know what my chances are with you."

"Your chances?"

"In another life, Rivka, I might ask you to marry me."

No, this couldn't be happening. "You? I always thought you were sweet on Olga."

He snorted. "No chance."

"You were always hanging around her."

"It was you I came to see."

"But you never showed me the slightest attention. You drew my portrait just once. You must have drawn her in every *pas* known to Nijinsky."

"I wasn't sure I had any chance with you. You never gave me any encouragement, and I was afraid of insulting you."

"By showing an inclination for me?"

"I didn't want to push myself forward if—well, if your interest is toward women."

"Toward women?"

"Rivka, you needn't admit anything to me." So he said, but his eyes were searching her bewildered face. "You don't know what I mean?"

"Enlighten me."

Bewildered himself, now, he chose his words carefully. "Sometimes women prefer to love other women, and men other men. Really, you've never heard of this?"

"Of course I have. Like David loved Jonathan in the Bible. They were friends, but more like brothers." Sadly, she added, "Closer, even, than my twin brother and me."

Gena cleared his throat. "I'm not talking of brothers, Rivka. I'm talking about a man who makes love to another man as—well, as he would a woman."

She stared at him. "Nonsense!" she said.

"Truth!"

She paused, considered. "But how—." She stopped again, blushing. Physically, the whole thing was impossible.

"He lies with a man as he would with a woman."

Rivka had known a boy whose parents could not find a match for him, though he seemed such a nice fellow. Behind his back, people called him *faigeleh,* a little bird. Was he…?

"I don't mean to insult you, Rivka, but your closeness with Yashka—well, let us say it raised questions."

And women, too? "I've never heard of such a thing."

"I can see that."

"Yashka, then—is one of those women?"

He shrugged. "If you don't know, how would I?"

"People said I was sweet on her. I feel so stupid."

"You're not stupid."

"How would I know if I'm one of those women?"

"Well, let's see," he said, scratching his head vigorously. "Who do you dream about, men or women?"

"No one," she said.

He looked skeptical. In his youth he'd survived typhus, and its fevered, gaudy dreams had troubled his sleep for months afterward.

"The other night, it's true, I dreamed of Gittel."

"Oh," he said, downcast.

"She was licking my ear." "Don't give me the details. I understand."

"Gennady," said Rivka, giggling. "Gittel is a goat."

Ah, Rivka, clearly, you've never heard of zoophilia, either.

They stared out over the water to the shores of the port, flat and sandy as far as the eye could see, lighter sand meeting darker sky at the sharp horizon, the sky vaulting impossibly high and wide overhead.

"Rivka, no one knows when this madness will end. The war looks like it's going on into 1919. In Russia, who knows how long before order and sanity are restored?"

Restored? Order and sanity no one ever had in Russia to begin with, but this was no time to point that out.

He took her hand, turned it over and kissed her palm. She felt a stirring deep within. Was this love? It must be, for Gena was so sure about it. How very strange. How strange to be here, to be now, to be feeling whatever it was she was feeling. Two weeks ago, none of this had been possible. Gena was off to fight, and she was off to America. Two weeks. There had been so much of her life when nothing had happened in the space of two weeks. Things had gone on in the same old way. Mischa had studied; Papa had gone to work and come home and complained about his workers; she had helped Mama do the laundry, bake the bread. Shabbes had come and gone and come again. Two weeks: what was two weeks? Nothing. Yet look here, in two weeks one could cross half a continent. Another two weeks, be on the brink of death and come back to life. Or sail halfway around the world to places where everything was unfamiliar, even the trees. In a period of two weeks, nothing could happen, or anything could happen. Or everything. One could fall in love.

She wanted to have a child. Not to replace Dudie, no. What child would ever do that? In her heart now there was room for another little *vantz* to bathe and feed and play with and ply with kisses. Another child, another moist little hand cupping her cheek, squirmy little fingers squeezing her nose to make her honk like a goose. Gena was dear to her, but he was not what she pictured when she pictured being married to him. The child was.

VII

Aaronsohn

GLAD TO BE quit of his female passenger, the ship's captain arranged transportation for Rivka from Port Said to Cairo in a motorized jalopy that was held together with whipcord (the driver's) and prayer (Rivka's). An eternity of jouncing across an empty landscape, devoid of people, trees, everything but sand, brought them finally to the marshy delta of the Nile. Rivka gawked at its muddy brown waters, at houses with grass roofs, at farmers ankle deep in rice paddies, at stands of wild reeds, at fields of ripening cotton, at long-legged birds in the marsh. The heat, which she thought could not get hotter, steamed up as they entered the city. Rivka took a mouthful of water from the flask Gena had handed her as she stepped off the ship. Dear Gena, he thought of everything.

The driver slowed to a halt and uttered something guttural.

"Take me to the British consulate," she said in Russian. With Britain in possession of Egypt, that seemed the logical place to start.

"*Baksheesh*," he said.

She tried Yiddish.

"*Baksheesh*," he repeated.

Then English, doing her best to pronounce the words correctly. "Breeteesh. Kone-sool."

"*Baksheesh. Baksheesh.*"

She didn't know this word baksheesh and could not have provided the proper bribe if she had. The driver left her there in a street packed with pedestrians, donkeys, bicycles, trucks going in whatever direction they wished, vehicles honking horns and mounting the sidewalks; camels braying and spitting; men standing in the middle of the traffic arguing at the top of their voices. A donkey relieved itself, its redolent pile barely missing her right foot. Had she been wearing a skirt, rather than army breeches, the load would have plopped onto her clothing. Do Not Faint, she ordered herself. Do Not.

Overcome by the heat, the dust, the noise, the odors of human sweat, oriental spices, petroleum exhaust and animal filth, she retreated into the shadow of an archway—and was instantly surrounded by half-naked boys, all sizes and ages, their palm-up hands waggling in her face. "Baksheesh," they caterwauled. "Baksheesh!"

"No baksheesh," rumbled a deep male voice from the courtyard behind her. The boys scattered, and she very nearly threw herself into the arms of the British soldier coming forward to save her, a complete stranger, a friend. He was a sandy-haired corporal with a lisp, who took her through the courtyard to his commanding officer.

"Breeteesh konesool," Rivka said, and the corporal was ordered to escort the lady there.

The consulate was housed in a handsome colonial building not far away. The man who spoke Russian with her there had fleshy cheeks and swollen eyelids that drooped over his pupils. The musk of habitual boredom wafted off him. He made no effort to disguise his lack of sympathy for her history or her plight. He probed at his ears and rubbed his chin with pudgy fingers, the nails bitten down to the quick. She had the distinct impression that if he had had any other work to do at that moment he'd have picked up his pen and proceeded with it, completely ignoring her. She did not want to stay in this country. In desperation she dropped Mrs. Pankhurst's name, for all the good it might do. *Och*, worse than none at all: the man regarded her with the distaste one reserves for disruptive children and surly wives. He told her he had more important things on his mind than getting the likes of her to America. America could go to the devil. The great President Wilson hadn't even had the decency to declare war on the Turks, but only on Germany. Here, they had an Ottoman war to be won, with Johnny Turk to be routed and these blasted Arabs to be kept in their place. You'd think the weight of it were on his round shoulders, and not the military's!

"The best I can do," he said, "is get you a place for the night in a women's hostel."

"You are very kind," she said.

The lodgings were simple and clean, a dormitory room shared with women who went silently veiled in the street, but indoors among themselves chattered incessantly, tossing their long black manes.

In the night, she dreamed that she and Yashka wheedled their way onboard a mammoth ship and sailed through unfathomable blue spaces. A sailor in a dark cap handed her a nameless, yellow fruit that tasted thick and sweet. She ate and ate until they landed in America. Palm trees crowded the shore, high mountains rising behind them. Yashka was feted by women in feathered hats and men in bowlers. From coast to coast, people flocked to see them, Rivka sharing in Yashka's heroic status as a living symbol of the Battalion. At the White House, President Wilson greeted them kindly. Yashka went down on her knees and begged him to intervene in Russia. He looked pale and stricken. Then they were among tall buildings. Rivka stood on a New York pier waving her damp handkerchief, Yashka at a ship's rail, disappearing beyond the horizon. Then Rivka alone in a dark compartment, alone with the sound of the chugging train, all the way to Chicago. Her uncles, her aunts, her cousins, all living like nobility there. They sent her to school and helped her find work in a glove factory. If her Uncle Seymour was a little overbearing and her Aunt Ruth too chatty by half, these things were of no importance. In her dream, she knew how blessed she was. Yet when she awoke out of the vividness of her dream-built Chicago into the insubstantiality of the steamy Egyptian dawn, she found herself at a loss. In vain she tried to identify something, anything, just one little thing in her dream of America that she wouldn't happily have given up to be back in the shtetl with her family, sleeping soundly in the shadow of the stove on a frosty, moon-drenched night.

RIVKA HADN'T HAD much appetite for the food aboard ship, though she'd eaten whatever was put in front of her, first broth, later rice, dried fish and beans. In her illness, she'd lost a lot of weight. Her joints bulged, and every bone showed. Her breasts were mere nubbins against her chest wall. Of muscle there was little. In the morning, she followed the hostel's chattering women to breakfast and found a banquet spread out for the taking: eggplant cooked three different ways; ground chick peas; yellow cheese; some kind of thick, white buttermilk; flat, round pancakes of bread; and fresh cucumber, onions and tomatoes. Years had passed since she'd tasted a tomato. Some wary people in her village wouldn't eat them at all, calling them witch fruit and slow poison, but her parents scoffed at this narrow-mindedness. She picked up a chunk and bit down. A juicy red sweet-tartness burst on her tongue like a bomb. For a full minute, she was all mouth. No tomato she'd ever had was like this, dense and rich, bringing tears to her eyes. The luxury of it. One slice of tomato.

Rivka loaded up a plate, said a hasty prayer of thanksgiving and tucked into the fresh, succulent fare. She sampled everything, and the more she ate the hungrier she got. Even when she was too stuffed to swallow another thing, she still felt hungry. She sipped at a cup of sweet, minty tea and wondered what to do with herself next. She'd been instructed not, under any circumstances, to go out alone. The rest of the day was featureless, and she felt like a vacancy in it. Aimless, she spent most of her time sitting or wandering about in the leafy little courtyard garden of the hostel. In the worst heat of the day, she went to her cot to rest. Later, with the evening's relative coolness, she practiced drills she'd learned while training with Yashka.

That night, her second in Egypt, she dreamed again of America. Her boy cousins were calling her Becky and treating her to the moving pictures. Her girl cousins told her she needed fattening up and took her for malted milks. She'd begun thinking of Russia as the "old country." Almost, she felt part of her cousins' merriment; except their laughter was light, hers deep and harsh. America did not feel like her country.

The next morning, just as she was finishing another epic breakfast, her corporal arrived. The British Army had not abandoned her. He'd been sent to collect her and take her to the Americans. She was to see a minor official in the Department of State who might be able to do something for her.

They waited in a stuffy room. Men came and went—some in light-colored suits, others in khaki uniforms—disappearing through a door into a warren of offices. Thankfully, the American uniforms have long pants, Rivka mused. It flummoxed her to behold the corporal standing before her in his short pants, with his sturdy legs on show, and his hairy knees. She closed her eyes and leaned her head back against the wall. The delay was long. Eventually the corporal took his leave of her.

Had she dozed off? Vaguely, she heard a voice chirping, "Oh, good morning, Mr. Aaronsohn, good morning. Right this way, sir. He's expecting you." The name startled her out of her reverie. *Aaronsohn*? She jumped to her feet. A door closed. The room was empty except for the young secretary who had told her to wait. Rivka approached and asked for Mr. Aaronsohn.

No one here by that name, she was told.

"But he's just come in," she insisted in a broken jumble of languages. She tried to explain her connection. "I am the best friend of Rachel Aaronsohn, you see. She is cousin to the Aaronsohns of Palestine." She reeled off the names of the four brothers and two sisters who were Rachel's cousins. The secretary was either unimpressed or uncomprehending. Rivka rattled on, feeling ever more foolish, her mashed-up words tripping upon themselves. "If I can only meet this Mr. Aaronsohn, he might be related, he might help me, he might be…well, a friend to me on account of Rachel."

Without a further word, the secretary went away. She returned after a few minutes and took Rivka to a closetlike room without windows. "Wait here," she said coldly, and left Rivka by herself. Every tick of the clock on the wall eroded Rivka's confidence. Perhaps she shouldn't have spoken up. The less you talk the better off you are. A miracle you shouldn't expect. People who stick their necks out can't expect to keep their heads. In slow increments she retreated to a corner opposite the door. She'd begun to feel it would be best if she'd been forgotten altogether.

At long last, a tall and beefy mountain of a man strode in. He left the door open, his hand on the knob behind him, making clear that he wasn't planning on staying more than a moment or two. "You asked to see me?" He looked her up and down. "Madam?" If he'd been swatting a fly he could not have been more abrupt.

"Your name is Aaronsohn?" she said in Yiddish.

A stiff nod.

"Might you be a son of Ephraim Fischel Aaronsohn, formerly of Rumania, now of Palestine?"

He shrugged. "It's common knowledge."

"May I ask which of the sons you are?"

He stepped backward, never taking his eyes off her as the door slammed behind him. His gaze was hostile. Rivka said, "I feel I know the four brothers and two sisters like my own family."

He didn't look anything like Rachel. He had a broad forehead, topped with a shock of unruly, light-colored hair going gray. His fiery eyes were deep-set beneath two slashes of eyebrow. He said, "You'd best stop the charade."

"What?"

"Admit straight out who you are and what you want. It will go easier for you."

What had she done? She took in a long breath and began repeating the explanation she'd tried to give the secretary outside. "Your cousin, Rachel Aaronsohn—"

He cut her off. "Where is your proof?"

"My—my proof? Of what?"

"You claim to be my cousin."

"No," she cried. "No, I do not. I am Rivka, Rachel's friend. Rivka Lefkovits. We're like sisters," she said, holding up two fingers tightly together. "Since earliest childhood."

His rigidity washed out of the man, his watchfulness did not. "They told me you were Rachel Aaronsohn."

"I don't have much English. I might have said it wrong."

He grunted.

"Rachel is home in the Ukraine, living in my papa's house—what used to be my papa's house," she corrected herself. "She was well when I saw her. Thin, like everybody, but healthy. Your aunt and uncle were alive as well."

"When was this?"

"A year ago. More."

"They're dead."

"I'm sorry to hear. They were always kind to me, both of them."

He shook his head. "All of them. Gone."

Rachel? Her knees buckled and a wail rose in her throat. "No-o-o!"

He helped her to a low stool, the only furniture in the room, and awkwardly patted her shoulder while she wept. No longer the suspicious wretch who had come through the door, he spoke quietly, telling her about the mob of hungry peasants that had terrorized the Jews of Rovno and Dubno and all the countryside around, about the Ukrainian pogroms that had enveloped village after village in flames, and about the attempt by the Jewish agency afterward to identify the dead and see to their burial. According to rumor, he said, as many as a hundred thousand Jewish lives had been lost in attacks by the Poles, the Austrians, the Russians, and the Ukrainians—as many Jewish lives as were lost soldiering in both sides of the fighting on the Eastern Front.

She gasped, "Is this true?"

"There's no proof as yet. The facts will take time to amass."

All the better: she was spared from believing this terrible thing until those facts were amassed. She said, "Rachel's brothers—did they make it all the way to Cuba?"

She'd surprised him. "You know about that? You must have been a dear friend, indeed. A trusted one."

"The boys?"

"They got to Cuba, and I arranged for them to enter the United States."

"You can do that?"

"I have connections."

"You're Aaron, then."

"I am."

Aaron Aaronsohn was the star in the family firmament, an agronomist of worldwide renown. "Can you arrange it for me to go to America?"

He frowned. "What I can arrange for you is an invitation to Shabbat dinner this evening with friends." He reached into his pocket and pulled out a fistful of foreign money. "You'll need a dress," he said.

She demurred.

He insisted, trying to force the cash into her hand.

Sternly, she crossed her arms and repeated her refusal.

"The money is not my own," he said. "It was donated for relief of the *Yishuv*."

"Of who?"

"The Jews of Palestine. Most live in abject poverty from years of persecution by the Ottoman Turks. On top of that, all of *Eretz Yisrael* has been picked clean by locusts. Agriculture barely exists there anymore."

Rivka pointed out that she was not of this Yishuv and had not been picked clean by locusts, and therefore not a pittance of his money was rightfully hers. "If not for Rachel, you wouldn't be offering it."

He acknowledged this with a slow nod. "Accept it, then, in Rachel's memory. She wouldn't want you out gallivanting around Cairo in men's clothing. It isn't wise."

The very idea of "out gallivanting" was so preposterous Rivka couldn't help laughing, even as her tears again spilled over. The way he said "it isn't wise" sounded just like Rachel.

THE MAN TO her right had loose, spittle-flecked lips eager to spill words. The Sabbath blessings weren't even over before she came to suspect that she and he were the two least important people at Aaronsohn's table. They were ten in all, nine men and

Rivka around a cloth strewn with flowers. The men spoke in Hebrew, English, Yiddish, German, and a few other languages Rivka couldn't identify.

She speared a bit of stringy meat in fiery sauce onto her fork. "What is this called?" she asked. Almost nothing here was familiar. Candles, yes, and sweet wine and challah, but little else reminded Rivka of Shabbes dinner at home in Russia. No gefilte fish was served, no roast chicken or golden soup-and-noodles with carrots and parsnip. Instead came a succession of unfamiliar dishes like the spicy meat stew accompanied by fragrant rice, hummus and fresh vegetables.

Her question went unanswered. The man's face flushed as he jabbered on, pressing his superiority over her by showing off his knowledge of the others. He was being indiscreet, but his Yiddish was not good, his Russian even worse than her English, and he mumbled. Still, the little that got through to her was shocking enough. She had known from Rachel's family that Aaron Aaronsohn was a prominent scientist, an expert in agriculture and water resources. Now he seemed to be saying that her host was also a spy! If she understood him correctly, the entire Palestinian branch of the Aaronsohn family were spies.

"The British count on NILI for their intelligence," he said. NILI, evidently, was the group the Aaronsohns had organized to help rid the land of Ottoman rule. In this they'd been highly successful, though at devastating cost. "Sarah paid dearly." Sarah, Rivka knew, was Aaron's sister. The man said she'd been captured by the Turks and tortured, revealing nothing to her tormentors for three long days before finally escaping them.

"How did she escape?"

He plucked at Rivka's sleeve. "By suicide."

Rivka's stomach turned over. Horrid man to tell such a horrid story.

She tried to capture the attention of the fellow to her left, but he was deep in conversation with a heavily beribboned officer on his other side and could not be distracted. And the boorish man still plucking at her sleeve! Sternly, she instructed herself *there's something to be learned from everyone*. Mama's lesson.

"You know, T. E. Lawrence takes all the credit," he told her, "but if not for Aaronsohn's information, Allenby wouldn't be sitting in Jerusalem now." She had no idea who T. E. Lawrence was, but Allenby she did. Allenby was the British commander who had pushed the Ottomans north, conquering Jerusalem. She'd seen the photograph of his triumphal march into the city, which had been published around the world in December of 1917. In deference to the holiness of the city, the general had dismounted from his horse and entered on foot. That had been six months ago. Since then, the Allied forces in Palestine had not moved forward so much as an inch.

There was more from her garrulous neighbor, much more, a tiresome amount of it completely unintelligible to Rivka. No one interrupted, certainly not Aaronsohn. Her host barely spoke to her all evening. Not until he saw her back to the hostel did Aaronsohn show the least interest in her well-being.

"How did you enjoy yourself tonight?" he asked.

"Do you ask for purposes of your own intelligence," she snapped, "or the British?"

He sighed. "It makes you angry, intelligence-gathering?"

"Not at all." Being stranded with a putz made her angry. NILI was his own business. In Russia one never knew who was trustworthy, what could be relied on, where spies might lurk. Why should she expect things to be different here in *Mitzrayim* of all places?

"I don't know what you've heard," he said stiffly, "but as for me, I'm working on alleviating suffering in Palestine. People are starving.

I'm establishing agriculture around Beersheva. You know where it is, Beersheva? Southwest of Jerusalem. The soil is rich there."

Now he was full out lecturing her, a *melamed* to a dimwitted schoolchild. "Longer term, I work on the economic development of Palestine. The Balfour Declaration—you've heard of it?"

She nodded. "It promises a Jewish state—if the Allies win."

"It promises nothing, but it makes room, let's say, for a Jewish state. We must labor for its fulfillment. Laboring for its fulfillment, Rivka, is what I do."

They had arrived at her door. "Shabbat shalom," he said curtly, and left her standing there.

Her Sabbath rest was anything but peaceful. In the night she dreamed for the third time about America. Again she was pampered by her uncles, her aunts, her cousins. Again came the food and the parties. She was no longer lonely or homesick. She knew her way around on the streetcars. She was doing well in the glove factory. She wore pretty dresses purchased with her own earnings. They were of good wool in vivid shades of blue and green, and she spent hours with her girl cousins shopping for matching hats. "Life is good," said her Aunt Ruth.

She awoke already sobbing, threw off her coverings, got out of bed and went to the window, where a soft light sifted through the old-fashioned grille. Now what is wrong with me? Nothing. I'm fine. What was wrong with the dream, then? Nothing. Nothing at all.

Her restless day was spent in the garden, wandering. She tried to read, or to learn some English. Concentration was impossible. It was too hot, and the dream had upset her. She felt hollow inside. But what was wrong with the dream? Life was good in America. Every Jew wanted to go to America.

The next day was the same. She wondered: what would Mama do in my position? What would Rachel do? She thought how beautiful her red-haired Rachel would have looked in the dream, wearing the blue wool dress with its short jacket and folded-back cuffs. If I should dream that same dream again, maybe I can somehow arrange it to see Rachel there.

But the dream, what was wrong in it? Life was good.

"Except—" came Rachel's calm voice, clear and incisive inside her head, "—except that life in America bored you to tears."

SHE'D HAVE PHONED if she'd known how. Instead, she arrived on foot at his office at the Savoy Hotel early the following morning. Aaron Aaronsohn was already at his desk, pen in hand. He offered her a seat. "I was just sending a message around to you," he said. "An American who can help you emigrate."

With a flick of her wrist she brushed the offer aside. "I no longer wish to go."

His eyes narrowed. There was a lengthy pause. Nothing else moved in his face.

"I've changed my mind, you see." How could she explain to him that America no longer felt like an adventure, still less like her future? *Follow your future,* Mama had said. Whatever that meant, it was not a glove factory and earnings spent on hats. Mama still wanted the best for Rivka despite everything Rivka had done to break faith with her. Mama had not deserted her, as Yashka had. Yashka had gone to America. Since Yashka was in America, it followed that Rivka must not go there after her, like a forlorn puppy. She must find her own way into her future. She said, "At Shabbes dinner I was told of a man, a Russian. He lost an arm in the war, but still he fights."

"Yes, I know him. And?"

This fellow had managed to convince the British to form a regiment of Jewish soldiers, officially identified as the 38th Battalion of Royal Fusiliers, but better known as the Jewish Legion. Her companion at dinner (that odious man) had told her something useful, after all. He'd said the Legion was going into action in Palestine. "And I want to join up," she said.

Aaronsohn snorted.

"I know how to fight. I've seen action."

"Yes. We've heard how Russian soldiers fight." Derision written all over his face.

"If I were a man you'd take me, even if I were a drunk and a scoundrel. You'd take me with one arm."

"It's not up to me, in any case. But Rivka, why do you want to do this?"

"For the adventure, I guess."

"Going to America is not sufficient adventure for you?"

A shrug was her only answer. How could she explain something that wasn't clear to herself? She detested war, the killing, the maiming. Yet there was something about the field of battle that made her feel exquisitely alive, as nothing else did. Had war made normal life impossible for her? She was simultaneously troubled and exhilarated to think so.

Aaronsohn said, "Three years were required to convince the British to let us Palestinian Jews fight, not just herd their mules. They won't accept you." It was a pity, really. The girl reminded him of his sister. Not physically: physically she was nothing like Sarah. But her spirit and strength of will were the same, and they touched him deeply.

"Is there a law against my service?"

"No doubt there is."

She stood. "Who can controvert this law?"

VIII

Allenby

GENERAL EDMUND HENRY Hynman Allenby, Commander of the Egyptian Expeditionary Force had a lot on his mind this June morning. It had been six months since the campaign that brought him to Jerusalem, and here he sat—still in Jerusalem and no further. Meanwhile, the German General Liman von Sanders had been made Commander of the Ottoman forces, and Sanders was a fellow to be reckoned with. Sanders did not, like his predecessor, prefer to retreat. He had dug in, biding his time. He was an old hand at commanding Turkish soldiers. Before the war, he had overseen their training and in 1915, commanding the Fifth Army at Gallipoli, he'd systematically taken apart the attempted Allied invasion. If anyone could get the most out of the war-weary Turks, it was Liman von Sanders.

Making matters worse, two-thirds of Allenby's trained and trusted infantry had been taken from him to fight against the German spring offensive on the Western Front. Only inchingly was he beginning to bring his troops up to strength again. Except that the replacements were coming out of India. They were untested. They lacked discipline, and discipline was Allenby's obsession. Not for nothing was he called "The Bull." Behind his back, he knew his officers whispered that he'd been known to chew out dead soldiers for disobeying orders. Let them bellyache all they liked, so long as *they* followed orders. But they were like a pack of children, intriguing for their own interests, jockeying for position, for the old man's best handouts. Sooner or later this war would end, and when it did, they wanted to be in the position of best advantage.

Not that he himself was immune from such thoughts. The capture of Jerusalem had perhaps wiped out his earlier failures on the Western Front. He was a hero now in Britain. The next campaign would be crucial to the repair of his reputation and his future in the Army. He needed to plan it out to the smallest detail, using every asset at his disposal, even the Arabs, who were as ragtag and fickle as the shifting desert sands. Their revolt, led by that silk-robed vulgarian T. E. Lawrence, was useful to him against the Turks. He had to keep it simmering, always simmering, never boiling over, never bursting out of control of the Allies, all of whose promises to the Arabs and the Jews could not possibly be fulfilled, for they were contradictory. It helped that *Al Nebi*, his name in Arabic, resembled the word for prophet.

A fortnight ago, Lawrence had facilitated a meeting between Chaim Weizmann and Emir Feisal near Aqaba, and the two leaders, Zionist and Arab, had worked out Arab support for a Jewish national home in Palestine. But many's the slip twixt cup and lip. Besides, what the Arabs and Jews might work out between themselves would not necessarily go to the best interests of Britain and France.

These worries were burdensome today of all days. The anniversary had come 'round. One year since his son died. First thing this morning he'd written the boy's name all over a piece of paper. Then he'd folded the paper and done it again. Michael Allenby. Michael Allenby. Michael Allenby. Killed in France by a splinter from an exploding shell. Goodhearted Michael, a veteran soldier who had survived a year and a half of service on the Western Front. Rough-and-tumble Mickey, who had been awarded the Military Cross for his bravery. Coltish Mikey, sweet little Micks. Allenby had sent many soldiers to their deaths both in France and here in Palestine. But Michael (Mickey, Mikey, Micks) he missed every day of his life. Michael Allenby, his son, dead one year at only nineteen years of age.

The last thing he needed today was another somebody wanting another special favor. Aaron Aaronsohn, though, was not just another somebody. If not for Aaronsohn's close knowledge of the land, his ability to map out water sources through the Sinai and Gaza, Allenby would not be sitting in Jerusalem now, plotting the defeat of the Ottoman forces. Outlandish as the man's request seemed to be—a woman seeking entry into his forces!—he'd devote ten minutes of his time. Aaronsohn seemed to think it would be worth the general's while, and though not politically astute, though often an irascible pain in the rear end, Aaronsohn was nobody's fool.

A LAND FLOWING with milk and honey it was not. Could her forefathers really have arisen in such a hot, dusty place, where mosquito-infested marsh alternated with blank stretches of sand? It was inconceivable to Rivka that this filthy outpost of hell could be what her ancestors spent two thousand years weeping over and pining for. She'd been traveling for over a week. Aaronsohn had brought her through the Sinai by car, a scarred and creaking Ford, entering Palestine north of Aqaba. He'd taken her first to Beersheva to show her the new planting fields. He spoke glowingly of the fertility of the soil, a future of abundant harvests. The soil had none of the rich, moist, dark promise of the Ukrainian farmland she knew. She saw only underfed people, ill-clad and dirty, scraping at meager ground. Aaronsohn was quick to explain that whatever structures had been there before, whatever order, whatever competence, had been swept away. Starting from scratch was not what she was witnessing here. They were starting from utter ruin, cleaning up the mess left by the Ottomans, who had raised neglect to an art form.

She kept her thoughts to herself when she saw a military installation going in, all wrong. Not enough latrines for its size. The place would be a sewer, worse than the Russian lines. If this was the British idea of sanitation, then she wasn't at all sure she wanted to join up, after all. If the Western Front was the same, it was a wonder the Tommies weren't all lying blue-faced in their trenches, dead of the cholera. She pitied poor Gena on his way there.

They drove west and north, where the land was richer, the air humid, past groves of olives, grapes and oranges. She saw Arab villages and Jewish settlements, their squat houses fronted with unfamiliar plants and flowers, the shapes and colors peculiar. This country with its brown-skinned, robed and fezzed inhabitants, this "Palestine" was alien to her. Half the time, she could not tell Arab from Jew.

And yet, this country dotted with places from scripture, this "Eretz Yisroel" filled her with a holy dread. With every step she might tread in the footsteps of Abraham, Isaac or Jacob, of Sarah or Rebecca, of Leah or Rachel. When Aaronsohn stopped along the road and went off behind some rocks to relieve himself, she was afraid to step away from the car. What if, in relieving herself, she should chance to violate a sacred spot? Bad enough that in Jaffa they peeled an orange and gobbled it down on a dune overlooking the sea. On that very dune the prophet Jonah might have sat pondering before he boarded ship for Tarshish. Papa would surely have laughed at her for the thought, and Mischa would scoff, "A sacrilege, *takeh*?" Maybe Mama would understand. These were places she'd thought were seated in her imagination through the stories told and read on *yontiv*. Now, Rivka was stumbling across them robed in sand, stone and sky.

Aaronsohn, she knew, would not sympathize if she voiced her befuddlement. He was touchy and seemed irritated by her. Not an easy man to get along with. Moody, he sometimes went silent for hours on end. Then would come a rush of words, a scientific theory exploding out of him, or a long thought about the future growth of Palestine. He could be biting about the aims of people he disagreed with, people like Ben-Gurion, the young firebrand of a socialist who wanted to "liberate"—the word like acid in Aaronsohn's mouth—the Arab peasant from the land. He could be passionate about the promise of wild, undomesticated wheat, which he himself was world-famous for having rediscovered in a chink of limestone in a vineyard. He could go on and on about nothing but dry farming, rebuffing her every attempt to change the subject. She found him difficult, maddening, though she also found him bluntly honest and never devious.

That night they stayed in a settlement near Rishon L'Tsion. Rivka was given a small chamber of her own. Exhausted, she fell instantly into a dreamless sleep. In the morning, Aaronsohn gave her no time to look around. They were on the road early, finally making their ascent to Jerusalem. The road wound upward, the hills steepening, the air freshening. Off to the left were ruined vineyards, the vines lifeless; to the right, a boy and his flock of sheep. As they drew nearer the city, the traffic increased. The twisting, rising road grew noisy with the clopping of horses' hoofs, the ringing of camel bells, the clatter of cart wheels, the songs of the drivers, the *whish* of the wind. It came into view, shimmering in the light, and she gasped. How beautiful it looked from afar, how very beautiful.

As soon as they got inside the city walls, she fell to her knees and kissed the stone pavement. She hadn't meant to do so, she just felt unable not to. "That's a Roman stone you're worshipping," observed Aaronsohn dryly.

They entered a maze of filthy alleyways, where people wandered barefoot and seemingly aimless among the cramped, dreary houses. Stray dogs and cats were everywhere, rooting in meager caches of garbage. Old men in maroon fezzes sat at the curbside smoking pipes of red and gray pottery, gossiping. Veiled women in loose robes balanced huge packages on their heads. Camels shambled under their heavy loads. Half-naked children ran shrieking beneath dingy lines of drying laundry. High above were golden roofs and the blue, unending firmament, but the old city below was mean and poor. The war had been hard on it.

He took her down a staircase, beggars on every step grasping her skirt and pleading for alms. At the bottom was a narrow, oblong veranda where stood an ancient wall sprouting tufts of weedy grass. Pigeons strutted here and there among the men in their black coats and hats who rocked back and forth, *davening* at the wall, kissing its stones and the books in their hands. Arabs in *kaffiyehs* strolled by, their homes stacked up nearby. Rivka touched the stones and wept, and this time Aaronsohn made no caustic remark. Without a word, he handed her a small piece of paper and a pencil. Without a word she wrote a prayer and tucked it into a crevice in the wall.

AT LONG LAST she was brought to see General Allenby. For once, she heeded nothing of her surroundings, for she was terribly nervous. This was her moment to prove herself the woman she wished to be—strong, confident, unshakable. Devorah and Yael rolled into one, with a bit of Yashka thrown in, too. Allenby rose when they entered and shook Aaronsohn's hand. Rivka held her head high and with military bearing faced the arbiter of her future. She resolved not to be cowed by the medals on his khaki uniform or by the goyish flat straightness of his features or by his august middle-agedness or even by the sadness crouching in his eyes.

The introduction was made. Why, she's just a girl, thought Allenby. No more than eighteen or twenty, despite her height and self-possession. I'll have to let her down easy.

"I want to fight," Rivka said. "I am a trained and seasoned soldier. I require no special treatment. I can live as an ordinary footsoldier, and when the men see what I can do, I will have their respect."

"I don't doubt it," said Allenby. "You've already gained mine."

She smiled, though she didn't necessarily believe him. Such words were easily said.

"But I'm afraid it's impossible."

"May I ask why?"

"You may not."

"I know you need every able hand you can get. You are even now training new troops, and you have bases that are empty of personnel." Something tightened in his face. She had said something that—what? Interested him? Perturbed him?

"What else have you seen?" he asked, and for the next twenty minutes he quizzed her on her observations and surmises—the installations she'd seen, the troop movements, concentrations of horse, mule and motorized vehicles. Specifically, he wanted to know what looked odd to her, or out of the ordinary. She answered all his questions of fact as fully as she possibly could, while trying to skirt his inquiries into her suppositions. Be smart, she instructed herself. The last thing any general wants is a soldier who thinks for herself.

Finally, he sat back in his chair, fingers tented. He glanced up at Aaronsohn, nodded and stood up. "Thank you for coming in," he told her. "I'll bear you in mind."

She kept her seat. "What does that mean?"

"It means precisely that. If there is a role for you, I'll let you know."

"When?" she pushed.

He said, "Whenever the moment comes."

He came around the desk. The interview was over, and she had failed. She got heavily to her feet and followed Aaronsohn to the door.

Allenby watched her go, a very observant young woman. "Miss Lefkovits," he called. "Where will you be staying?"

Oh, she hadn't thought of that.

Aaronsohn answered for her. "Near Rehovoth."

She frowned. When had this been decided?

"You'll be safe there," he explained. "As soon as the war's over, you'll go wherever you please."

"And you?"

"On my travels. As usual."

In other words, he was dropping her, a piece of surplus with no say and no choice.

REHOVOTH HAD BEGUN thirty years earlier with a handful of determined Polish Zionists. After a dicey start, they had prospered, and, with an influx of Yemeni immigrants, planted vineyards and almond orchards and citrus groves. Rivka lived in a barracks that housed fifteen women. Each had a bed, several cubbies and a squat wooden stool of her own. Their clothing was provided each week from a communal laundry; their food was served in a communal dining hall. The men shared barracks across a dusty compound, and married couples had small apartments to themselves. They rose shortly before dawn every morning except Shabbat and worked until noon. There was a break after lunch in the heat of the day, when Rivka wrote letters to Mama, Mischa and Gena. Then a return to work until the sun hung low in the western sky.

She worked in an orange grove wrapping the fruit for export. Each orange was wrapped individually with a thin tissue and set carefully in the crate. She herself had received such an orange every Hanukah, for its golden color was a reminder of the miracle of the oil that burned for eight days, and its sweetness was the sweetness of freedom from oppression. In Russia, the tissue made it a treasured gift to be unwrapped slowly and lovingly. The paper, too, had seemed to Rivka a soft, crinkly gift, one that she would spread and smooth. When she'd hold it to her nose she'd catch a faint, enticing scent, which she'd imagined was the essence of Eretz Yisroel.

Her bitterness at being Aaronsohn's castoff faded rapidly as she worked. With each orange, she pictured a girl or boy in Russia, in Spain, in China or in America unwrapping the orange, peeling it, separating it and taking that first ecstatic bite, the juice running down the child's chin. Perhaps her own relatives in Chicago would eat this very orange. Perhaps Gena, on leave from the front, would be handed that one. In this way, her first days at Rehovoth passed quickly.

Eventually she tired of the game, running out of countries she could think of and fresh costumes for the boys and girls. By then, she was taking an interest in the circle of five women who worked alongside her, their hair tied back from their faces with cotton babushkas, their sleeves rolled up to the elbows, their arms darkened by the sun. They gossiped together in Sephardic Hebrew while they worked. Rivka's ear had been attuned since birth to Ashkenazic Hebrew; she hadn't been taught it, but all the same, she'd absorbed its sounds. When first she attempted to speak to the women they laughed at her *oys* and *aws* until she learned to replace them with *ohs* and *ahs*. That part was easy, compared to learning when to replace the *ess* sound with a *tee* and when not to. While they chattered, she listened for sounds and meanings. She listened until she could understand much of what they said, even those newly coined words never found in Torah. Then she began to make herself understood. She asked questions. They clucked at her for her ignorance, but their amusement was lighthearted, even affectionate, and they told her what she wished to know.

She wished to know how things worked, how people got along, the Jews among themselves and the Jews with the non-Jews. Papa had a favorite joke back in the old country. "There was once a desert island," he said, "home to two Jews. Three synagogues on that island. Why? Because of a fight in the first synagogue, each went off and started a new one."

Nu, and why should Rivka have believed that things would be different in Eretz Yisroel? If you had two Jews, you had three opinions, at least. Here, she learned, lived Jews whose families had never left the Land of Israel, who had been here since time immemorial. You had Jews of the Old Yishuv, elderly and pious. You had the younger Jews of the New Yishuv, who had been arriving and starting settlements since thirty-five or forty years ago, Petach Tikvah and Zichron Ya'akov and Rishon L'Tsion and the newer ones popping up everywhere.

Such disagreements among them! You had the Yiddish speakers versus the Hebrew speakers. You had those who wanted a Jewish state now versus those who thought the time was not ripe—not to mention those who wanted to wait in patience for a state until the Messiah should come, not try to bring him before his time. You had those who thought a Jewish state precluded the Arabs, who outnumbered Jews by a large margin in Palestine, versus those who maintained we could live in peace with our Arab neighbors, as we had done more or less successfully for hundreds of years.

Of the five women who worked beside her in the packing shed, two were sabras, meaning they'd been born in the land. She found them brash. Like other Jews, sabras seemed to expect to be disliked, to be mistreated. But instead of cringing in the face of this, sabras walked around with a chip on their shoulder. "I dare you," they seemed to be saying in the jut of their chins, the set of their shoulders, the shrill force of their voices, even the henna with which they reddened their hair. One of them, Tsipi, often seemed to go out of her way to annoy the others, standing too close and arguing positions that Rivka was fairly sure she didn't hold, just for the sake of stabbing her finger in someone else's face. The other one, Shoshanah, had a milder disposition, but she pranced about half naked in sandals and short bloomers and light, loose blouses that might have suited the weather, but certainly not her modesty. These two made Rivka uncomfortable. She did not admire them, but she envied their boldness all the same.

Of the other women, two had made *aliyah* as children, with their parents, and could only remember snitches and snatches of the lives they had led in Europe. The third had come from Bessarabia as a bride with her husband. Of her previous life she spoke little, and from this Rivka learned that no one was interested in who you had been before, only in what you were prepared to do now. Rivka spoke little of her adventures in the Imperial Russian Army. If she thought of them at all, it was like remembering something she had read in a book, and not what she had lived on the Eastern Front only a year ago. Every sight, every smell, every sound and taste was new to her in this world and different from what she had seen, smelled, heard and tasted in that old one. Even the sweat of her body was different here, for it mixed with a different, sandier grime on her skin and dried to a saltier film on her face and arms.

In August, letters arrived from Mama and Mischa. Nothing from Gena. Mama wrote that she was well, she was regaining her strength, and her cousins were generous to a fault, sharing whatever they had. The war had gone away from Grodno, and the countryside around her was peaceful. She did not say what she was regaining her strength from. She did not say how much or how little her cousins possessed to share, or whether there was enough food for them all. Her handwriting was spidery. Still, it was her own hand, and it carried all of her love and all of her prayers in it for Rivka.

Mischa was well. He could not tell her where he was or what he was doing. He could not say that he was out of danger, as long as the Revolution was imperilled by its foes. Rivka understood this. The news coming out of Russia boded ill for the Reds. On all three fronts—south, east and northwest—they were in retreat. There was more to the letter, three pages of closely written philosophy and argument, almost nothing in it personal, almost all of it political: concerning the Marxist future, how would the state wither away? There was sharp disagreement in Moscow as to whether the interim government ought to be consolidated or diffuse, concentrated in the hands of a few, or spread across the land in local soviets. It troubled Mischa that what was realistically expedient could run at cross-purposes to what was philosophically apt. Something of all this *narishkeit* she understood, but it made her sad. The brother she knew was absent in it, gnashed up by the jaws of revolution, his vitality sucked out like marrow from a bone. Mischa, my eager linguist, where are you? Languishing in Russia, speaking only Russian, for who would dare be so impolitic as to know an imperialist tongue? And here am I, untalented in languages, garnering bits of English, of Hebrew, even a little Arabic, needing to speak them every day. What a sense of humor God has.

THE HIGH HOLY Days came early that year. There was a bustle in the markets, women buying fruits and vegetables, meat and fish and poultry and flour and wine to celebrate the new year. People said how good it was to feel the weather turning cooler. This was news to Rivka. Hot was hot, and she felt no nip in the air, none of the crispness of autumn, the start of a new time.

To her mild surprise, she was invited to join Tsipi's family at dinner on Erev Rosh Hashanah, the evening of September 6. Rivka suspected the sabra of harboring particular hostility toward herself, an interloper with good connections. Of course, Tsipi was prickly with everyone, so having nowhere else to go, Rivka purchased an armful of flowers as a gift for her hosts and set out with Tsipi, wearing the Shabbat outfit Aaronsohn had bought for her.

Tsipi's parents lived just outside Jaffa in the settlement of Neve Tzedek, in a neat white house with a red-tiled roof. The front door stood open in welcome. The rest of the street was deserted, for, as Tsipi explained, theirs was the first family to have moved back. In the spring of 1917, Djemal Pasha, the Turkish governor, had ordered the banishment by the eve of Passover of all Jews from Jaffa and Tel Aviv. Ten thousand people had been uprooted. Some left in carts sent by Jews from the Galilee, but most were on foot. They went north to Tiberias, to Safed, to Zichron Ya'akov; some to Kfar Sava, to Petach Tikvah, now in no-man's-land. By the first morning of Pesach that year, Tsipi said, the only Jews remaining were two Yemenis hanging from two trees.

Her family had fled east to Jerusalem with nothing but the clothes on their backs. "Whatever has become of our friends who went north will not be plain until the cursed Turks are defeated." But the things her father had learned from Armenians in Jerusalem—about the horrors their people had endured at the hands of the Turks—left little reason for hope. Armenians had been slaughtered. Armenians by the thousands had been herded into rivers to drown. Armenians had been evicted from their homes, marched into barren wildernesses and left to die. Why should the Jews, an equally despised minority, expect any better treatment? The December day that Allenby marched into Jerusalem was the very day Tsipi's father made arrangements to move back to Neve Tzedek. Despite its proximity to the front?—No, because of its proximity. Every day they occupied that house was a poke in the Ottoman nose.

Tsipi's father and brothers were at home when the two young women arrived. Evidently, they had not gone to the evening service. Odd, Rivka thought, how in Eretz Yisroel people did not seem to go to shul very much. As if by the act of living here they had lost the need to show up someplace special for the purpose of worshipping God or attending to his commandments. Every Jew in Palestine would be celebrating the holiday. At once solemn and joyful, every Jew would greet you with a wish for a *Shanah Tovah*, a good year. Not one in ten would set foot in a synagogue.

Had she ever yearned for new places, new people, new experiences? Rivka went to the dinner wanting apples and honey, then a little stuffed cabbage or gefilte fish, then roast chicken and carrot *tsimmes*, then honey cake and *teglach*. It was tradition, and in a land filled with new names, new faces, new languages and a new geography to learn, Rivka hungered for the familiar meal. It was not Tsipi's tradition. Tsipi's grandfather, a sinewy old man with a face like a walnut, had been born and raised in the hills of Afghanistan. At the age of twenty-three he'd left his native village on foot and walked—all the way to the Land of Israel. The trip had taken him a year. His only possessions of any value were his traditions, which he'd protected on his trek and joyfully installed in his new home. His children had learned to respect and follow them, and his children's children had come to love them. Which is how and why Rivka, as their esteemed guest, was presented at table with the severed and roasted head of a sheep. *Gutt in himmel.* Its sightless eye sockets stared at her. She had no choice but to stare back. When offered the honor of carving, she barely managed a gracious demurral. She couldn't possibly: her merit didn't deserve it.

Tsipi's derisive lips pursed and curled and twisted. The rest of the family—grandfather, parents, three brothers and a sister—exchanged wide smiles of unmixed delight. Like our patriarch Abraham, like our matriarch Sarah, they relished this opportunity to please a stranger in their home. For their sake, Rivka girded herself to eat whatever was put in front of her. Even when the sheep's eye turned out to be the greatest of delicacies, specially reserved for their guest, she got it down her gullet for their sake—and with a show of enjoyment. The enjoyment was for the sake of spiting Tsipi.

ANOTHER LETTER FROM Mischa: perhaps she had already heard that the Tsar and his family had been assassinated at Ekaterinburg. He knew this would hurt Rivka's soft heart, but he himself was convinced it had been unavoidable. The sacrifices we make are such as scar our souls, he wrote, and yet we must make them, for this is a fight for the souls of all men, and no sacrifice is too great, ~~if~~ when the outcome is large enough to warrant it.

He had crossed out "if" and substituted the less doubtful "when." Because he'd found a better word? Or because he was being prudent? Rivka knew from the newspapers that Czech troops now occupied Ekaterinburg; that they held a line from the Pacific all the way to the Volga and had captured Simbirsk, Lenin's birthplace; that an attempt upon Lenin's life had been made by Social Revolutionaries who accused him of betraying the peasants with his class warfare. The ferocious Bolshevik reprisals were being called the Red Terror. It was hard for her to believe that things could get even worse than they had been, but the papers said no one was safe now, and death lurked around every corner. One could be accused and executed on the spot for almost anything, for treason or for looting, for desertion or for drunkenness, for mutiny or for robbery, for espionage or for insubordination, for counterrevolutionary activity or for having syphilis, for ducking military service or for prostitution. A person might be executed for cause, and two innocents thrown in with him as an example to others, or on account of mistaken identity. *Oh, so sorry, we killed your daughter by accident. You must understand, these things happen when there are so many miscreants to keep track of.* Because Mischa mentioned none of this, she understood that the New Russia, like the old, employed censors, secret police who monitored even those most faithful to the party. *Och*, Mischa, where have your dreams gone to?

YOM KIPPUR, THANKS be to God, involved no eating of sheep or anything else. Kol Nidre evening, every Jew showed up for services. The place overflowed, and still people came, for everyone loved the ancient chant with its haunting melody. They loved it despite the misunderstandings it caused with the goyim. Legalistic in form, the prayer announced the community's intention to disavow all vows we might make in the coming year. Rivka had to admit that if, God forbid, she were not a Jew, she, too, would think this a slippery way of squirming out of any dealing, and that it proved a Jew had no inkling of honest commerce. Go try to convince them that this thrice-repeated utterance proved, to the contrary, the great seriousness with which a Jew made any oath, for his soul was bound up in it.

That night, she went to bed hungry. The hunger would recede, and the morning would be easier. She would feel emptied out, yet she knew from experience that she would not crave food until the moment she took a nibble of *challah* at the communal break-the-fast. Then, she'd be ravenous.

Except she never made it to the *motzi* and that enticing, delicious, famished nibble. Just as the morning services were concluding, someone tapped her shoulder and told her she had a visitor outside.

On Yom Kippur who visits?

Who else but Allenby, in the shape of his adjutant, an apologetic young officer who claimed to know what an imposition this was on her holy day. Nevertheless, he begged her to go with him.

Her face flushed. She had never given up hope of joining the Legion. Now Allenby was sending for her—and the Yizkor service was starting. "Go away," she said. "Come back for me after sundown." She ducked back into the huge tent that had been set up to accommodate the crowd.

Before the war, shuls had emptied out when the memorial service started. Children played in the sunlight while young mothers and fathers formed small knots and chatted idly. Now, though, barely a person moved from a seat anywhere under the tent. Everyone had a relative or a close friend who had died since the war began, if not by a bullet on the field of battle, then by starvation, by disease, by mistreatment or by misery. Rivka swayed in unity with the other bereaved in that congregation, praying God remember Papa and Rachel, pledging herself to good deeds in their memory, grateful for the gift of tears. Afterward, she moved toward the exit for a breath of air.

Jews stand and talk wherever they happen to meet, especially on yontiv, and who pays any attention to where you are or who is behind you, even if the tent is like an oven, even if you happen to be jamming the opening and nobody can get in or out around you? No one objects. They're all busy talking, too, to whoever is beside them, or behind them, or in front of them. The crowd heaved back and forth like an arthritic elephant relieving the pressure on its knees. It must have taken Rivka half an hour or more to make her way out.

There stood the adjutant, on the spot where she had left him. He said nothing, just nodded to her and touched his cap. Not a salute, but cousin to it. She said, "Why are you still here? I told you, I won't leave until the holiday is over."

"General Allenby ordered me not to leave without you."

"It's a long wait in the hot sun."

He shrugged, a hitch of his right shoulder, barely perceptible. This Brit, she thought, you'd think it costs him money to swing an arm. It would be nice if he'd exhibit a little urgency. Then, maybe….

She considered, and said, "Is this a matter of life and death?"

"I believe it is, Miss."

"All right. All right, then, I will come now." To save a life, any of God's commandments could be violated, even on the holiest day of the year.

SHE MADE A smart salute as she was ushered into the General's field headquarters, a whitewashed house, tree shaded and airy, and close to the front lines. The generals she'd known had run their battles from so many versts behind the combat zone that the battles they fought were invisible to them. It impressed her that Allenby's lines seemed to be within hailing distance. The General stood when she came in, towering over her, self-assured and unsmiling. She was still dressed for the holiday and wore a broad-brimmed lavender hat with a bright feather. He didn't return her salute. Gravely he offered her a seat and gravely he returned to his chair behind the cluttered desk. For a full minute he stared at papers on his blotter, his lips pressed tightly together.

She waited.

"What do you know of Sarah Aaronsohn?" he asked finally.

"She was a spy. She was caught. She committed—an unholy act."

"You mean suicide."

Rivka nodded. Sarah Aaronsohn was a murderer. She had murdered not only herself but all the generations that might have arisen out of her.

"Let me tell you how they tortured her," he said quietly. "First they pulled her hair out. Magnificent, her hair—a mass of red-gold curls. They yanked it out by the roots."

"Why are—"

He shot her a look that warned her off. "Then they moved on to her teeth, and then her fingernails, extracted, each one, by the roots. Yet she refused to answer their questions. That was the first day. On the second day, they applied the bastinado—the soles of her feet beaten with sticks hour upon hour. Then they made her dance on burning bricks. I'm told that her roasted flesh could be smelled everywhere throughout Zichron Ya'akov."

"Why are you telling me this?"

"On the third day of her interrogation, the skin was flayed from her legs and torso, but even that wasn't the worst of it. Do you like eggs, Miss Lefkovits? They boiled eggs and inserted them, scalding, into the umm—the most sensitive areas of her body."

Rivka's fingernails cut into her palms. Had she stayed at services instead of coming here, she'd be reading the martyrdom, a yearly ritual. *Rabbi Akiva recited the Shema as the Roman executioners raked his flesh away from his bones. So much did he love the Lord our God with all his heart and with all his soul and with all his might.*

"I tell you this because I need you. I have a special mission for you to carry out. From what I've seen of you, I believe you to be uniquely capable of doing what needs to be done. But you must know the risk you take."

Rabbi Chanina ben Tradyon, caught teaching Torah in public, was wrapped in the Sefer Torah and set alight, wet wool over his heart to prolong his suffering. "The parchment is burning," he cried as the flames rose around him, "but the letters fly free."

"And by the way, Aaronsohn doesn't know the details of Sarah's ordeal, so don't mention them to him."

Ah, poor Aaronsohn.

"I will give you as little information as possible, but that won't save you if you fall into their hands."

"I'm a soldier, not a spy," she protested. And yet, she already knew his "information." She'd done her own kind of snooping and surmised his battle plan. Allenby was going to great lengths to create a gigantic trick. Those empty installations she'd seen after leaving Beersheva, anyone not right on top of them would think troops were being massed there for an onslaught. A small corps of soldiers could be marched up the Jordan Valley by day, secretly taken back to their starting point by night, and marched again the following day. Whole battalions would appear to be on the move. Mules could drag harrows along the roads to raise great clouds of dust, and agents could be sent to buy up forage in the area for horses and camels that didn't exist. Meanwhile, a canny general could conceal his real strength among the groves and vineyards along the coasts. Rivka had spotted trucks under the branches of date palms, pup tents among the orange trees, horse lines next to the building that held the wine presses in Rishon L'Tsion. By these signs it was plain to Rivka that Allenby was planning a breakthrough on the western end of his front, near the sea, and all of his actions for the past couple of months were meant to deceive the enemy into thinking the attack, when it came, would come from the east.

She even had guessed the date when the offensive would be launched. The newspapers and kiosks were full of advertisements for a horse race in Gaza to go off this very week, on September 19. But Tsipi's father happened to work in Gaza, and at dinner on Rosh Hashanah he chanced to remark that he'd seen no preparations being made for such a meet. With luck, Rivka thought, on September 19 the Turks would be at their ease: no war this day, their enemy on holiday at the races.

"Last night," said the General, "north of Jerusalem, one of our sergeants crossed over into the Turkish lines."

"He deserted?"

"A damned wog. Heaven knows what he's told them."

"No matter what he's told them, why should he be believed?"

"We have an entire section of people whose job it is to interview deserters and evaluate their information. I daresay the other side has the same capability."

"Still, would you take the word of some Arab showing up here today, claiming to have crucial intelligence from beyond the lines? I wouldn't."

"My dear young lady, you insist you're a soldier and not a spy. As a soldier, I'm afraid you can make very little difference to the outcome of this war. As a spy—though I don't see what's so terrible about espionage—"

"Be a Jew in Russia and then tell me what you think of those who take up informing on others for a living."

She thought she saw light dawn in his eyes, but who knew? He and his kind never had to worry about a blood libel. He said, "This is the decisive moment in the Holy Land. You have the opportunity now, tonight, to make the difference between victory and disaster."

So you say, she thought, for she'd heard this gilded kind of talk before, with regard to the Battalion of Death. She was silent.

"On the Western Front, the tide has turned against the German. In Mesopotamia, we've pushed him back beyond Baku. He is pinched for oil, food, matériel, everything. If we, here, can take away his access to the sea and the eastern railways—don't you see? You must do it."

"For the sake of the Allied cause?"

"For the sake of your own people in Palestine, if not for mine. You must."

An adventure, and one only she was fit for. "But why me?"

"Because you're a woman who notices things. Because you're a soldier who can distinguish between normal troop movement and an unusual flurry of activity. The Ottomans won't suspect a woman to have the courage for intelligence work, not after the example they made of Sarah Aaronsohn. They might not even recognize you as a Jewess because of your coloring, your fair skin, light hair and eyes. And finally, being a Russian soldier, you know how to live off the land." Though he said it evenly, she suspected this was as much an insult to the Tsar's Imperial Army as a compliment to her. Living off the land in Europe was one thing, in this forsaken land another, but she decided not to mention that.

IX

The Land

THE MOON, HIGH and almost full, cast shadows across the ribs of the rowboat. "Unlucky the night is so bright," the sailor whispered. In the bluish light, loose curls glistened across his dusky forehead. Rivka was keenly aware of the danger of being spotted, but she also knew the opposite difficulty of finding one's way in inky darkness. Just as well to have moonlight. Just as well it wasn't rainy season, with clouds piled one atop another and driving winds and the little boat bobbing helplessly in stormy waters. The air was clear, the sea calm, their destination close by.

It was nine hours since she'd left Allenby's office. Brigadier General Bartholomew, Allenby's chief of staff, had himself seen her to Port Said. "Call me Barty. Everyone does," he said by way of introduction. Then he went over instructions with her all the way to the *Managem*, the steamer that would take her up the coast, deep into enemy territory. If anything, Bartholomew was even more concerned than Allenby about the Indian sergeant's defection. "All our elaborate ruse may be for naught," he fretted, his gloomy face with its loose jowls and down-curving eyes reminding her of a large and fleshy dog. "The campaign rises or falls with what the enemy believes. The Turks can save their fighting strength simply by retiring seven or eight miles up the coast. If they do that, we'll be left like a fish flapping on dry land with our railways and artillery, our dumps and stores, our installations all misplaced—and without groves of oranges and olives to hide our preparations for the next assault."

"I'll find out what he's told them," said Rivka.

Barty shook his head. "No time for that anymore. The attack goes forward in any case. The Bull—" he smiled ruefully, "Allenby will not call it off. If need be we'll fight without ruse, but we must know to a certainty where the enemy will be met and in what strengths. That's where you come in."

She was surprised when he boarded the *Managem* together with her. While he went off to consult the captain, she was handed clothing, food and *bishliks* to tide her over for three days. Immediately, she wolfed down two days' rations, for she'd been fasting and hadn't had a morsel in her stomach for twenty-seven hours. In a cramped cabin, she changed her clothes into the simple dress of a workman's wife and a sturdy pair of boots. It was not the best disguise, considering her height and coloring and the fact that she could speak neither Turkish nor Arabic with any fluency. She was not likely to blend in if blending in should become necessary.

Barty, when he returned, looked her over thoughtfully and then said, "Trust no one. Suspect everyone, Jew and non-Jew alike. NILI is destroyed, and Hashomer"— the group which had guarded Jewish settlements—"Hashomer, too, is just about extinct. Any of its members who wasn't deported has by now been hanged."

"How will I get word back to you?"

He hemmed and hawed. Now it became clear why he'd come aboard with her. It seemed this part of the operation had not yet been arranged, quite. However—he assured her, rubbing at his mustache—they had some promising ideas.

God should only bless me so that I don't need these people, thought Rivka. Her life was at stake, and they were improvising. Her stomach knotted in dismay, though she was inclined to blame the food ration eaten too quickly.

One plan, Barty hastened to add, producing a map, was for her to return to her landing spot on the coast and signal the ship, which would linger offshore below the horizon, returning every eight hours to look for her. If by day, she would hoist a piece of clothing, and if night, then lanterns. But the danger of discovery on the beach would be great. A better plan for her would be to head north to Aaronsohn's agricultural station at Atlith, where she could wait in safety for a rendezvous. He tapped the spot on the map with his forefinger, about sixty miles north of Tel Aviv on the northern coast just short of Haifa. But as she could see, time would be lost in travel, and along with it the usefulness of her intelligence. She studied the map for a better place of refuge. Zikhron Ya'akov, where the Aaronsohns lived, was closer, if somewhat inland. She pointed to it.

Barty shook his head. "Assume nothing, not even the safety of Aaronsohn's name. It could prove to be a liability, especially near his home."

"For what reason?" her sharp tone more accusatory than she'd intended, but she was confused now, and trying to divert attention from her pointing finger, which had begun trembling.

He answered mildly. "Fear, jealousy. A quarter of the population of Zikhron Ya'akov have been involved in some way with the Aaronsohns and NILI. That leaves three-quarters who have not. To these people, NILI's activities against the Turk are a gnawing vulnerability. Through no fault of theirs, calamity could befall their community."

"But to win the war, sacrifice is necessary."

"Depends which side you take. Not a few Jews still think themselves better off playing along with the Turks, as your people have done for hundreds of years. Why should they trust themselves to us and the French? The Dreyfus affair wasn't that long ago, you know. Though I expect it was back-page news by the time you were born."

It was, but she'd heard about Dreyfus, the French officer who'd been framed for treason and persecuted because he was a Jew. "Barty," she snapped, "a Jew could be born yesterday and yet understand that anti-Semitism has no borders." He looked instantly chastened, a wrinkle-faced, damp-eyed hound of a man, and she regretted her sharpness. After all, they were here to complete the same mission. She said, "Is there no trace at all of the old spy networks I can contact?"

"Forget them. Any remnant might very well be hostile to someone connected with the Aaronsohn family."

What had she gotten herself into? "But I thought NILI— "

"One of the NILI group babbled every secret he knew to his Turkish captors."

"Impossible! No Aaronsohn would do that."

Barty shook his head. It was all rumor, he acknowledged, a carrier pigeon blown off course into the garden of none other than the chief of police. In the container attached to the bird's foot was a message implicating a NILI operative, Naaman Belkind. He, under torture, gave up everyone else working to undermine Ottoman rule.

"And this man Belkind was an Aaronsohn?"

"No, but NILI and the Aaronsohns are considered virtually synonymous."

Hadn't she herself thought them identical? "Fair enough. That accounts for the fear you spoke of. What about the jealousy?"

"Oh, well, you know how tongues will wag. I'm told there are those who always thought the Aaronsohns too high and mighty, and were glad when Sarah got her just deserts."

A shudder ran through Rivka. "No one deserves what Sarah got."

"I daresay," murmured Barty, keenly aware that Rivka was putting herself at the same risk. He rubbed clumsily again at his bristly mustache, then returned to business. "One result of all this," he said, "is that carrier pigeons no longer are looked upon here in Palestine as valiant soldiers risking feather and wing to bring intelligence home—although in your case, you know, the distance the bird would have to travel is minimal. We have a pigeoneer aboard ship who has a dozen birds trained to go that far."

"Without stopping to pay a call on the chief of police?"

The problem was not the bird's return home, Barty said. They returned with 90 percent accuracy. The problem was being found in possession of the bird. Rivka could not risk carrying a pannier containing a sleek homing pigeon. "It's simply out of the question. You'd be safer writing *spy* across your forehead."

"You have no one in the north who raises birds and could give me one?"

"I'm touched by your faith in us, my dear," he said, smiling. "It's true, at one time we did, but he's long dead, and as to his pigeons, I've no doubt they provided some pasha with a sumptuous dinner. So you see, we're stumped."

Had she come all this way for nothing? Was Barty going to cancel the mission? If so, surely he'd have done so already. He stood there watching her, his tongue repeatedly wetting his indrawn lower lip. She saw that the way forward, if there was to be one, was up to her.

"I'll have to carry the bird—it's the only alternative."

"If you're seen with a homing pigeon, a quick execution on the spot is the best you can hope for. The very best."

"We'll have to make the bird invisible."

"How?"

"I don't know yet, but if all goes well, it's only for eight hours or so."

"Too dangerous."

"You have a better idea?"

Thoroughly chapfallen, he shook his head. No other solution offered the speed and directness of a pigeon. No one else could be trusted with the pigeon but Rivka.

A TINY FELLOW was brought to them, no more than five feet four inches in height and skinny as a sapling, with the apple cheeks of an angel. This was the pigeoneer. Rivka didn't know whether to return his crisp salute or to pet him. He looked like a child who'd raided his elder brother's closet. His uniform hung on him, the shorts flapping around his shanks. A golden cowlick stood at attention just above his right temple.

Though his looks didn't inspire confidence, his work with homing pigeons, Barty assured her, was first-rate. "Observe how expertly he handles them." She observed, not that she had any basis for comparison. The birds strutted and ruffled out their feathers, making soft sounds in their throats, behaving not unlike the gray denizens of the squares in Petrograd that pecked for scraps in the dung. To her mind, only their coloring set these apart, two each to a wicker cage, fourteen in all, yet the pigeoneer evidently knew each one individually by name and temperament.

He chose a bird for Rivka, delicately removed it from the cage and held it in his hand. "It's lovely," she said—pure white, richly feathered and small. "But not invisible. We need you to make it invisible."

The pigeoneer's angelic expression never changed. Unfazed by Rivka's outlandish request, he produced a small length of cloth in which he wrapped the bird. Then he inserted it into a little bag of black cotton, and pulled the drawstring tight. The pigeon, which had been fluttering and cooing, went quiet.

"Presto," said Rivka.

"How long will it remain still?" asked Barty.

"As long as you need it to." The pigeoneer's eyes shifted, coming to rest neither here, there, nor anywhere. This was not a fellow used to prevaricating.

Don't ever play pinochle with Papa, Rivka thought, before it came to her—came as a fresh shock—that Papa was gone.

Well, what difference did it make now that the handler was unsure of his bird? Rivka didn't challenge him, nor did Barty. They had run out of room for any more improvising. In the quick half hour while the ship steamed up the coast north of Jaffa, they had to devise a pocket for the bird to lie hidden beneath the fullness of Rivka's skirts. The handler had to teach her how to remove the bag and wrapping, how to attach her message, how to release the bird into the air with a smooth upward toss. He had to warn her against disturbing the feathers of its wings or tail. He had to catechize her as to proper care of its feet and its beak. He had to caution her against feeding it, since food and water would be its reward for returning home. By the time they reached the drop-off point, he was fussing and fretting over Rivka just as if she were one of his flock—albeit of a somewhat inferior breed. She yielded gratefully to his tutelage, impulsively throwing her arms around his thin shoulders as he handed her down into the rowboat. She had not felt so cossetted since taking leave of Gena.

SHE WAS DROPPED on an abandoned bit of coast well south of the ancient ruins of Caesarea. The rowboat immediately pushed off for the *Managem*. She had orders to head further south, but under no circumstances to go below El Tire, five miles from the battle lines. Under no circumstances was she to approach the trenches or head inland. After releasing the pigeon, she was immediately to make her way north to Aaronsohn's agricultural station at Atlith. The war would swing eastward, away from Atlith, and the *Managem* would rendezvous with her there. Those were her instructions.

In the night she trudged through sand and muck, making her way steadily southward toward the enemy lines marked in red on the map she'd memorized. She skirted Hadera and by 4 AM had reached the Alexander River. She was making good time and could afford a couple of hours' rest. She found a lonely spot, rolled herself in her cloak and shut her eyes.

By seven she had breakfasted on a handful of dates and was walking along a treeless road. All was quiet. Not a truck, not a car, not a horse or mule passed. Not a man in uniform. How could it be so utterly dead quiet? She'd been ordered to stay near the coast, but if she followed those orders, how could she make her report? If Barty had been trying to provoke her, he couldn't have done a better job. The coastal plain gave her no vantage from which to make her observations.

To the southeast rose a line of small hills. She pondered them. From up there, one would see further than the couple of miles to this flat, still, unchanging white horizon. From up there, she might discover something of consequence, and then who in the world would care about her orders? She left the road and traveled eastward toward the hills, following a narrow byway that was little more than a camel path. Two Bedouins in blue cloaks passed her, staring openly. Was it because she was a woman alone, out at this hour without any obvious purpose in her hands—a bucket to be filled at a well, a basket of produce to be brought to market? She could feel their eyes on her, boring into her back. Did something else about her—her clothing, her gait, her closed face—proclaim her mission?

For a very long time the rises and hills that had looked so close grew no closer. About one minute short of eternity, sand finally began giving way to stone, and stone to bramble and briar. It became hard going over the rock-strewn, scrub-choked ground. Twice she tripped and fell. Her dress caught and tore among the nettles. The creature sequestered in its cotton wrapping slapped against her hip bone. She smoothed her skirt and kept on going.

As the sun rose higher, the footpath she was following widened until eventually it became a pocked roadway. A few carts went by, each one drawn by a scrawny donkey and driven by a wizened old man in ragged clothing. They paid her no attention. Spread out in all directions were fields of thorns and briars, of lizards and scorpions. In the midst of this desolation, she passed through an Arab village that seemed to her a vivid mirage, with its vegetable gardens and faded wheelbarrows and wandering chickens and goats at rest with their heads in the road. The houses were ornamented with lucky horseshoes or with hamsas, those stone-studded, hand-shaped amulets meant to ward off the evil eye. She'd meant to leave the evil eye behind, in Russia. A *muzhik* superstition, utter nonsense from top to bottom. Still and yet, she murmured, today of all days let evil cast its shadow on somebody else.

At the far outskirts of the village a young mother, little more than a child herself, offered Rivka a seat on a dusty rug and a glass of mint tea, syrupy and delicious. The baby wore a long dress with fancy needlework at the yoke. It regarded Rivka solemnly out of round, dark eyes like olives, and its lips glistened with drool. Rivka had a sudden recollection of Dudie when he could just barely sit up on his own, hunched like a little old *zaideh,* a lush beard of drool bubbling down his chin and across his shirtfront, soaking him to the skin. The sharpness of the vision jolted her, Papa laughing, Mischa turning away in haughty disdain. Under her skirt, the pigeon shifted and let out a soft moan. The Arab woman, busy tending to her baby, appeared not to notice.

AT AN HOUR after noon, she climbed to the top of a rise and looked out over the rooftops of El Tire. Beyond lay the village of Qalqilya, and beyond that the enemy lines snaking across the land. The air shimmered in the heat. The sun's rays were so strong they'd make a rifle barrel too hot to be touched. Here and there she spotted the dust of a solitary moving vehicle, and that's all. No large troop movements. A lull in the trenches and behind them. What could she conclude from this? Either that the Indian hadn't talked, or he'd talked but hadn't been believed. This business of spying was easy. Why did people make such a tsimmes of something so tame?

Ottoman troops are not on the move, neither into the lines, nor back from the lines. That was her report. With a quick glance around to make sure she was alone, Rivka reached under her skirts and carefully untied the cotton sack holding the pigeon. The bird was so still while she extracted it and unwound its wrappings that she held her breath, fearing it had died. As the last wrapping came off, though, it cocked its white head and regarded her with eyes like jet beads. *Nu?* it seemed to be thinking. *What took you so long?*

Clasping it gently, she attached the tube to its foot. Then she launched it into the air. Her arms swung. The bird fluttered and flapped, circling her head. It landed on a stone not far away. Four steps it took, strutting and cooing.

"Fly, why don't you?"

It ignored her.

"Go home. Go!" She shook her skirt at it. She shooed it with her hands. It hopped onto the breeze and rose, dancing into the air. "Go," she called again, and it sped south. Soon enough, it was spotted by an enemy soldier. She could not see him pointing, but she heard the shots. The bird swayed aloft, a bright shiver against the sky. She willed it to keep flying into the blue until it became a mere point and she could see it flickering no longer. "Easy," she breathed. Then she buried the sack and the wrappings and started walking northward.

FROM BEHIND CAME the clattering of wooden wheels, the braying of a donkey, the creaking of a cart. She moved aside and watched him approach. The driver looked to be under thirty, a Jew in worker's garb and wide-brimmed hat such as farmers wore. The cart slowed to a halt beside her, and he offered her a ride. Sorrow was mapped in the creases of his face, yet the man's eyes held the light of hope. Trust no one, Barty had said, but such a face, how could she not believe in it? He was a pioneer on the land. She climbed up, thanking him in Yiddish for the lift.

Immediately, he switched to the mother tongue. "Where are you going, little sister?" he asked her.

"To Tulkarem."

His eyes widened, and his chin swiveled in her direction. He studied her, but said nothing.

This was her reasoning: why head directly to Atlith, as she'd been instructed, when the ride afforded her extra time to search out some vital piece of intelligence, perhaps changing everything? At Tulkarem was the headquarters of the Turkish Eighth Army. She asked, "Have you heard any news?"

"Of what?"

She shrugged. Of whatever.

He drove on in silence. Finally, he said, "In the coffee house there are whispers of an Arab assault on Amman, though others say it's Deraa and others Hejaz."

"An assault."

"So it would seem."

"Successful?"

"So it would seem."

The man was not very forthcoming. "*Nu*, and is this good for the Jews?"

He offered a noise from the back of his throat, half laugh, half snort.

At the side of the road, a patch of green shoots appeared, an elfin oasis. The donkey stopped to graze at it. Halfheartedly, the man slapped his reins against the animal's back. Dust flew up. The donkey kept chewing.

He studied the backs of its ears. "What takes you to Tulkarem?" he asked casually.

"My cousin," she responded, a cover story she'd hastily concocted since climbing up onto the seat beside him. "He and I came up to the land of Israel six months ago. From Odessa. We've settled in Haifa and are looking for work. This is not so easy. Two days ago, just before sundown, he left the house dressed for the holiday. I haven't seen him since."

"What makes you think he's in Tulkarem?"

She shrugged. "One has to start somewhere."

"You've come south of Tulkarem."

"Have I?"

"Perhaps you are acquainted with Rosenberg. He, too, is from Odessa. Isaac Rosenberg, who lives by the slope of Mt. Carmel."

"Who doesn't know him?" She had no choice but to say this. According to reason, there were so few Jews in the land that every Jew must know, or at least have heard of, every other Jew.

The donkey raised its head. The man slapped the reins, and the cart started. "Listen," he said. "I am from Qalqilya. You are from Qalqilya."

"I—"

"Never mind. You are from Qalqilya. I am your cousin. My name is Avram Ben Yohanan."

"And why do I want to be related to you?"

He said, "Me, at least you know I work the land. As everyone knows, the land deserves every sacrifice, for without it, every Jew is doomed to eternal wandering. Also, as everyone knows, Isaac Rosenberg from Odessa, now of Haifa, runs a brothel."

She didn't blanch. Whether or not he was bluffing, she could put up a creditable bluff of her own. She said, "Oh, *that* Isaac Rosenberg. I thought you meant the young one, who studies Talmud."

He grinned, white teeth neatly aligned.

She pushed it further. "He, too, lives near Mt. Carmel."

"A Talmud *chochem*? Earns his allotment turning simple words into unfathomable phrases?"

"Ah, you know him, then."

"Him and all his thousand *oysgeputst* relatives." Once more he grinned.

He was handsome in a bearish way, with a full dark beard and long-fingered hands that sprouted small, glossy curls on their backs. She liked the way he held the reins loosely, comfortably. She felt he knew his own strength and had no need to exert it just for show. She said, "I was told to trust no one."

"That's good advice."

"Can you be trusted?"

"Have you a choice?"

She studied him thoughtfully. Where the bridge of his nose met his forehead there was a small, star-shaped dimple. His eyes were shrewd, but not unkind. Even covered in the dust of the road, he gave the impression of good order, for his hair and beard were neatly trimmed, as were his fingernails and even the nails of his toes showing through the straps of his sandals. And he worked the land, still, despite the depredations of Turks, Arabs, locusts, drought, war and whatever else God had thrown at him in the way of personal tragedy. She smiled inwardly. If she hadn't already decided to trust him, she couldn't have asked him the question.

The road they traveled twisted through the rough Judean hills. When the donkey wasn't stumbling, the cart was jouncing, and when the cart wasn't jouncing, the wheels were shimmying. The sun seemed stuck in its track across the sky, unable to continue its westerly fall toward the horizon. They talked together and fell silent, and talked again, or not, their interplay as rambling and patchy as the route they followed. Beside her now, Avram was whistling a tune through his teeth. Some men's silences she found uneasy, but not his. He wasn't a chatterer, no more than she. When he spoke, it was because he had something to say worth listening to. If she spoke, he would pay her his grave attention, and if she grew pensive, he would respect her silence. Her eyelids drooped. Her head was a round and heavy melon. Except for the hour's catnap before dawn, she'd had no sleep in, let me see….

THERE WAS A sharp cry. The donkey brayed. The cart swayed, skidded, stopped. Rivka was jerked awake.

"Trouble," Avram muttered.

Six Turkish soldiers with rifles trained on them were closing in on the cart.

Who had accused her? "You picked me up on the road," she whispered. "I said nothing to you." An innocent farmer must not be arrested as her accomplice.

The soldiers' uniforms were shabby. They wore no boots, but only makeshift strips of thin leather—or was it paper?—tied with string to the soles of their feet. They prodded Avram and then Rivka from the wagon and inspected its contents. Rivka recognized in them the signs of sinking morale. Often enough in Russia she'd witnessed men taking commands dully, as these did now, no readiness to their movements.

The squad's leader spoke to Avram in Arabic. The crevice between Avram's eyes deepened. He grunted, shaking his head.

The Arab woman must have alerted the Turks. Remorse filled her. She should have been more alert. For her moment's weakness over mint tea and a bright-eyed baby, she had jeopardized both her mission and the life of this man. "You don't know me," Rivka prompted. "Tell them. They'll let you go."

He gaped at her. "It's me they want. I'm trying to convince them to let *you* go."

No one was let go. Both were taken prisoner and hauled in. Why, she wasn't sure—but it did seem to be Avram, and not she, who interested them. What was he involved in?

They were taken into the town. The road was quiet, except for a group of Germans who rode past on fine horses, sitting their mounts with the kind of authority that comes only from high command. The German General von Sanders and his staff were headquartered well north of here, in Nazareth. What exigency would bring high-ranking Germans to this comfortless spot near the front? Could it be the warnings of a certain turncoat Indian sergeant? Too late now, she thought smugly. Too late for your troops to be moved in strength from the eastern to the coastal sector. They wouldn't be in time to meet the attack. Those already in the line could be put on alert, of course. Troops prepared for battle would fight better, especially poorly fed, poorly uniformed and demoralized troops far from home, like the Turks who'd taken her prisoner. If caught by surprise, they might collapse and run.

The hope of this rose in her and struggled with fear, for they might as easily turn savage, wreaking their anger on noncombatants like her. She'd witnessed this, too, in Russia, and it was ugly beyond all imagining.

At Tulkarem, she was taken into a low wooden building and shut up in a room with a Turkish guard who ignored her. Avram was led away, she knew not where or for what purpose.

SHE CROSSED HERSELF as Sanders strode in. No mistaking the commander; though he was not tall, he bore himself like an emperor. Never had she seen a man dominate the space around him as this one did. She made the cross using the open-handed Austrian method rather than the three-fingered Russian method. Long ago Mischa had pointed out to her how they differed in manner and direction.

"What is your name?" the general asked in English.

She lifted her eyebrows. He asked again, and when still she said nothing, her Turkish guard came growling at her with raised arm and clenched fist. The German barked a single, sharp word. Like a tide receding, the menace backed away.

"What is your name?" This time in German.

"I don't know," she replied. She could say very little else in his tongue without exposing herself as a Jew. From any Jew, Sanders would assume treachery, but a Jew who could speak no Turkish in an Ottoman land he would know to be his enemy. With her blond hair and straight nose he might take her to be a Christian, but only so long as she kept her German locutions simple.

"Residence?"

"I don't know."

"What city are you from?"

"I don't know."

A mirthless smile. "Well, then, my girl, what *do* you know?"

She shook her head. The guard, glaring, flexed his fingers. She offered one of a handful of proverbs she'd learned in German, the only one she could speak without a Yiddish intonation. "*Das Gluck suchen wir, das Ungluck sucht uns.*" It had none of the saltiness of Yiddish proverbs. German maxims all seemed to be about bad luck or stupidity or evil intentions. In proper German she'd said, "We seek good fortune, misfortune finds us." In Yiddish she might have told him *A kluger farshtait fun ein vort tsvei.* A wise man hears one word and understands two.

The commander gave a clipped nod. "She'll go with us," he ordered. Assuming he was going up to headquarters, this was good news to her ears on two counts. First, she'd be out of the hands of the Turks and their brutalities. From the Germans you might at least expect civilized behavior. Second, the general's headquarters were in Nazareth, well away from tomorrow's plan of battle, and also near to Atlith. Looked at in the right light, Sanders was offering a convenient northbound taxi service across the Judean hills beyond Nablus, through Jenin and El Afula.

But why had he said to bring her? What were his suspicions, and what was he planning to do about them? He struck her as a man without pity.

When they took her outside, Avram ben Yohanan was nowhere to be seen. Had he, too, been questioned? Had he, God willing, been let go? It was not a good sign that his riderless cart was being loaded with barrels for the journey northward. Before she could make out what the stores were, the men covered them with a tarpaulin. The German party mounted their horses. She was given a donkey and a guard. As they set out, the reddening sun was dropping toward the sea.

THE SKY DARKENED, and they mounted into the hills, picking their way slowly northward, the air growing crisp and much colder. Sanders with a few others went on ahead. The rest seemed in no hurry to get back to their base. They made frequent stops to water the horses and have a bite themselves. She was offered a bit of sausage at the point of a soldier's knife. When she shook her head, the soldier chuckled low in his throat and leered at her. Had she failed a test, he offering pork, she proving herself a Jewish spy by refusing? Rivka, shivering, drew her shawl closer around her.

In the early morning hours, they reached Jenin. Dimly through the darkness the boxy outlines of German biplanes could be made out lining the airfield. Rivka automatically counted them, though there was little chance now that she could get the information to Allenby. When the faint booming of cannon reached them, coming from the south, she concealed her quick smile. The bombardment must be starting, the pounding of enemy lines that always preceded an advance, the aim being to destroy the enemy's defenses and his will to fight. For half an hour, Rivka, listening, allowed herself to gloat. Then the sound died away. The Germans glanced uneasily at one another. They seemed as mystified as she. Sometimes in the stasis of trench warfare, a sector might suffer a brief, heavy bombardment of half an hour's duration, but these were meant to harry the enemy and were launched in daylight. When the bombardment preceded an attack across no-man's-land, the cannonade was more likely to begin in darkness, as this had, but in that case it ought to continue far longer. On the Eastern Front, such bombardments typically lasted two or three days. On the Western Front, they'd been known to go on for as long as a week. This one, like those, was broad and thunderous. While it lasted it lit up the dark southern sky. Then it stopped abruptly, setting everyone's teeth on edge.

LIGHT CREPT BACK into the world. Rivka, who'd been lulled almost to sleep by the rocking of her saddle, awoke to find that the gray rocks were turning yellowish-white and the gray trees were turning brown and green, and the dark sky had become pearlescent, turning rosy at its eastern edge. Dawn on the 20th of September. Nazareth was just ahead, a scattering of small mud-and-wattle houses climbing a hill with a larger, longer building at the very top. Jesus had lived in Nazareth: the Christian Messiah, much good had he done! Keep an eye on the goyim, she instructed herself. Do whatever they do. There might be a special ritual for entering the city, or when passing its sacred sites. Watch them, and if they cross themselves, do likewise. If they—

The thought remained unfinished as she did what they did: kicked her mount hard and raced pell-mell with them up through the town's narrow streets. To their rear, El Afula had burst into flame. Less than an hour ago they'd been passing through Afula. Despite her sleepiness some unblinking part of Rivka's brain had noted a house with its lights blazing: not the lonely lantern of someone awakened in the night by chance, but the solid, comfortable light of those accustomed to working by night. Communications, she'd guessed. A hub. Her eyes had searched for, and found, the telltale wires going south toward Nablus and Tulkarem, and those going north toward Nazareth. Now, British planes were swooping over the city, dropping bombs, destroying the Hun's ability to telephone Johnny Turk.

Other explosions targeted Afula's railway junction connecting the far-flung cities of Constantinople, Aleppo and Damascus with the line to Haifa. As the Germans dismounted at the hill's summit, Rivka turned to search the horizon for the bursts. Behind her, the long building was disgorging men in uniform. One of them cocked his head, listening to a fainter thunder of detonations from even further south.

"Jenin," he said.

Another contradicted him. "Nein. Nablus."

The guard dragged her to an empty pen, the kind used for keeping domestic animals. She sat down on the ground inside, he outside. For two hours, the planes came and went, relentlessly dropping their ordnance on Afula, Jenin and Nablus. Then, silence. If all was going according to plan (though when, in war, did things ever go according to plan?) Allenby now owned the skies; communications between the Turk and the German were crippled; and near the coast the Allied cavalry at this moment were smashing straight through Turkish lines and wheeling right, opening a sluice through which the Allied infantry would pour eastward. Yet here, with the breeze riffling past her ears, with the sounds that reached her of birds singing, horses snuffling, and even occasional shouts of children playing somewhere in the streets below—here at German headquarters all seemed routine.

No one showed the least bit of interest in her, a good sign. Still, it would be nice if someone would remember to feed her. She began to regret how she'd turned her nose up at that chunk of blood sausage, even if it did resemble a clod of flesh on the tip of the man's knife. She was thirsty and chilled, and her body ached from the long night's ride.

In the afternoon, Sanders came out to look at her. She pretended indifference, humming softly to herself until her guard entered the cage and forced her to her feet in front of the great man. Sanders had a long face with crafty eyes and hair cropped as short as a new recruit's. Like a stalking panther he studied her. Studied her until she was pierced through with his gaze. Her eyes felt gritty, her tongue swollen inside her mouth. Silently, doggedly, she telegraphed, *If all goes well, you'll be gone in a week. If all does not go well—sooner or later you'll still be gone.*

He uttered not a word, merely nodded to the guard and turned away.

And now her mind raced with worries: Has the attack succeeded? Are Allenby's troops bogged down, or do they make progress against the Turk? Is the Jewish Legion performing in such a way as to bring us pride? She fastened onto this as an issue she could safely ponder: Who seriously believes a Jew can fight? Not the British, not the Turks, not the Arabs, least of all Jews themselves. Everyone thinks us weak and cowardly, despite the evidence of scripture. She tried, as night fell and the cold crept up from the ground into her bones, to concentrate her mind on the question of Biblical victories. But underneath and behind and around all her musing nagged the question of fate that would not be silenced: what does the German commander plan to do with me in the morning?

Rivka's wartime experience told her a week at best was needed for Allenby's troops to advance this far north. Only God knew if she'd still be alive by then. "Hassan Bek, Hassan Bek," her guard was taunting her, his sibilant whisper hissing in her face. Herr Doctor Hassan Bek, he jeered through mossy brown teeth, is a physician and chief officer in the Turkish Fourth Army here in Nazareth. A man of distinction—you understand?—renowned among the most skillful Turks for the elegance of his—ah—interrogations. She shivered, and now it was not from the cold. A week from now, would she still care to be alive, or like Sarah Aaronsohn…? Tomorrow, she thought. Tomorrow will begin my ordeal.

SHE AWOKE OUT of a troubled sleep in the early hours of September 21 to the thunder of horses' hoofs, shouts in German, lights swinging, men running. There was a bonfire, stacks of paper ablaze, and more stacks being dumped on top. Sanders' horse was brought around dancing and snorting in the commotion. As Rivka watched, the great man rushed out onto the porch, unmistakable by his military bearing, his close-cropped head and the obsequiousness of the men he brushed past. She laughed out loud: the general, wearing nothing but his riding boots and a pair of striped pajamas, mounted his steed and galloped off north toward Tiberias. A half-dozen rumpled members of his staff trailed behind.

Rivka crouched in a corner of her cage, forgotten. Her vile guard was gone. Everything she knew about the stasis of war in Europe said that it was too soon, far too soon, for Nazareth to be threatened by Allenby's troops. Not a single shell had burst, not a shot fired. It was impossible that the offensive could be moving so fast, impossible. Yet what else could account for the men's obvious confusion and fear? What other crisis could explain them scrambling to set up a machine gun nest on the rim of the hill?

In such perfect incoherence, it was hard for her to know what to do. If she'd really been forgotten, immobility would appear to be her best hope for survival. Move from this spot, and she might be remembered, then summarily executed. On the other hand, don't move, and someone racing past might still take notice and decide to shoot her. Shut as she was in this cage, she was defenseless.

From the southwest came a rumbling of horses' hoofs and a scattering of rifle fire. Rivka didn't suspect and wouldn't know until much later that the sound heralded the last great cavalry charge of the war, indeed the last in history. She did suspect an oncoming storm, one that would present her best opportunity to escape unnoticed. She threw herself against the gate. Once, twice. It squealed, and she assailed it again. It gave way, toppled, she rolling to the hill's edge. Below, a group of Turkish soldiers went running from British horsemen. The Germans—only nine of them left—huddled together in their machine gun nest, spraying bullets across the field. The attacking cavalry took aim from their horses. They threw grenades. The hill vomited showers of earth and flame.

She had risen to her feet and now jumped up and down like a child cheering the home team. In the deafening clamor, a bullet whistled past her. Not from the Turks and Germans—they were too busy defending themselves to bother with her. The shot had come from one of the Brits. A rider had aimed right at her, she was certain of it. She being at enemy headquarters, he'd seen ENEMY written all over her. You shoot first when approaching the enemy, and ask questions later. *God willing I'll live long enough to be asked questions!*

A tall bay mare had come back from the Tiberias road with a lone boot hanging out of its stirrup. It was trotting nervously in a ragged circle near the cage where Rivka had been penned. Rivka whistled for the horse and began edging toward it. It stopped, eyes large and watchful, ears pricked. Rifka neared, and it shied. She had all she could do to hold still and wait, speaking soothing words, doubting the horse could hear her in the din. She inched closer. The mare tossed its mane. Not far away a grenade exploded. She lunged and caught the bridle, the mare prancing, the boot bouncing heavily against its flank. No time left for stroking and calming. Rivka disengaged and tossed away the boot, which had a foot still inside it. In one fluid motion, she bent, pulled the back hem of her skirt forward, tucked it up into her waistband, and mounted. As the first wave of British cavalry overran the German machine gunners, she turned the horse's head and gave the animal a powerful kick.

She had become a prophet. *You will not be here long,* her defiant eyes had warned Sanders' probing ones. That had been only yesterday. Who could have imagined how swiftly the British would advance? Unbelievably, in a single day they had covered forty miles and more. Only yesterday Rivka had foretold the German general's demise, and today the man had fled in his nightclothes like a panicked little rabbit, transfiguring Rivka into a judge and seer. Devorah, speaker of truth.

The thunder of hoofs was Sanders' first inkling of the enormity of the Turkish defeat. As she picked her way southward, Rivka was determined not to be caught dozing like him. She carried no papers. Without papers she was done for. No one would accept her identity on her say-so alone, and a demand to see Allenby or Bartholomew would surely be scoffed at. With every pore and muscle alive to danger, she moved in an undulating line skirting settlements, villages, anywhere that launched a human sound out into the air.

It was a journey she would never forget, made glorious by her combat-ready senses. The rising day was piercingly beautiful, the air intoxicating. She traveled through dry scrub, and she stumbled upon miracles: gurgling water, gay carpets of wildflowers, verdant trees, tumbled piles of stone that might have been ancient signposts or walls or houses. Birds sang to her, birds with saffron throats, with turquoise bellies, with dark masks across their eyes or tail feathers of orange and green. A needle-beaked bird with a yellow crown across its head called *oop-oop-oop* as she passed, and then rose into the air on black-and-white striped wings.

The mare was good company. She had been well trained and followed commands instantly. She was sure-footed in the hills and could pick her way through rock-strewn defiles. She had deep eyes, this horse. Rivka talked to her along the way, and she nodded her head as if she understood.

At Afula, Rivka crept forward to view the Turkish telephone and telegraph offices in ruins. Farther south, she caught sight of two British bombers circling Jenin. The slightest movement on the airfield below sent bombs careering down, while machine guns rat-a-tatted the hangars. The fighting will soon be over, she assured the horse. The British rule the skies. Hear that noise? That's the bombing and strafing. Roads, railways, troop concentrations…and not the least challenge from enemy pilots, is there? I don't hear any. You don't either, do you? It won't be long before we have all the ground as well, and then I can go home. Wherever home might be. She'd had a home, in a fine village, peopled with neighbors she knew, with friends who cared for her. All of that gone. The Russia she knew (no picnic to begin with) had turned unrecognizably savage. Then Yashka, in whom she'd found a kind of home—or so she'd thought—had deserted her. And with Gena? Could she make herself a home with Gena?

Never mind. Just let it be over. Then everyone can go home, all the soldiers and all the refugees, and all the horses, too, and even the mules.

If something still exists anywhere called a home.

The refugees would be gaunt shadows moving along the road, tired, hungry, silent in their suffering. She remembered them that way from 1915 coming eastward out of Galicia, the children with stick limbs and swollen bellies, silent in their illness, silent in their deaths. They'd been that way in 1916—so Avram ben Yohanan had told her as they rode together in his wagon—the Passover refugees whom he'd helped coming northward out of Tel Aviv through Qalqilya, too weak or too exhausted or too indifferent to flap away the mosquitos and flies from their scabrous faces. They'd be that way for a time even after the war was done.

"I worry about the farmer," she told the horse. "I don't know, he said it wasn't my fault we were captured. But he had no idea how foolishly I stopped to take tea with an Arab woman. What do you suppose has become of him?" At that moment they were navigating a particularly tricky turn, and if the horse had an opinion, she didn't share it.

That man, Avram, was a Zionist unlike any of those Rivka had known in Europe. They were boys whose fathers were tailors or bakers or merchants, and they'd never once held a hoe in their soft hands, much less a plow. They talked unvaryingly about The Land, how to till it, how to tend it, to raise funds to get to it, to organize it and on and on and on. Nothing else interested them except Eretz Yisroel, and you itched to say, "So go, already. Who's keeping you here?" Those who wanted to leave usually found a way. A few were forced to stay because of a wife who was sick, or a father, or worst of all a child. That left the numbers of boors who chattered forever but never managed to get up on their hind legs—pardon the expression, horse, no offense meant—and depart. Armchair Zionists, Papa called them. Avram, by contrast, seemed a man of action, a man who toiled for the land, whose sweat and blood were mixed in with the soil, but whose mind roamed widely, and whose lips spoke of other people's deeds, not his own.

If not for Avram, Rivka would have taken the horse westward to Atlith. They'd be there now, safe and sound at the coast, waiting for the *Managem*. Except she couldn't leave Avram in Turkish hands knowing the chaos that comes when a weak and dispirited army is in retreat, knowing the danger for him, the opportunity for her. It was toward him she'd turned the mare's head. Toward the place where she'd last seen him. Southward they went, alone together in the land, avoiding Germans, Turks and Britons equally.

THEY'D BEEN ON the move for many hours when they came across a ridge to the uncovered remains of a Roman road. For a length of twenty feet or so, flat white stones were laid six across in the earth, crisscrossed with ruts. The sun was high in the sky, and she was tired and sore from riding. Nablus, headquarters of the Turkish Seventh Army, could not be far to the south, Tulkarem not far to the west. She got down to inspect the stones. She imagined the iron wheels of chariots clattering over them, gradually furrowing them out: Roman chariots on a Roman road crossing Judean hills on their way to put down the rebellious Jews. Running her finger along the ridged edges, she recalled a newspaper article Rachel's father had handed her before the war. "The triumph of archeology," he'd said dryly. The article told of a startling excavation just east of Nablus, where the ancient ruins of Shechem had been discovered close by the known site of Jacob's well. Shechem was the city in which Jacob's daughter, Dinah, had been violated, by one man, a Hivite prince. Then all the men of Shechem had been killed by Jacob's sons in revenge. According to the article, the bloody slaughter and spoliation were all there in Genesis 34 if you cared to read.

She stood, stretched out her arms, tightened and released the muscles of her thighs and calves. Compared to the stones of Shechem, these beneath her feet were young, yet these were two thousand years old. "Bloodshed, it's ancient," she told the horse. "Older than Rome, older than Shechem, older even than Genesis." The mare's moist brown eye swiveled toward her. So can this war end bloodshed forever? You're the prophet, Rivka. What is your prediction? She sighed, foretelling only that she ought to remount and get moving again. She bent from the waist to ease out the tightness in her back. The clenched muscles relented, and she reached for her toes.

Now comes the sharp smack on her horse's rump. Next, a thick arm circling her waist, the breath knocked out of her as she is dragged, gasping and scrabbling, into darkness.

He pins her to the ground. Arms pin arms, legs pin legs, and as she starts to scream, his mouth comes down on hers hard, as hard and unyielding as the thing she feels through the folds of her skirt, swelling against her thigh. She hasn't been listening, hasn't been hearing, doesn't know what he said, a hoarse whisper in her ear as he pulled her into the cave. Fight was all she knew. Scratch, bite, batter and kick.

But now she begins to hear him, now with his mouth on hers she finds herself listening, and now she hearkens even though he is uttering not a word. Is it the grassy smell of him, the briny taste of him? Is it the soft roughness of his beard against her skin, the curling of his gentle fingers through hers? These are not the fingers of an enemy. She feels his tongue against her lips. With his tongue teasing her lips, she stops fighting. She opens to him, and he leads her through a lingual dance. It starts as stately as a minuet, quickly changing to a waltz, then a wild mazurka. Delirium fills her mouth, delirium behind her eyes, delirium deep in her groin.

He rolls off of her, gasping, penitent. Can she forgive him? He rubs at his face. He didn't mean to take advantage. He only meant to silence her,

She nods, wishing he wouldn't apologize. She is not the least bit sorry, certainly not with the taste of him alive still in her mouth. Ought she to tell him so? She folds her arms. She'd die first.

He says, "What in the name of God are you doing here?"

"I came to rescue you from the Turk."

In the gloom of the cave she can scarcely make out the astonishment in his face. "Nice job." He's only barely whispering, but she cannot mistake his irony.

She splutters, "You've probably lost my horse for me."

Avram shrugs. With any luck, the Turkish scouts he'd spotted have gone off following the animal. Didn't she know the entire

Seventh Army was on the move? He'd been up above and had seen the scouts making straight for the spot where she stood, climbing hand over hand straight up the hill. Any minute now, a mass of Ottoman soldiers running for the Jordan would be passing along the road, and short work that bunch would have made of her.

Had he been spying on her?

Well, yes, in a manner of speaking. Guarding her was the term he preferred.

"Did they hurt you, the Turks?"

He shook his head. He'd been able to escape with minor injuries only.

"And here I'd been thinking to rescue you."

He took her hand in his and kissed her open palm. "So you have."

"What did they…." Outside, the growl of motors.

"*Shah! Shah!*" An armored vehicle ground its gears. They heard it lurch forward, picking up speed. It was followed by wagons, first those hauling cannon, then the supply train. Finally came column upon column of enemy soldiers trudging past. None of them took any notice of the cave. These hills were pocked with caves. Limestone was like that, all sorts of holes in it big and small that not one of them wished to explore. What every man devoutly wished was to be out of there and safely beyond the river, behind sandbags and packed earth and thick rolls of barbed wire.

After the last vehicle had passed, after the clank and thud of the last passing troops had disappeared on the breeze, after the air cleared of dust and the birds came twittering back, they stole from their hideout. Rivka blinked in the sunlight. "Come with me," said Avram.

They climbed up to the top of the ridge. From there, all the country to the east spread out before them. Striated brownish ridges stepped all the way to the horizon, utterly barren of vegetation. What a grim, harsh beauty, the starkest kind of grandeur, breathtaking in its otherworldliness, aloof and troubling. Overhead a lone plane circled and then headed west. A hawk circled and then dove. Out there, the long column of the Turkish Seventh Army made its slow way forward, nothing more now to the two watchers on the ridge than a tiny, segmented tan worm wriggling among the deeper tans of the cliffs. The worm entered a gorge. Rivka's eye traced the ribbon of road winding through it. How had mere men cut such a road in the steep cliff, with sheer rock towering above and a sheer drop canyoning below? Whatever else might be said about the Romans, they were astonishing builders.

From the south came the buzz of a biplane, then two, three, four. Their canvas wings were the dun hue of moths, the only brightness coming from the red, white and blue insignia of the British or Australian air corps. They flew to the far side of the defile, where the head of the column was advancing by inches. Airplanes had rarely been used in Rivka's sector of the Eastern Front, and then only for reconnaissance. She watched dumbstruck as these swooped down to attack. Black columns of smoke rose, long seconds before she could hear the crump and boom of the explosions. Tiny licelike things raced away. A plane dipped, and yellow flashes plumed from its rear. Below, the insects shook and went still as the tattoo of machine-gun fire reached Rivka's ears.

The planes emptied themselves of bombs. They strafed the column with their guns, wiping away the men who tried to escape from the road by climbing up or down the cliffs. As they flew away, in came another squadron and dipped down and did the same. Then another. Then another. Within an hour it seemed nothing could still be living out there, yet the planes kept coming.

X

Avram

IN THE DEEP stillness after the battle (if you could call it a battle, and not a turkey shoot), Avram said, "Come, let's go."

"Go where?" But she knew where.

They were not first to reach that place of panic and devastation. The burnt air was thick with thousands of thrumming flies. Stones and sand, black with blood, churned with flies. Their drunken buzzing sickened Rivka. The carnage shocked her. Wagons had run into trucks, trucks into wagons, crushing men, horses, donkeys, everything. In its momentum the pile-up had sent the living in their vehicles over the rim into the gorge. What wasn't smashed to pieces was torn to bits. Avram was able to estimate about a thousand transport vehicles along the six-mile route. Neither one of them could begin to guess the numbers of slaughtered men and beasts, so shattered were the corpses. Where this morning they had seen an army—thousands of men in their long columns streaming westward toward the river—by evening there was none. The destruction was total. Some men had perhaps managed to scale the cliffs, evading inexorable death. Against them, there would be mop-up operations: more bombs in their tons, more machine-gun rounds in their thousands assailing the survivors as they stumbled toward safety. Some few stunned and leaderless individuals might still manage to make good an escape across the river. But their army itself? The Seventh Army was no more.

Avram squinted at the sky. "The next war," he said, "will be fought in the air."

"The next?" She shuddered. This one was not even over yet, except nominally in Russia, where civil war had replaced the Great War, and seemed to her a mere extension of it.

"You think this war will end all wars?" he said, mimicking the American President Wilson.

"One can hope."

"Then we shall hope," he said, nodding.

They had turned and begun retracing their steps. "You're humoring me," she chided.

He peered at her, the crease deepening between his eyes. "Why would you say that?"

"Because people always seem to find something to fight over."

"And yet we all long for peace," he said.

"Do we?"

"Most of the time."

They walked on a while in silence, sobered by the carnage they'd witnessed. Avram had not touched her since the cave (kisses still fresh on her lips and prickling the warm palm of her hand). For this reserve, she was grateful to him. If he should try to embrace her again, she could not allow it, and things would be awkward afterwards. He was acting in a thoroughly decent fashion. Yet as he marched them southwestward, rarely stopping except for water, she found herself sorely vexed. Why hadn't he tried? For example, at the moment she'd shied in horror from the terrible slaughter. Would it have been such a big deal for him to give comfort in her distress? He hadn't so much as grazed his fingers across her huddled shoulder. Well, if avoidance was his game, she supposed she could play it, too. She resolved there and then not to speak to him until he broke the silence.

Avram, lost in thought, gazed steadily forward. They reached a road, and then a nearly dry streamlet, where a pocked and crooked cup hung suspended by a piece of crumbling twine from the low branch of an ancient olive tree, its trunk gnarled and hollow. He rinsed the cup and scooped up a mouthful of clear water for her to drink. "And you?" he said finally, as if there'd been no lapse at all in their earlier conversation. "For what do you long? Other than peace?"

It was the last question she expected from him, and for that reason it burst the truth out of her. "God alone knows! All my life up till today I've longed for adventure, and this is what led me here." She glanced around as if contemplating herself in the landscape of Palestine for the first time.

"All your life? Truly?"

She spoke then about her early years, her home and family, Mischa, Dudie. He prodded her for more.

"Ancient history," she said. "Who cares anymore?"

"I do."

So she told him about Yashka and becoming a soldier, and about the October Revolution, with all its terror. She told him about the journey to Vladivostok, about the two Filippovs and the ship to Egypt. She did not mention Gena's proposal, nor her engagement. She described her decision to come to Palestine and her acceptance of Allenby's invitation to spy on the enemy. "A woman of valor," he said gravely, and she blushed. She said she wasn't sure anymore that such adventures were what she ought to long for. She belonged nowhere, and she would soon be eighteen.

"If adventure is your heart's desire, age won't change it."

"Then must I become heartless, do you think?"

She was being saucy, but he seemed to take her seriously. His lips pursed. "Not if you redefine what you mean by adventure."

"I could become a prophet."

"You could."

"You're laughing at me again."

He put his hand to his heart. "On the soul of Djemal Pasha, I am not."

She happened to know—because he had told her—that he deemed the Turkish governor 'the soulless whelp of a soulless whore.'

She merely said, "And you? For what do you long? Other than peace?"

Avram was not a man of many words. She managed to get out of him that he had been born in the land of Israel to parents who had made aliyah in their youth, distant cousins traveling from Russia with an older cousin in the wake of the pogroms that followed the assassination of Tsar Alexander II. He had been raised in Petach Tikvah and from a small boy had loved farming. "This is not a Jewish occupation," said his father, a schoolteacher who had quickly become disenchanted with the mud-spattered ideals of the pioneers. Avram's three brothers had gone into business, one leaving the land and returning to Europe as a trader. When the family moved to the new city of Tel Aviv, Avram had stayed behind to work the soil. That was all there was to his story, he claimed: twenty-five years old, twenty of those a farmer.

He got to his feet, saying they needed to keep moving. "Someday," she told him, "I'll make you tell me the rest of your story."

THERE WAS NO official debriefing, not even a pat on the back and a "well done, brave warrior." Allenby was far to the north, Bartholomew with him. The old headquarters were pretty much deserted, and even the pigeoneer, when she sought him out, was nowhere to be found. Just an empty coop and a pile of guano. The war had shifted north. She had played her part, and the knowledge of it was to be her reward.

At least the girls she worked with were excited to see her. They crowded around as if she'd been gone for months, begging to know where she'd been and what had happened to her, wanting to tell her how changed she looked, or not changed at all, depending on who it was peering into her face. She said little. She did feel a change, initially, some kind of separation, or disconnection, or disjunction she couldn't quite put her finger on…yet within only a couple more days she found she'd slipped seamlessly back into her old routines, almost as if she'd never left at all. Funny what the mind can do, how the clamorous present and the insistent immediate world make every other reality vague and dreamlike. Try to conjure up mountains of stiffening flesh, rivers of darkening blood, the sharp crack of a corpse-bone in a wild dog's mouth: in her nightly dreams these became vivid again, but by day, amid the lushness of orange groves, nothing concrete or tangible remained of them.

The speed of Allenby's victory was staggering. On October 1, Damascus fell. On October 26, Aleppo, Syria's northernmost Arab city. Pressed on all sides, the Ottoman Empire capitulated on October 30. Under the terms of the armistice, Turkey's sea-lanes were opened, its forts occupied, its army demobilized, its prisoners released, its Middle Eastern provinces relinquished. Its surrender was total.

Mind you, the same could be said of Avram, and also of Rivka: total surrender. Sometime around the first of October, he came to her at her barracks in Rehovoth. They walked out together into the stillness beyond the settlement, the night a soft blanket wrapping them close. He nuzzled her neck, his breath warm against her skin. "You smell like fine linen," he murmured. She touched the deep crease between his eyes and watched his eyelids fluttering closed. He smelled of grass and laundry soap. She touched the massed muscles of his shoulders. He kissed her ear, her chin, her quivering lips. Her tentative hands slid to his slim waist. He folded her in his arms and talked about the future he foresaw for himself and Eretz Yisrael. For Jews, the chance of a homeland, finally, after two thousand years of wandering. For him, personally, a chance of happiness. She hesitated to ask whence his happiness would come, for fear his plans did not include her—and for fear they did. He left so much unsaid that night, as did she. But there were more nights and other days, filled with their chatter and their laughter, their sighs and deep silences. He found them shelter from prying eyes, where they spent hungry hours in each other's arms. What had she known? Only Nachum's peck at her hand, only Gena's chaste kisses on her cheek and closed lips. Lust, she hadn't imagined. Now she tugged his shirt up out of his trousers by handfuls, her fingers burrowing for the spot just beneath his waistband where the matted hair of his torso gave way to the silkiest of skin, whiter and more tender than any infant's flesh. He pressed her against himself, his strong hands cupping her from behind, while she, feeling the heat of him through her skirt, thrust herself even closer.

The hours away from him were a luscious agony; the hours with him, lying out under the stars, fully clothed, unbuttoned, hardly less so. Longing, she learned, had a pungency to it, had a tart flavor, had a hollow sound that buzzed in her ears, had a pressure that congested every atom of her being and agitated her soul. Oh, but it was intoxicating to learn how to please him, how to set her fingers just where he wanted them and stroke him so that he moved to her caress, moaning. Avram, for his part, seemed to intuit how her pleasure would come, learning all that he needed to know about her at the same moment she came to know it.

THEY WERE DRINKING tea in a three-table café when the news reached them that the Ottoman Empire, for all practical purposes, now ceased to exist. Cheers went up. The grim centuries of Turkish rule in Palestine had come to an end. People hugged, people wept. "It's over," breathed Rivka, relief washing through her. A clarinet appeared, then a fiddle, and there was dancing in the street outside, a wide circle of delirious revelers. In the center, four men lifted Rivka in an armchair and danced with her above their heads while she crowed in tottery triumph. In this giddy hour, she had become their heroine. The Battle of Megiddo—as Allenby had named it, conjuring the biblical Armageddon—would go down in history as the last and the first. The last great cavalry charge and the first great air attack in the history of warfare. It had won them the war in Palestine, it had freed Eretz Yisrael from the Turkish yoke. And word had spread that she'd been part of it. So they danced and they danced until finally she tired of her celebrity, for she had caught sight of Avram standing alone, stock still in the midst of the whirling crowd.

His hands were at his hips, his eyes hard upon her. Conquest was in his gaze, the joy of this one, and the promise of another sort. She begged her admirers to put her down, and when they did, she reeled toward Avram. He caught her in his arms, steadied her. And then they ran all the way to the packing shed, she leading him down crisscrossing lanes of orchards. It was emptied of workers, everyone gone celebrating. And there, on the packing room floor, their clothes tossed aside, naked and without thought or care of being caught, they made love. They made love ravenously, and they made love tenderly. They were shy, and they were joyous. He entered her, and she filled him; and they were all that existed, there was nothing else, a universe unto themselves; and they were the sum total of creation, encompassing all other existence. How could an act of love possibly be more bountiful?

"So this is what it's all about," she sighed afterward, sated and drowsy.

Sweet laughter rumbled up from his belly.

Later in the afternoon, as they lazed under a tree sharing a bite of food, a parade passed nearby, an impromptu parade by the look of it. Children were beating pot lids with spoons and sticks and other pot lids; dogs were barking and jumping and running in circles; horns and bells were sounding, along with a snare drum and a pair of maracas; and British flags slung on poles were flapping in the air. Rivka jumped to her feet. "Let's go," pulling at him. "Come march with me."

"Why?"

"Why? Because it's over."

He shrugged. "I'll parade if you want. But it's not over."

"What then? Germany's troops are in retreat. Her home territory is being torn apart by riots. Everyone says the war in Europe is in its last days."

"For us it has hardly begun," he said.

Four years of war, four years of upheaval, unimaginable suffering. Nothing will ever be the same, and he thinks it's not enough? "A plague should come to you," she growled. "How dare you say such a thing?"

"Because here, there's work to do. We must secure the pledges made in wartime."

"By more fighting? More shooting?"

"Who said shooting?"

"We have the promise of a homeland. It's in writing."

"A promise made by whom? By God?"

"By the British. In the Balfour Declaration. You know that as well as I do."

"By men, then. Men make all sorts of vows, especially in war." His gaze shifted away from her, toward his toes. "Maybe women do, too."

She flushed. Did he know about Gena? What had he guessed? She herself had avoided any mention of the romance aboard ship. For one thing, she hadn't heard a word from Gennady Fyodorovich since her arrival in Palestine, and this worried her. She prayed he was safe, neither wounded nor ill. With Gena she had never felt desire such as she had for Avram. Nor, she'd begun to realize, did she feel the same exquisite pleasure in his very existence. This perhaps Gena might come to understand if she sought his forgiveness. He would be hurt, of course, and jealous. He'd likely try to win her back, reminding her of the awful privations they had shared, of the tribulations life brought and would always bring. With his pouted lips he would represent himself as the better partner for the long run. "This man Avram," he'd argue, "what do you really know about him?" Next to nothing. And that was another thing that worried her. She was—what? Playing at love? Falling in love? Already long gone in love?—with a stranger. A hundred times over she had already told herself all of this, lectured and chastised herself to no avail. All her heart wished Gena to be happy—happy, that is to say, without her.

XI

Home

AARONSOHN WAS BACK. He'd been abroad in Europe and the United States having strategic meetings with dignitaries and magnates and the biggest of *machers*. Now he came to see her. "There'll be a peace conference in Paris," he said. "Bargaining and haggling, threats and promises, some broken, some unbroken. I plan to be there."

Rivka nodded. Where else would he be?

"Will you come with me?"

She stared. What could he mean by such an invitation? He was an old man, almost as old as her father, had he lived.

Aaron gave a shout of laughter at her obvious shock and confusion, shaming her all the more. "I meant as my secretary," he said.

Maybe, but he had a reputation as a ladies' man. "I can't go, but thank you." She wanted no part of what would go on in Paris. She could have no real part in it even if she went. It would be just like in Russia. She'd look on, seeing the waste of energy, the cynical toying with ideals, and she'd be sick at heart, and there'd be nothing she could do about it. Maybe Aaronsohn could achieve something, but he didn't need her. Anyway, she was too busy.

"What can I say to change your mind?"

"Nothing, really. You make your own maps, you do your own talking."

"Come, Rivka, think what an adventure you'd have."

Very true, she would. But she was needed here in Eretz Yisrael, building the land and staking the Jewish claim. As a for-instance, thousands of eucalyptus trees had been cut down in Hadera to support the Turkish war effort. In the 1880s those trees had been planted by Jewish settlers to drain marshlands, and now the work had to be done all over again. It was the same everywhere in the land, as he well knew, as he had so often told her. Work to be done, and not enough hands to do it. She could accomplish more good here—and even see more of life—than if she sat hemmed in and useless among prattling diplomats in Paris. She didn't need to run far off in order to run into adventure. She'd begun to see that the wide world she craved emanated here, from herself, from her ability to discern and put a name to it. So she turned him down. Not long after, Aaronsohn left for England, and Rivka had the awful feeling she'd never see him again.

A letter arrived from Mischa, the soiled envelope practically falling apart in her hand. Dated September 12, 1918, it had taken months to reach her. He had been in Moscow over the summer, he wrote, and met up with an old family connection. Her heart turned over, jumping ahead of her eyes to the conclusion he'd found Dudie; but no, only Brusilov. The aging general still cut a dapper figure in his polished cavalry boots, Mischa said. They had a drink together, and Mischa talked of his decision to work within the Bolshevik party for the betterment of Russia. Not only did Brusilov support Mischa's position, but he put Mischa in touch with—Rivkeleh, you'll *plotz*—Lev Davidovich Trotsky!

"The Commissar for War is a man whose prodigious intellect is evident in his prominent forehead and riveting gaze. I was privileged to join him and a cadre of dedicated men much like myself traveling south-eastward toward the Volga. I can tell you now, dear sister, that the Red Army was at that moment crumbling. Our soldiers were everywhere retreating, and the cause of Bolshevism was in dire threat of destruction from its enemies.

"Commissar Trotsky is a master of organization. Our railroad train carried a telegraph office, a radio, a printing press, several automobiles and gasoline, even our own bathhouse. We brought boots to our war-sick soldiers, we brought food, medicine, weaponry, tobacco—and we brought Trotsky, a man of sublime fervor. Every time the Commissar spoke, his words of inspiration healed the men's weariness, stirred them to hope and courage.

"When we reached the Fifth Army west of Kazan, he immediately went about restoring order in the ranks. He is a man of strictest discipline, and yet only by pitiless means could this be accomplished. During those days I came to understand (most reluctantly, Rivka) your old friend Yashka's point of view on capital punishment. As Commissar Trotsky says, the soldier in battle must be placed between the *possibility* that death lies ahead and the *certainty* that it lies behind. So, with discipline restored and his thrilling exhortations in our ears—*Allow the enemy not a step further! Drown him in the Volga! Tear Kazan from his hands!*—we went forward on the attack.

"It was half past three on the morning of September 10. From three sides we stormed the city's walls, and by early afternoon the enemy had folded, and Kazan was ours! Simbirsk and Samara followed easily after. Thus has the tide turned. The Revolution is saved, and now, the great work can truly begin!"

Rivka scratched her head. So. The tide has turned. If Mischa lived by the sea like me, he'd know that tides turn every six hours or so. Wait a little, and a tide that has come in always goes back out. His revolution for the sake of the masses was now turning bloody, taking its own barefoot soldiers and executing them as examples. How could Mischa extol such "pitiless means" in the name of the people's revolution? "Most reluctantly," he'd said. This was more than Rivka could work out.

Troubled, she glanced at a news clipping he'd enclosed. It was from *Pravda,* trumpeting "the first truly major victory of the Red Army," and quoting Trotsky's address to the crowd that, it reported, had gathered spontaneously at the Kazan Theater to hear him: *Why do we fight? We fight to settle the question of whether the homes, palaces, cities, sun and heavens will belong to the people who live by their labor—to the workers, peasants and the poor—or whether they will belong to the bourgeosie and the landlords.* Intuition told Rivka that her brother still had a heart as big as all Russia, that his grandiloquent letter had been penned in a ripple of jubilation following the battle, that it did not reflect the whole of who he was, or was becoming. Hopefully, her intuition was more acute than the evidence to be found in this newsprint. She crumpled it in her hand.

She had other worries. Something was going on, or had gone on, between Tsipi and Avram. Rivka saw it in their furtive eyes one day when Avram came to walk out with her. As they were leaving the barracks, Tsipi was just coming in. Her glance met Avram's and darted away, startled into hardness. Sweeping past, Tsipi bade Rivka a peaceful Shabbat, her wide lips faking innocence. Meanwhile, Avram devotedly studied the clouds. Something, definitely, was there between them, something they had agreed to hide from her.

She was keeping a sharp eye out now for any clue to their alliance. Often she'd mention each to the other in a manner she hoped was offhand. Nothing came of it. Avram showed only mild interest, the same as when she talked about any of the girls at work and their doings. His failure of candor did not in the least abate Rivka's passion for him, a fact that infuriated her all the more. Tsipi was even less demonstrative, if that was possible. When Rivka mentioned Avram's name, she might just as well have been specifiying a chair, for all the interest Tsipi showed. Rivka considered getting them together and confronting them straight out, but why bother?

She was sure they would deny any connection. All the same, they were thick with each other. She could see it plainly enough, persist though they might in feigning ignorance and indifference.

Then, at the turn of the secular year, the shoe she had been waiting for finally dropped. A letter came concerning Gena.

Dear Miss Lefkovits,

My name is Eleanor Simons. I am a nurse at Val-de-Grâce Hospital in Paris. I work with Dr. Morris Toby, who specializes in reconstructive surgery. Gennady Fyodorovich Filippov is my patient. He was brought to the hospital several months ago, morose and uncommunicative, as are many of the men with wounds such as his. Many spend weeks staring off at nothing. Gennady, when he thought no one was looking, stared at a slip of paper that he carefully protected from the view of others.

One day, I asked him what it was. He shook his head, but it seemed to me his eyes were begging me to ask again. During the next few weeks, I did so, several times over. You might say I made such a nuisance of myself that he had to give in and let me have a look! I'm sure by now you've guessed that the drawing I saw on the carefully unfolded sheet was a portrait of you. When I learned that he was the artist, I brought him drawing materials. Since then, his attitude has changed, and he is busy about the wards and grounds making pictures.

He has asked me to explain to you the nature of his injuries, sparing no details. He assures me that you will welcome plain speaking in all matters.

On his first day in action near the Marne, Gennady was among a group of eight who were gassed. Gennady's lungs were affected, though not his eyes, thank Heaven. The others were more or less blinded, and he was leading them in a line to the aid station when a shell caught them. Five men died instantly. Gennady lost half his face.

In the best of circumstances, his injuries would require years of reconstructive surgery employing new and often untested procedures. Given the delicate condition of his lungs, his treatment will be even further protracted. Dr. Toby estimates it might be as long as a decade before this patient can begin to think about pursuing a normal life. In that, he is lucky. Many of the injuries I see will never allow for anything approaching normalcy in life.

Under these circumstances, Gennady releases you from any and all promises you have made to him. He asks you not to write to him and not to try to visit him. He wishes me to tell you specifically that should you come to France he will not see you. He has had months to think about it and will not change his mind. I cannot say I concur in his decision, but I believe he means this with all his strength and stubbornness. You will honor him by honoring his wishes.

Through a family friend, I have been able to show Gennady's artwork to a reputable art dealer. I think you will be relieved and pleased to know that a few of his pieces have already attracted attention. He has a future as an artist, and this prospect tickles him pink.

I'm sure you have questions. If you direct them to me I shall do my best to answer them. I regret the circumstances that have caused this letter to be written, but after all, things could have been so much worse.

With all best wishes,

Sincerely,
Eleanor Simons

WINTER IN REHOVOTH was dreary. There was little for her to do in the groves. Rain fell day after day, sometimes in a drizzle, often in heavy sheets driven sidelong by the wind. To walk in it, Rivka had to slant herself against it, holding her coat closed with one hand and her hat on with the other. Chilly water trickled under her collar and into her sleeves. Accustomed as she was to frosty winter days, bright with snow that gleamed in the sun, she felt like a dishrag moldering under a dripping spigot. Dry, bracing cold and blustery winds might have invigorated her. These dank, soupy days and nights weighted her with gloom. Little to do suited her just fine. Precious little was exactly what she wanted to do.

If only Avram would leave her be. But no, he'd wrap an arm around her waist, and she'd move away. He'd burrow his nose in her neck, and she'd push him away. He'd say, "What is it now?"

He knew full well what it was. "Gena."

"He doesn't want to see you. Does that mean no one should see you?"

"I'm his intended."

One day, Avram pointed out that she had also been Gena's intended when they two had.... She slapped him and ran away and refused to see him the next time he came, and the next. She took to her bed to find refuge in sleep.

Tsipi, of all people, wouldn't allow her the slumber. Tsipi found chores requiring her help: sweep out the shed, inventory the stockpiled crates. One day, Tsipi's appeal for help was so transparent and lamebrained that Rivka threw a pillow at her, then rolled herself into a tight ball beneath the covers. Tsipi said, "You wouldn't have married the Russian, you know. I'm sure he's a fine boy, and you were too kindhearted to let him go off to war without your encouragement; but he's not Jewish, so you had no intention of becoming his wife."

Rivka snapped, "I wouldn't be the first Jewish girl to marry out."

"Some do. Not you."

All the more reason why she couldn't abandon Gena now, when he needed her. All the more reason.

She had sent Mama a copy of the nurse's letter, with a brief explanation. Mama wrote back, quoting the letter: "'*You owe him the honor of honoring his wish.*' Because his wish corresponds with your own, dear daughter, you think he has made things too convenient for you. Why should your life be made easy? Why should you have happiness when all the world is suffering? But Rivka, my darling, it is wrong to think this way. You must take happiness where it comes. You wrong no one by it, and you increase the sum of the world's joy. There's something to be said for that." Rivka tossed Mama's letter aside, muttering, "If Gena were Jewish and Avram a goy, it would be another story."

Day and night she slept. When next Tsipi came to find her, Rivka ignored her, and when Tsipi persisted, "Rivka, you can't go on like this," Rivka countered, "What is between you and Avram?"

Again with the sliding eyes. "Nothing."

"Liar."

"Ask Avram, then."

"I'm not seeing Avram."

Tsipi shrugged her shoulders and walked off.

The girls brought back food for her from the communal dining room. She didn't much care whether or not she ate.

"She can't go on like this," the girls said.

"Apparently, she can," said Tsipi.

Every evening, Avram came by and asked to see her. Every evening she refused. The other girls shook their heads and clucked their tongues. Such a nice fellow, they murmured to one another—and she turns up her nose. Where does she think she'll find another like that? Rivka played deaf, even when Shoshana warned, "I'll be glad to take him off your hands, since you don't want him." Shoshana went so far as to parade herself and her naked long legs in front of Avram. He seemed not to notice. Shoshana struck up conversations with him that lurched to a halt. He waited for Rivka to come out, and when it was clear that she would not leave her bed, he went away, only to return like clockwork the next evening, every evening the same.

Finally one evening she got out of bed, threw on some clothes and ran a brush through her hair. The girls stared.

"Look who's up," said Tsipi.

"How are you feeling?" said Shoshana.

"Tell him I'll see him," Rivka said.

There were conditions, of course. He must not make love to her, not in any way, not in a look, not in a word, not in the smallest deed. She would meet him for fifteen minutes in public. Though the air was fogged and drizzly, they must sit out on a bench in the open. Fifteen minutes only: the ache in her heart was too heavy for anything more.

Avram waited for her on the damp bench. He was happy just to watch her treading the puddled ground toward him, grimly determined. Something was on her mind, that was sure. Whatever it was, he was glad of it, since it brought her out to see him.

She stood over him. If only she'd take one step closer, she'd be between his knees. "Have you had an affair with Tsipi?" she demanded.

"With Tsipi?" Feeling for his eyebrows. "Do I look singed?"

She didn't crack a smile, just fixed him with her saucer eyes and waited.

Avram rubbed his thick, dark beard. He cleared his throat. "With Tsipi it's not what you think," he said. "Not at all. Another time, when you're feeling better, I can explain."

"You can explain right now."

"There's no time. Fifteen minutes, it's not enough."

"You'll make do."

"I warn you, it's complicated, not a short tale at all."

"The truth never takes long to tell." Like Mama, she sounded. Like the best of Mama.

Avram's dark eyes searched her face, its bleak smile. "After the war broke out," he said at last, "I joined a band of young men like myself. We organized for the security of the Jews in and around Tel Aviv, where my parents and theirs had settled. We're small, and we work in secret. The Jaffa Group, we call ourselves."

"You're a spy?"

"I try to keep Jews alive, that's all. Whatever it takes to keep a Jew alive, I'll do. Pass information, steal medicaments, smuggle arms or people."

"You love war, is that it?"

"No, Rivka, I'm at war with no one—not the Turk, nor the British, nor the Arab. But my loyalty—my only loyalty—is to the Jews."

"As if the Jews are on our knees begging you to fight for us."

"You want to argue about this? I thought you wanted me to tell you about Tsipi." He glanced at his watch, a plain, unornamented silver timepiece that he kept in his pocket. It had been his father's. "Only five minutes left."

"So tell."

In the Jaffa Group he'd met Tsipi and her brothers, he said. They trained together, went out on patrol together, and became fast friends. When the Jews were forced out of Jaffa and Tel Aviv, Avram's parents managed, through their connections, to get both families lodgings in Jerusalem. Jerusalem had fallen to Allenby without a shot being fired, but neither of Avram's parents had lived to see it. His mother died of leukemia in January of 1917, his father of pneumonia later in the year. Tsipi and her mother had helped nurse them both, day and night, day in and day out. "Tsipi can be a *klipeh*, a demon," Avram said. "Bossy, insolent—but she is always there when you need her. Always."

Bitterly, Rivka cried out, "Is any Jew in this country what he seems to be?"

Avram grinned. "I would hope not, or else we'd be a sorry lot."

THE NEXT EVENING she was there at the backless wooden bench waiting for him. With an accusation: "You knew about me, didn't you? You knew of my mission. It was no accident, you passing by in your wagon. Innocent farm boy with his innocent donkey. I should have asked myself what you were doing out there in the middle of the day, no market nearby."

"That was meant to protect you," he said gravely. "I didn't mean to get you arrested, quite the opposite." But the Ottomans had him dead to rights on charges of helping young Jews evade the Turkish draft. "A capital crime. They meant to hang me."

She gave him a sullen scowl. And here she'd gone and laid the blame for their arrest on that Arab woman—not to mention scolding herself for dereliction of her duty, when all she'd done was take a rest and a cup of tea with a young mother and her happily drooling baby.

"It could have ended badly for both of us," Avram conceded. Allenby's swift advance had come not a moment too soon.

"It most certainly did end badly. For me." It had given him to her, though she didn't say that aloud.

The next night she refused to see him.

On the next, he didn't come. And the next.

She'd grown used to his coming and didn't like the change in habit. Habit, was it? Standard procedure? Pure reflex, now overcome?

Shabbat eve, a gorgeous, clear night. Three stars shone in the sky. Would he show himself? A fourth star appeared, six, eight. He wasn't coming. He wasn't ever coming again. Served her right. She'd driven him away. She'd thought he was made of better stuff. She kicked the dirt, raising brown dust on her way back inside.

"Rivka!"

Out of the velvet darkness he emerged with long strides. Warily she joined him, circling the bench like an adversary.

"Talk to me," she said.

"I intend to."

She shook her head. "About peace."

"About peace? What do you want to know?"

Not a thing, in point of fact—she just wanted to pick a fight with him. "It's Shabbat."

"So?"

"So tell me how we'll have peace with…." She just wanted to fend off the appeal of his eyes, which were bright as a child's. "Oh, with the Arabs, let's say."

He sighed. At this moment, what did either of them care about Arabs? Or Turks, or Fiji Islanders, or little men from Mars, for that matter? He wanted to reach for her hand, but stopped himself in time. He said, "The Arabs will be our friends until they're our enemies. They'll be our enemies as soon as we're strong enough to claim this land for our own. We have ancient claim to it, yes. So do they."

"Aaronsohn believes we can live together with them."

"Aaronsohn is a scientist, not a politician, nor an economist, nor a historian, nor a particularly good judge of human character."

She bristled. "He likes me. He thinks well of me."

"The exception that proves the rule, obviously," Avram said with a smile. "Look, Rivka, I have many friends among the Arabs, as does Aaronsohn. But I have no illusions as to their loyalties. We both love the same piece of land. There will come a time when it will prove too small to support us both."

With a zealous fury, she said, "I don't believe the land is holy to them, as it is to us."

He shrugged. "How can you measure what's in men's hearts? Many a Zionist in 1905 would have given up Palestine for security in Uganda."

"So you say."

"It's a fact."

"Yet you yourself would give your life for the Jewish homeland in Palestine."

He dipped his head, and musing on some inward vision, nodded soberly. "I would," he said. "In an instant." His gaze came back to rest on her. She looked awful. Her hair was lank and lusterless. The skin of her face was a relief map crowded with pimples. She'd lost weight, her arms and legs gangly. "So would you," he added.

"You're making love to me. That's not permitted."

"Oh, so now it's my fault you've been wooed and won by the land?"

"The land at least I can count on," she spat back.

Now he did take her hand, and though she recoiled, jerking it away, he promised, "I won't fail you again."

"And what makes you think I was referring to you?"

EVERY EVENING AFTER that Avram made the trip without fail to claim his quarter hour with her. On Tu B'Shevat he brought her a cypress sapling, which they planted together. That night, the smell of pine filled her dreams, Russian groves of pine trees giving way to white forests of birch, Papa, Mama, Mischa, Dudie waving from beyond the forest edge. Branches stretching to the sky, Gena ghostly among them. But where is flame-haired Rachel? Here, beside her in a shadowy field beneath a pale moon. Telling her, "You're angry because Gena doesn't want to see you. How dare he spurn you?"

"That's crap."

"Well, then, it must be you're angry because you don't want to see him. He knows it, and he lets you off the hook. How dare he treat you well?"

"That's crap, too."

"Rivka, it's all crap. You know it, he knows it, I know it. What are you going to do about it?"

Good question.

WEEKS LATER, ON Purim, Avram came dressed as a yellow-crowned hoopoe flapping his black-and-white wings, going, "Oop-oop-ooooooooooop." Costumed thus as a gargantuan bird, he made her laugh. "At long last," he whispered.

Slowly, her appetite returned. She slept less. She began hiking alone and came back with handfuls of wildflowers, which she dried and pressed and sent to Gena, care of his nurse. It was a relief to her to send them, and a further relief to receive no response. Soon after, she shipped a crate of oranges.

Every day except Shabbat she went to work. Every evening without exception she met Avram, and they sat together. No one else used the bench anymore, though it stood only steps away from the barracks. Tacitly, it had become theirs. Sometimes she stayed out with him talking for hours. Sometimes he was late, and she waited.

ONE FINE SPRING day, at the new moon before Pesach, Tsipi said, "It's time you got involved."

Rivka said nothing. She was packing fruit.

"Think about it. We need you," Tsipi added.

An hour later, Rivka went to the door of the shed. The sun felt warm on her face. Pollen floated on the breeze and coated the windowsills. In the last few days, it seemed to her all the world had burst into flower. Everything bloomed. Everything. Color had come back, filling her heart with wonder: yellow, pink, red, violet, green greengreen. All the world greening. Over her shoulder she called back to Tsipi, "Okay. When?"

SUNSET. BARELY TIME for her to splash her face with water after work and grab a morsel to eat. They followed the road to Jerusalem, Tsipi hurrying ahead, barely glancing back to check that Rivka was keeping up. Rivka would gladly have besieged Tsipi with the hundred things she burned to know about being "involved." Tsipi's flinty eyes warned her off. At Ramla, they stopped at a rundown caravansary to use the facilities, which were primitive. Then they continued straight on for a while until, at no particular landmark Rivka could discern (so much yet waited to be learned about this country!), Tsipi angled them off into the brush. They crossed the old battle line on rising ground. Jerusalem was somewhere off to the right above them. What looked like a shepherd's dwelling gradually took shape in the murky darkness up ahead. It was a daub-and-wattle hut sheltered by a single tree and with a single covered window, light leaking around the edges of the curtain.

A handful of people crouched in a tight circle on the packed-dirt floor inside. A lantern shone in their midst, illuminating their faces orangely. She recognized the suntanned features of two of Tsipi's brothers, whose toothy grins greeted her. Avram was at the top of the circle, a smile touching the corners of his mouth, his eyes crinkling. He shifted to make a place for her next to him.

"Meet Rivka," he said softly. The others, who were strangers to her, nodded their welcome. She sat at Avram's side, their shoulders brushing, their arms, hands, fingers. Home: she'd found her way there.

Author's Note

THERE REALLY WAS a Battalion of Death, formed in mid-1917 and led by the indomitable Maria Leontievna Bochkareva. Her autobiography, *Yashka, My Life as Peasant, Exile and Soldier* (as set down by Isaac Don Levine, 1919), recounts her remarkable life before and during the Great War. I have mined from this and journalistic sources of the time to provide as faithful an account of her words and stances as possible. The same is true of other historical figures in this work; wherever possible, I have used their words, rather than my own, and I have sought to remain true to historical fact—except where it interfered with my aims in the novel. Any errors in fact or interpretation are my own.

Many thanks to Mark Wilson Parker, Barbara Taffet, Francine Medoff, and Bernie and Shellie Schneider for their insightful comments on earlier drafts, to Nancy Nicholas for her help in lifting this story up out of flatland, and to Jerry Gross for setting me on the right track and lending me his magnificent eye and ear. Maggie Cadman did an astute job of copyediting (Maggie, does that get a hyphen?). Betzie Bendis roughed in the maps, which Keith Bendis digitized. Ailian Price graciously rescued me from my graphic ineptitude, while the rest of the Price family—Eric, Ian and Liz—were, as ever, staunchly in my corner. I am grateful to Susan Isaacs for her encouragement and steady support. As always, the research librarians at Long Island's Port Washington Library have been a joy to work with, retrieving books for me from hither and beyond yon. To my friends who've cheered me on— including Michael Kasky, Jackie DeYoung, Louise Estrema, Choral Eddie and so many other good people; and to my family—Zach, Sam and Jordan—thanks is too little to say and more than you've asked for. Your love sustains me.

Rivka's journey has also been my own, and I hope neither of them is yet done. As to Yashka, in April 1918 she did, indeed, have her audience with Woodrow Wilson and then went on to England and met with King George V. By the spring of 1919, she was back in Soviet Russia, having entered with the Allies through Archangel. She was arrested and interrogated over several months; on May 16, 1920, she was executed by firing squad as an enemy of the people.

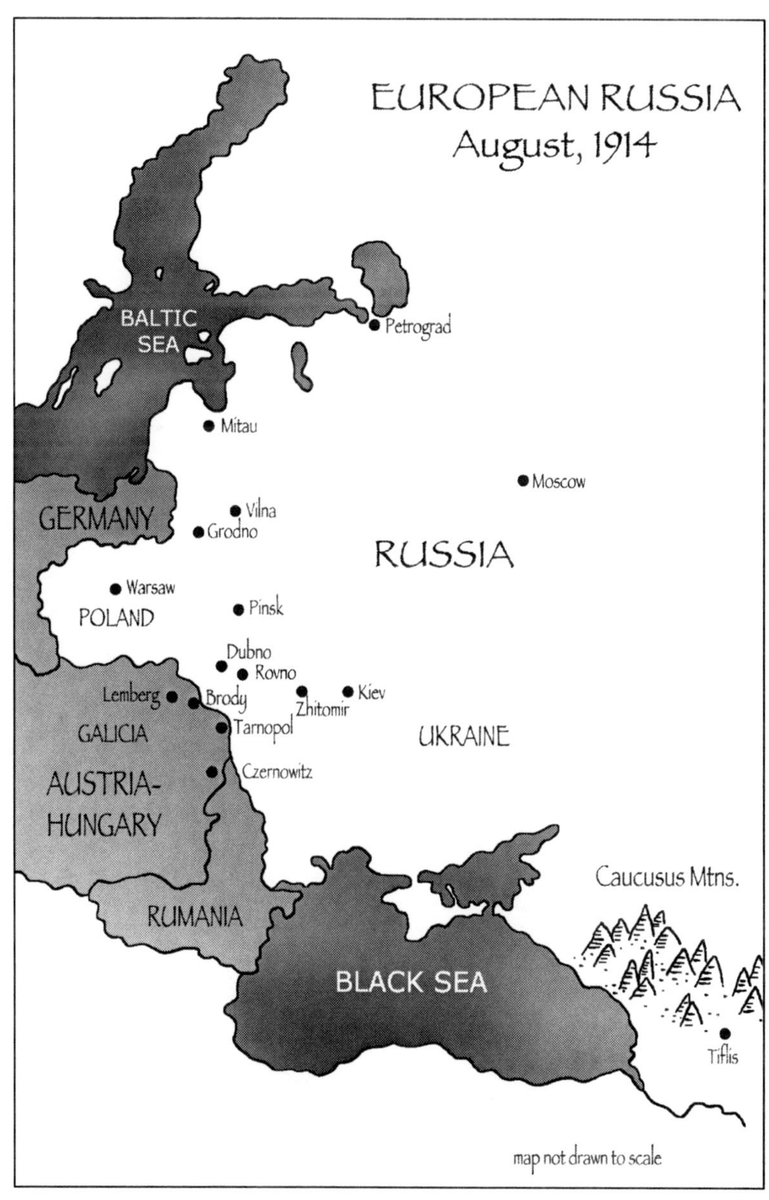
EUROPEAN RUSSIA
August, 1914
BALTIC SEA
Petrograd
Mitau
Moscow
GERMANY
Vilna
Grodno
RUSSIA
Warsaw
POLAND
Pinsk
Dubno
Rovno
Lemberg
Brody
Zhitomir
Kiev
GALICIA
Tarnopol
UKRAINE
Czernowitz
AUSTRIA-HUNGARY
RUMANIA
Caucusus Mtns.
BLACK SEA
Tiflis
map not drawn to scale

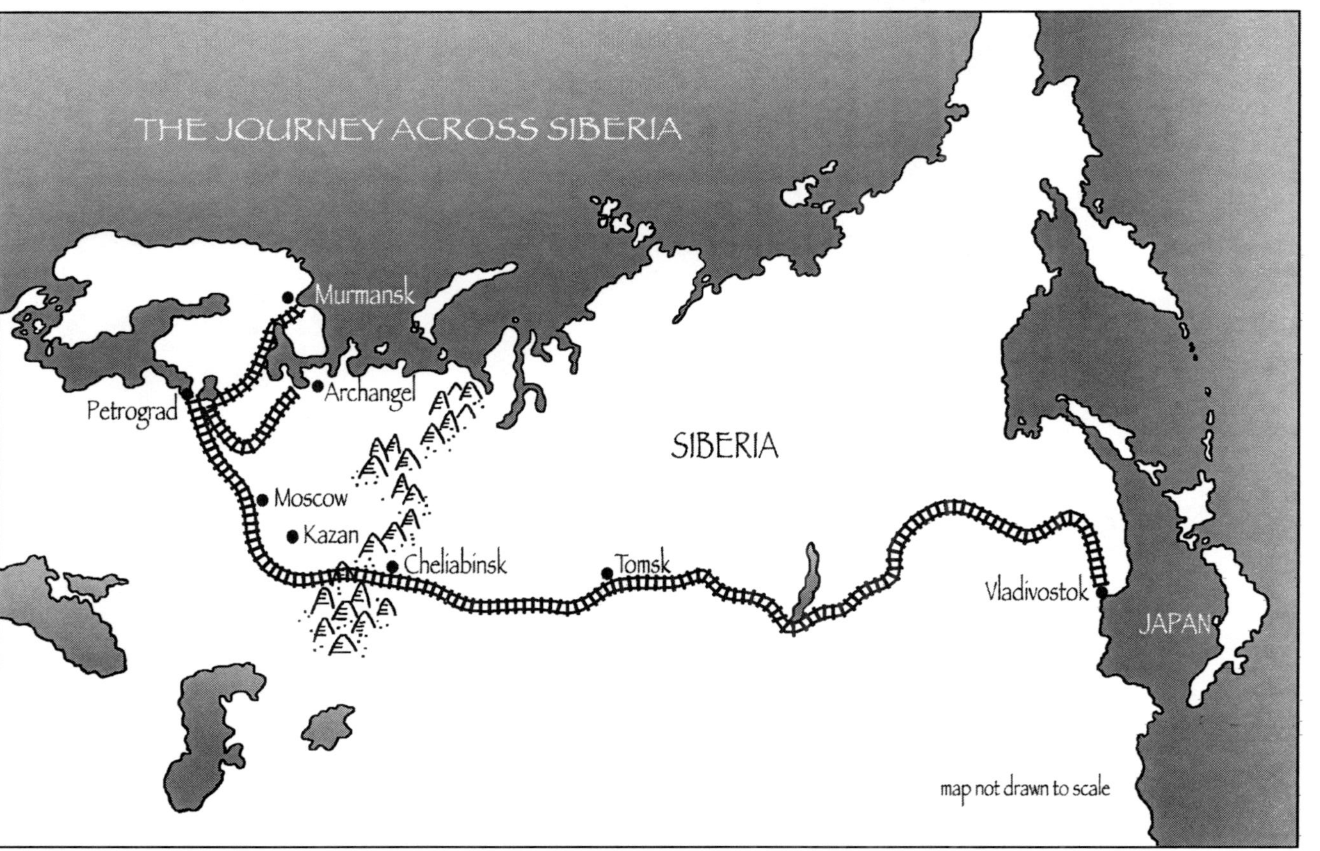
THE JOURNEY ACROSS SIBERIA
Murmansk
Archangel
Petrograd
SIBERIA
Moscow
Kazan
Cheliabinsk
Tomsk
Vladivostok
JAPAN
map not drawn to scale

PALESTINE, September 19, 1918
MEDITERRANEAN SEA
Haifa
Atlith
Nazareth
El Afula
Jenin
Deraa
Tulkarem
Nablus
El Tire
Jaffa/Tel Aviv
Front Line
Ramla
Jerusalem
PALESTINE
Beersheva
map not drawn to scale

Glossary of Foreign-Language Terms

abi gezunt	as long as you're healthy
aliyah	see "make aliyah" below
baba	woman
bimah	raised platform in a shul where Torah is read
bishlik	unit of currency equal to 2 ½ Turkish piastres
bobka	coffee cake
Bolshevik, Bolshevist	a follower of Marxist-Leninism; this narrative tends to use Bolshevik to mean a party member, Bolshevist an adherent to communist philosophy
bubba mayse	(lit., grandmother's story) old wive's tale
challah	braided egg bread made for the Sabbath
chasid	member of a sect following a strict form of Orthodox Judaism
cheder	school, often one-room
chevrah	group of associates
chochem	wise man, or wiseacre
daven	pray
Eretz Yisroel	the Land of Israel (in Hebrew, Eretz Yisrael)
farshtopt	cluttered
flanken	a cut of beef, usually boiled
Galitsianer	Jew from the area known as Galicia (eastern Poland and Austria)
gefilte fish	a mixture of white fish (pike, carp) that is ground, rolled in a ball, boiled and served cold
gevalt	a cry of distress
goyim	gentiles
Gutt in himmel	God in heaven
haftorah	a reading from the Prophets following the weekly Torah portion
kaffiyeh	traditional Arab headdress

keinahorah	(lit., no evil eye) may no evil occur
kvell	be filled with pride and happiness
landsleit	neighbors, fellow townspeople
lemeshke	bungler
macher	big shot, fixer
maideleh	little girl (term of endearment)
make aliyah	relocate to the Land of Israel
mameleh	little mother (term of endearment)
mandelbrot	(lit., nut bread) similar to a biscotti
mehitzah	curtain or other barrier separating men and women in an Orthodox shul
melamed	teacher in a cheder
Mitzrayim	Egypt
motzi	blessing over bread
narishkeit	foolishness, mumbo jumbo
natchalnik	commander
NILI	acronym for a phrase from I Samuel meaning "The Eternal One of Israel will not lie"
nu?	so? well?
oy vey	oh woe
oysgeputst	overdressed
pas	ballet step
pilpul	Talmudic argument about seemingly insignificant or nitpicking issues
plotz	burst
putz	obscene word meaning penis; derogatorily applied to a man
rebbetzin	rabbi's wife
rugelach	small, sweet pastries with cinnamon and raisins
schlemiel	fool, clumsy or inept person
schnorrer	moocher, a beggar who puts on airs

Shabbes	the Sabbath (in Hebrew, Shabbat)
shah	hush
shivah	seven-day mourning period
shnaps	liquor
shoychet	ritual slaughterer
shtetl	village
shtreimel	fur-trimmed hat worn by a Chasid
shul	synagogue
takeh	truly?
tallis	prayer shawl
tateh	father, papa, daddy
tateleh	little father (term of endearment)
Tsenerenah	properly Tsena Urenah (Come Out and See), a collection of biblical passages and commentary in Yiddish, based on weekly Torah portions
tsimmes	lit., sweet carrot pudding; a fuss over nothing
vantz	bedbug
verst	Russian measure equal to 3500 feet, about 2/3 of a mile
vey is mir	woe is me
yeshiva bokher	student of a Talmudic academy
yontiv	holiday
zaideh	grandfather

CPSIA information can be obtained at www.ICGtesting.com
Printed in the USA
BVOW081618050513

319850BV00002B/13/P

9 781626 520509